ART FAIR

'97 GuangZhou International

ART FAIR

'97广州国际艺术博览会

'97广州国际艺术博览会

主办单位：广州市人民政府
承办单位：广州市文化局
日 期：1997年12月6日至12月10日
地点：广州、中国出口商品交易会大厦
协办单位：

广州市人民对外友好协会
广州市文学界联合会
岭南美术出版社
广东占美广告有限公司
广艺博文化有限公司
深圳卷烟厂
永利发彩印有限公司
广美佛宝矿泉有限公司
广州市关键广告公司

'97GUANGZHOU INTERNATIONAL ART FAIR

Sponsor: The People's Government of Guangzhou Municipality
Organizer: Guangzhou Municipal Culture Bureau
Date: December 6-10, 1997
Place: The China Export Commodities Fair Building, Guangzhou
Co-organizers:

Guangzhou People's Foreign Friendship Association
Guangzhou Federation of Culture and Art
Lingnan Fine Art Publishing House
Jami Advertisement Co.Ltd.
Guangyibo Culture Company, Ltd.
Shenzhen Tobacco Factory
Yonglifa Color-Print Company, Ltd.
Guangmei Fobao Mineral Water Company Ltd.
Guangzhou Guangjian Advertising Co.

'97广州国际艺术博览会组织委员会

**The Organizing
Committee of the
'97 Guangzhou
International Art Fair**

顾　问

黎子流 —————————————————————— 于光远

主　任

—————————————————————— 林树森

副主任

朱小丹 —————————————————————— 姚蓉宾

委　员

陈纪宣 —————— 阎宪奇 —————— 杨苗青
陈万鹏 —————— 李文洲 —————— 刘青云
曾石龙 —————— 刘长安 —————— 陈永锵
张伯华 —————— 余卫新 —————— 俞昭道

秘书长

刘长安 —————————————————————— 陈永锵

副秘书长

王庆生 —————— 华　珊 —————— 乐润生

艺术总监

—————————————————————— 陈永锵

行政总监

—————————————————————— 乐润生

Consultants

Li Zi-liu ———————————————————— Yu Guang-yuan

Director

———————————————————— Lin Shu-sen

Deputy Directors

Zhu Xiao-dan ———————————————————— Yao Rong-bin

Members

Chen Ji-xuan ———— Yan Xian-qi ———— Yang Miao-qing
Chen Wan-peng ———— Li Wen-zhou ———— Liu Qing-yun
Zeng Shi-long ———— Liu Chang-an ———— Chen Yong-qiang
Zhang Bo-hua ———— Yu Wei-xin ———— Yu Zhao-dao

Secretaries-General

Liu Chang-an ———————————————————— Chen Yong-qiang

Under Secretaries-general

Wang Qing-sheng ———— Hua Shan ———— Le Run-sheng

Chief Art Inspector

———————————————————— Chen Yong-qiang

Administrative Inspector

———————————————————— Le Run-sheng

名誉主任

关山月 —————————— 黎雄才
郭绍钢 —————————— 廖冰兄
潘 鹤 ———— 王 琦 ———— 刘勃舒

主任委员

林 墉 —————————— 王玉珏
梁明诚 —————————— 陈永锵

艺术总监

—————————————— 陈永锵

艺术主持

—————————————— 王璜生

委 员

汤小铭 ———— 林 墉 ———— 王玉珏
梁明诚 ———— 陈永锵 ———— 张治安
邵增虎 ———— 张绍城 ———— 郑 爽
唐大禧 ———— 林抗生 ———— 潘嘉俊
皮道坚 ———— 沈 军 ———— 张从达
苏庚春 ———— 杨小彦 ———— 王璜生
梁 江 ———— 韩子定 ———— 郭 桓
关玉良 ———— 潭 天 ———— 李伟铭
曹利祥 ———— 马若龙 ———— 董小明

秘书长

—————————————— 陈永锵

Honorory Chairmen

Guan Shan-yue === Li Xiong-cai === Guo Shao-gang
Liao Bing-xiong, ==== Pan He == Wang Qi, Liu Bo-shu

Chairmen

Lin Yong ================= Wang Yu-yu
Liang Ming-cheng ========== Chen Yong-qiang

Chief Art Inspector

==================== Chen Yong -qiang

Art Manager

==================== Wang Huang-sheng

Members

Tang Xiao-ming === Lin Yong ==== Wang Yu-yu
Liang Ming-cheng =Chen Yong-qiang == Zhang Zhi-an
Shao Zeng-hu ==== Zhang Shao-cheng === Zheng Shuang
Tang Da-xi ==== Lin Kang-sheng ===Pan Jia-jun
Pi Dao-jian ==== Shen Jun ==== Zhang Cong-da
Su Geng-chun === Yang Xiao-yan == Wang Huang-sheng
Liang Jiang ==== Han Zi-ding ==== Ge Heng
Guan Yu-liang ==== Tan Tian ==== Li Wei-ming
Cao Li-xiang ==== Ma Ruo-long === Dong Xiao-ming

Secretary-general

==================== Chen Yong-qiang

行政总监
══ 乐润生
行政副总监
华　珊 ═══════════════════════════════ 邵杰明
黄雄伟 ═══════════════════════════════ 李健军
办公室主任
曾建成 ═══════════════════════════════ 李伟儒
副主任
林　宇 ══════════ 蔡亚忠 ══════════ 张　捷
招展部
乐润生 ══════════ 陈孝杜 ══════════ 高　玲
招商部
黄雄伟 ══════════ 张国鹏 ══════════ 余能勇
宣传部
邵杰明 ═══════════════════════════════ 张　捷
保　卫
连广生 ═══════════════════════════════ 罗晓风
外联部
李伟儒 ═══════════════════════════════ 亦　群
接待部
林　宇 ══════════ 毛　蓉 ══════════ 郑小敏
储运部
林　宇 ══════════ 陈孝杜 ══════════ 袁怀勇
财物部
陈小玉 ═══════════════════════════════ 吕冬红
会　刊
乐润生 ═══════════════════════════════ 李健军

Administrative Inspector
════════════════════════════════════ Le Run-sheng
Deputy Inspectors
Hua Shan ══════════════════════════ Shao Ming-jie
Huang Wei-xiong ═══════════════════════ Li Jian-jun
Office Directors
Zeng Xian-cheng ══════════════════════ Li Wei-yu
Deputy Directors
Lin Yu ══════════ Chai Ya-zhong ══════════ Zhnag Jie
Exhibition Business
Le Run-sheng ══════ Chen Xiao-du ══════════ Gao Ling
Business Contact
Huang Wei-xiong ══════ Zhang Guo-peng ══════ Yu Neng-yong
Publicity
Zhao Jie-ming ══════ Zhang Ji ══════════ Wu Jing
Security:Lian ══════ Guang-sheng ══════ Luo Xiao-feng
External Liaison
Li Wei-yu ═══════════════════════════ Yi Qun
Reception
Lin Yu ══════════ Mao Rong ══════════ Zheng Xiao-min
Storage & Transportation
Lin Yu ══════════ Chen Xiao-du ══════════ Yuan Huai-yong
Finance
Chen Xiao-yu ═══════════════════════ Lu Dong-hong
Bulletin
Le Run-sheng ═══════════════════════ Li Jian-jun

姚蓉宾副市长在97广州国际艺术博览会上的讲话

尊敬的先生们，女士们：

　　在天高云淡的初冬时节，'97广州国际艺术博览会又如期开幕了。97年是我国对香港恢复行使主权，党的十五大胜利召开的日子。因此，赋予了本届博览会以特殊的意义。籍此机会，我谨代表广州市政府，广州市全体市民，向来穗参加此次盛会的海内外艺术家，企业家，收藏家们，向莅临今天开幕式的各届人士和朋友，致以热烈的欢迎。广州是一座历史文化名城。秦代以来，一直是我国对外贸易往来的重要港口城市。汉唐时期，又成为我国联结西亚，欧陆的"海上丝绸之路"的起点。经济，文化发达，对外贸易活跃。

　　　从历史上看，广州文化艺术市场的形成有着得天独厚的条件。改革开放后，我市的文化艺术市场得到了蓬勃发展，大大促进了文化艺术的繁荣。美术界更是名家辈出，异彩纷呈，成绩喜人。本届艺术博览会是我市今年一项重大文化活动。它的举办对于加强中外文化交流，促进艺术创作和艺术市场的繁荣发展，具有重大意义。我们希望通过举办博览会，能为繁荣和规范我国的艺术品市场作出贡献，使我国艺术品市场与国际接轨，并使广州国际艺术博览会逐步立足于世界著名的艺术博览会之林。

　　'97广州国际艺术博览会是艺术品展示，交流和交易的盛会。参展作品既有名家大师的手笔，也有近年崛起的新秀之作。共有三百多位中外艺术家，画廊和企业参展，展出作品近一万多件。此外，拉萨市人民政府对本届博览会予以热情的支持，为藏族艺术家赴穗参展提供了帮助，使本届艺术博览会增色不少。对此表示衷心的感谢。对鼎力支持我们举办本届博览会的上级领导和赞助企业，致以诚挚的谢意！预祝'97广州国际艺术博览会取得圆满成功。

副市长 **姚蓉宾**
一九九七年十二月六日

Vice- Mayoress Yao Rong-bin's Address
at the '97 Guangzhou International Art Exposition

Respected Ladies and Gentlemen:

　　On this early winter day when the skies are deep andcloudsarethinlywan, the '97 Guangzhou International Art Exposition opens once againaccording to schedule. In 1997, we have resumed the exercise ofsovereignty over Hong Kong and have succssfully heldthe15thCongress ofthe CPC. Hence, this exposition has a special significance.I'dlike to take this opportunity, on behalf of the Guangzhou MunicipalPeople's Government and the people of Guangzhou, to extend a warmestwelcome to the artists, enterpreneurs, collectors, domestic and foreign;and to those who are present at today's opening ceremony.

　　Guangzhou is a famous historic and cultural city. Since the QinDynasty, she has been an important port city of our country for foregntrade. In the Han and Tang Dynasties, Guangzhou, a city with advancedeconomy, culture and active foreign trade, became the start-point of the"Silk Route at Sea", linking China with West-Asia and the EuropeanContinent. And in the Song Dynasty, there appeared "gou lan" and "washe" (public places of entertainment) and well developed book markets.From her history, we can see that there are advantageous conditions forthe formation of Guangzhou's culture and art market. With theimplementation of the "open and reform" policy, this market has beengrowing vigorously, greatly promoting the prosperity of culture and art.There have emerged numerous famous artists in the circle of fine artwith satisfactory achievements.

　　This art exposition is an important cultural activity of our city.It has great significance in developing Sino-Foreign cultural exchange,and in promoting art creation and the prosperity and growth of thecultural and art market.It is our hope that through this art exposition,we can contribute to theprosperityand standardization of ourmarket ofartwork, linking it with the outside world and making ours one ofthose world-famous expositions.

　　The '97 Guangzhou International Exposition is a grand event inwhich artworks are displyed, exchanged and traded. The works exhibitedinclude masterpieces by renowned artists and works by newly emergedpainters. There are altogether over three hundred artists andrepresentatives of art galleries and enterprises, with approximatelyten thousand pieces of work. Beside, the Government of LhasaMunicipalitywarmly supports this exposition, assisting Tibetan artiststo join us in Guangzhou, which adds attraction tothe exposition.I'd like to express my heartfelt thanks to them and to the authoritiesconcerned and enterprises that have supported us!

　　Here, I wish the '97 Guangzhou International Art Exposition agreat success!

Yao Rong-bin
Vice-Mayoress
Dec. 6, 1997

参展画廊/单位/画家及作品

赖征云 《崔小姐肖像》 油画 122cm × 80cm 1997 年
Lai zheng-yun "Portrait of Miss Cui"
122cm × 80cm Oil Painting 1997

广州画院油画展
参展画家：吴海鹰、熊德琴、黄坤源、叶献民、赖征云、何坚宁、徐兆前、陈铿、张伟。
广州画院地址：水荫路 130 号　邮编：510075
电话：(020) 87712631　87637148
Oil Exhibition of Guangzhou Academy of Painting
Paiticipating Artists : Wu Hai-ying,Xiong De-ging,Huang Kun-yuan,Ye Xian-min,Lai zheng-yun,He Jian-ning, Xu zhao-gian,chen Keng ,zhang Wei.
Add : No.130 Shui Yin Road,Guangzhou,china
P.C. : 510075
Tel : (020) 87712631,87637148

赖征云，６５年毕业于广州美术学院。作品多次入选全军美展，全国美展，常参加联展，出国展。８９年在广州美术馆举办个展。９７年应邀赴日本举办画展并出版纪念画册。出版《赖征云油画选》,《赖征云油画集》。

Lai Zheng-yun, a graduate of Guangzhou Institute of Fine Art in 1965.His works have been selected into the army and national exhibitions many times, and taken part in joint exhibitions. He held solo exhibition in the Guangzhou Gallery of Fine Art in 1989. In 1997 hewas invited to hold exhibitions in Japan and had his commemorative work collection published there. His publications include "Selection of Lai Zheng-yun's Oil Paintings", and "Collection of Lai Zheng- yun's OilPaintings".

叶献民 《生存空间》 油画 114cm × 86cm 1997年
Ye Xian-min "Living Space" 114cm × 86cm Oil Painting 1997

叶献民，中国美协会员，新加坡水彩画会会员，广州画院副院长。１９９６年修读于广州美院油画系研究生班。作品曾多次参加国际及全国大型画展。获全国画展铜奖、省及市画展金奖。出版有《叶献民集》、《叶献民水彩画集》、《叶献民作品集》等。

Ye Xian-min is a member of China Artists' Association, of Singapore Water-color Painting Society, and vice president of Guangzhou Academy of Painting. He has taken graduate courses in the Department of Oil Painting in the Guangzhou Institute of Fine Art. His works took part in many large scale exhibitions and were awarded a bronze prize in the national art exhibition, and gold prizes in provincial and municipal exhibitions. His publications include "Collection of Ye Xian-min", "Collection of Ye Xian-min's Water Color Painting", and "Work Collection of Ye Xian-min".

昊海鹰 《三色玫瑰》 油画 50cm × 50cm 1996年
Wu Hai-ying "Three-Colored Roses" 50cm × 50cm Oil Painting 1996

吴海鹰，广州美术学院毕业，中国美协会员，广东美协常务理事，一级美术师。作品入选第4、6、7、8届全国美展，获第6届全国美展铜奖，广东省美展金奖，第2届广东省鲁迅文艺奖，1987阿尔及尔世界文化荟萃特别金奖等。先后在广州、香港、台北、巴黎举办个展。两次出版《吴海鹰油画集》。

Wu Hai-ying graduated from the Guangzhou Institute of Fine Art, and is a member of China Artists' Association, director of Guangdong Artists' Association, and firstclass artist. His works have been selected into the 4th, 6th,(won a bronze prize)7th, and 8th National Exhibition of Fine Art, and a gold prize in the Guangdong Provincial Exhibition, "the Second Luxun Cultural and Art Award of Guangdong", a Special Gold Prize in the '97 Algeria World's Distinquished Cultrues Work. He has held solo exhibitions in Guangzhou, Hongkong, Taibei, and Paris succesively. His "Collection of Wu Hai-ying's Oil Painting" has been published for two times.

张伟《平淡的主题》 油画 140cm × 166cm 1994年
zhang Wei "Prosaic Subjects" 140cm × 166cm Oil Painting 1994

张伟，８８年广州美术学院毕业，现为广州美院讲师，广州
画院特聘画家，广东美协会员。作品多次入选全国大型画展。
曾获全国作品优秀奖和省展二等奖。其油画《加入》被国际
奥委会永久收藏。《香港早晨》被９７'中国艺术大展组委会
收藏。

Zhang Wei graduated from the Guangzhou Institute of Fine Art in 1988,
and is now a lecturer of it, a guest painter of the Guangzhou Academyof
Painting, and a member of Guangdong Artists' Association. His works
have been selected into many large scale exhibitions, and awarded
anational excellence prize and a second prize in the provincial exhibition.
His "Participation" is collected by the International Olympic Games,
and "Good Morning, Hongkong" by the '97 China Art Exposition.

陈铿 《西关老屋》 油画 180cm×180cm 1996年
Chen Keng "Old Houses In Xiguan" 180cm×180cm Oil Painting 1996

陈铿，８９年毕业于广州美院。作品入选国际青年年、中国青年美展，全国体育美展，广东省、广州市美展，获首届中国连环画"金杯奖"，省市美展优秀奖。多幅作品被海内外报刊发表并收藏。９７年获美国佛龙特艺术奖学金赴美交流和访问。现为广东美协会员、广东青年美协常务理事、广州画院特聘画家。

Chen Keng, a graduated from Guangzhou Institute of Fine Art in 1989. His works have been on show in international and national youths fine art exhibitions, and Guangdong and Guangzhou fine art exhibitions ascompetition, excellence prizes at provincial and municipal fine art exhibitions. Quite a few of his works were published or collected at home and abroad. He was granted a scholarship and went to the US for academic exchange and visits in 1997. He is a memeber of Guangdong Artists Association, standing director of Guangdong Young Artists Association and a guest painter of Guangzhou Academy of Painting.

熊德琴《闲》 油画 80cm × 60cm 1996-1997年
Xiong De-gin "Leisure" 80cmX60cm Oil Painting 1996-1997

熊德琴，６５年广州美术学院毕业。国家一级美术师，中国美协会员，广州美协理事。多次参加国内外大型美展并有获奖。作品在海内外专业杂志发表。在台湾、日本、加拿大、美国、香港均有收藏。

Xiong De-qin, a graduate of the Guangzhou Institute of Fine Art in 1965, is now a state first class artist, member of China Artists' Association, and director of Guangzhou Artists' Association. She has participatedin exhibitions at home and abroad for many times and was awarded. Her works were published by many professional magazines, and collected by people of Taiwan, Japan, Canada, America, and Hongkong.

黄坤源 《草棚与牛》 油画 125cm × 90cm 1976年
Huang Kun-yuan "Straw Shed and Cows" 125cm × 90cm Oil Painting 1976

黄坤源，中国美协会员，广州画院高极美术师。油画作品多次入选全国，省市美展，在广州等地举办个展3次。出版《黄坤源油画选》，《黄坤源画集（水彩）》等书著。作品被美国，马来西亚，意大利，台湾收藏家收藏。广东，广州电视台曾作专题播映。

Huang Kun-yuan is a member of China Artists' Association, and a painter of the Guangzhou Academy of Painting. His oil paintings have been selected into national, provincial, and municipal art exhibitions formany times. He has held solo exhibitions in cities like Guangzhou three times. His publications include "Selection of Hung Kun-yuan's Oil Painting", and "Collection of Huang Kun-yuan's Painting (Water Color) ".His works were collected by art lovers from America, Malaysia, Italy, and Taiwan. His life has been reported by the Guangzhou, and Guangdong TV Staions.

何坚宁　《山村小学》　油画 100cm × 100cm　　1992 年
He Jian-ning　"Primary School in a Mountain Village" 100cm × 100cm　Oil　Painting　1992

何坚宁，６０年生于海南省。８２年广州美术学院油画系毕业。现为广州画院画家，中国美协会员。出版《何坚宁油画》等。

He Jian-ning was born in Hainan Province in 1960. He graduated from the Department of Oil Painting in the Guangzhou Insitute of Fine Art in 1982.He is an artist of the Guangzhou Academy of Painting, and a member of China Artists' Association. His publications include "He Jian- ning's Paintings".

徐兆前《极顶》 油画 110cm × 120cm 1996 年
Xu zhao-gian "The Peak" 110cm × 120cm Oil Painting 1996

徐兆前，解放军艺术学院毕业。现为广州画院创作室主任，高级美术师，中国美协会员。作品１２次入选文化部及中国美协举办的全国美展，两次获奖。６件作品被国内外美术馆，博物馆收藏。９７年受日本丸龟市政府邀请赴日举办个画展。出版画册３集，挂历１册。

Xu Zhao-qian graduated from the PLA Art Instiute,and is director of the creation workshop of the Guangzhou Academy of Painting, a senior artist, and a member of China Artists' Association. His works have been selected into the National Exhibition of Fine Art for 12 times, and awarded twice. Six pieces of his works are collected by galleries and museums in and out of China. In 1997, he was invited to Japan to hold solo exhibitions. He has three painting collections and one picture-calendar published.

何东 《落日熔金》 国画 100cm × 100cm 1997 年
He Dong "Golden Sunset" Chinese Painting 100cm × 100cm 1997

天津国际大厦艺术展示中心
地址：天津市南京路７５号天津国际大厦１６０３室
电话：（０２２）２３３２３４８９
参展画家：王慧智，晏平，李志强，付羽，梁金琦，何东
Art Show Center of Tianjin International Mansion
Address: Room 1603, Tianjin International Mansion, No.75, Nanjing
Road, Tianjin
Tel:(022)23323489
Participating Painters: Wang Hui-zhi, Yan Ping, Li Zhi-qiang, Fu Yu,
Liang Jin-qi, and He Dong.

何东，８２年天津美院毕业。天津市美协会员，天津市青年
美协副主席，天津国际大厦艺术展示中心艺术总监。作品曾
参加国际，全国画展并多次获奖。

He Dong, a graduate from the Tianjin Institute of Fine Art in 1982, is
now a member of Tianjin Artists' Association, vice president of Tianjin
Young Artists' Association, and general supervisor of the Art Show
Center in Tianjin International Mansion. His works have been selected
into international and national exhibitions and awarded.

醉墨堂画廊展览厅
Show-hall of Zui Mo Tang Art Gallery

醉墨堂画廊，以经营名人字画为主，兼营古董文物，高级工艺品。定期举办画家精品展，代销天津美院教授书画作品。目前展出孙其峰、梁崎、爱新觉罗．溥佐、孙克纲、何家英、赵松涛、吕云所等名家精品。
地址：天津河北区天纬路 11 号增 7 （邮编：30014）
电话：022-26263051

Zui Mo Tang Art Gallery deals mainly in paintings and calligraphic works by famous people, curios, and high class art crafts. Exhibitions. of art works are held regularly. It is also a gallery commissioned to sell works of professors from Tianjin Institute of Fine Art. Now works of famous artists as Sun Qi-feng, Liang Qi, Ai Xing Jue Luo.Pu Zuo,Sun Ke-gang,He Jia-ying, Zhou Song-tao, and Li Yun are on sale in ZuiMo Tang.

卢津艺 《溪》 国画 200cm × 100cm 1997 年
Lu Jin-yi "A Stream" Chinese Painting
200cm × 100cm 1997

卢津艺，天津美术学院毕业。大量作品被美国、日本、韩国等友人收藏，多次参加省市级大展，各类报刊有发表。作品获"天津９７香港回归展"优秀奖、"天津八一建军节画展"获特别纪念奖并被收藏。参加９６、９７年中国艺术博览会，９７年作品参加"太平洋天津精品拍卖会"。出版有《琵琶记》。现任北方艺术公司环艺部经理。

Lu Jin-yi, a graduate of Tianjin Institute of Fine Art, is manager of Enviromental Art Department of the North Art Company. Many of his works have been collected by poeple from America, Japan, and Korea, taken part in large scale exhibitions and published by different kinds of journals. He has been awarded an excellence prize in the "'97 Tianjin Exhibition of the Return of Hongkong", and a special souvenir prize in the "Tianjin Art Exhibition of Army Day". He participated in the '96 and '97 China Art Fair, and "Pacific Auction of Tianjin's Refined Works". "Records of Pipa" is among his publications.

王根生　《夏》　国画　100cm×100cm　1997年
Wang Gen-Sheng　"Summer"
100cm×100cm　Chinese Painting　1997

王山岭《秋韵》　65cm×65cm　1996年
Wang Shan-Ling "Charm of Autumn"
65cm×65cm　1996

王根生，作品曾获"牡丹杯"国际书画大赛二等奖，中国文联主办的国际文学艺术博览会特级作品奖，首届青年国画家大展新人奖等。作品被郭沫若纪念馆，红军纪念馆等收藏。现为徐州书画院画师。

王山岭，天津美术学院毕业，中国美协天津分会会员。其作品在国内外许多大型美展中多次获奖并被收藏。９７年应邀赴新加坡、马来西亚、香港进行学术交流。艺绩收录于《中国当代艺术家名人大辞典》、《世界华人艺术家成就博览会大典》等。编著有《民族儿童》、《有趣的动物》。

Wang Gen-sheng won a second prize in the "Peony Cup" International Competition of Calligraphy and Painting, a super-class work prize in the International Exposition of Culture and Art sponsored by the China Cultrual Federation, and a New Artist Prize in the first Exhibition of Young Artists of Chinese Painting. He has works collected by the Guo Mo-ruo Memorial Hall, the Red Army Memorial Hall, etc. He is now a painter of Xuzhou Academy of Calligraphy and Painting.

Wang Shan-ling, a graduate from the Tianjin Institute of Fine Art, is a member of the Tianjin Artists' Association. His works have won prizes in many large scale exhibitions and been collected. He was invited to Singapore, Malaysia, and Hongkong for academic exchanges in 1997. His name has been listed in the "Dictionary of Famous Contemporary Chinese Artists" and the "Catalogue of the Exposition of Achievements of Chinese-Origin Artists in the World". His publications include "Children of Different Nationalities" and "Lovely Animals".

纪荣耀 《幽闲》 国画 65cm × 65cm 1997 年
Ji Rong-yao "Leisure in Quietness"
65cm 65cm Chinese Painting 1997

杨乾亮 《钟馗行猎图》 中国画
170cm × 90cm 1996 年
Yang Qian-liang "Zhong Kui Going Hunting"
170cm × 90cm Chinese painting 1996

纪荣耀，天津美术学院毕业，天津美协会员，天津工笔画研究会会员。其作品在国内外各类美展中多次获奖，部分被国内外收藏家收藏。编著书籍有《中国历代人物线描集》等。现为职业画家。

Ji Rong-yao, a graduate from the Tianjin Institute of Fine Art, is a member of the Tianjin Artists' Association, and the Tianjin Research Society of Gongbi Painting. His works have won prizes in many exhibitions at home and abroad, and many of them have been collected by art lovers. His publications include "Line Drawing Collection of China's Historical Figurews Through the Ages" and others. He is now a professional painter.

杨乾亮，４９年生于北京。师范学院艺术系毕业。现为职业画家。作品多次参加全国性及省市级画展并有获奖。部分作品在报刊发表。最近完成１００幅京剧系列水墨画。

Yang Qian-liang was born in Beijing in 1949 and a graduate of fine art in a normal university. He is now a professional painter. His works have been on show in municipal, provincial and national painting exhibitions and awarded. He has had part of his works published in journals. He has recently finished 100 serial inkwash paintings on Beijing operas.

王全力 《踏雪图》 国画 85cm × 85cm 1997年
Wang Quan-lin "A Walk in the Snowfield" 85cmX85cm Chinese Painting 1997

王全力，作品多次参加国内外重大展览，并被载入《二十世纪中华画苑缀英》和《当代中国名人宝鉴》。作品在国际中国画展大赛中获三等奖；在"明星杯"全国书画大赛中获银奖；"红军杯"全国书画大赛获二等奖并被中国红军纪念馆收藏。还有作品获"巴黎铁塔艺术杯"书画大赛特别纪念奖。

Wang Quan-li has had his works shown in many exhibtions at home and abroad and carried in the "The Best of Chinese Paintings of the Twentieth Century" and the "Introduction of Famous Contemporary Chinese Artists". He was awarded a silver prize in the "Star Cup National Competition of Painting and Calligraphy", a special souvenir prize in the "Paris Tower Art Cup Competition of Painting and Calligraphy", and a second prize in the "Red Army Cup National Competition of Painting and Calligraphy",with his work collected by the China Red Army Memorial Hall.

史玉《秋栖玉露微》 国画 69cm × 69cm 1997 年
Shi Yu "Autumn Scene" 69cm × 69cm
Chinese Painting 1997

高学年 《香金秋露华》 国画 69cm × 69cm 1996 年
Gao Xue-nian "Fall" Chinese
69cm × 69cm Painting 1996

史玉，女，天津美术学院毕业。作品获全国首届职工美展一等奖，世界牡丹杯大赛二等奖，参加９６'广州国际艺术博览会，９７'中国艺术博览会。曾举办个展。作品在国内外多种刊物发表，被多国人士收藏。

Shi Yu, female, graduated from Tianjin Institute of Fine Art. Her works won a first prize in the first national workers fine art exhibition, a second prize in the world "Peony Cup" competition, and were on display in the '96 Guangzhou International Art Exposition and the '97 China Art Exposition. She has held solo exhibitions and had works published in journals at home and abroad; many were collected by collectors from different countries.

高学年，大专毕业。现为天津炎黄书画院画师，天津炎黄文化研究会书画院画师。作品曾入选全国"卫生之光"美展，获天津，河北书画联展一等奖，"迎世妇会"华联杯书画大赛铜奖，天津首届扇面展等。作品在多种报刊发表。部分作品被海内外人士收藏。

Gao Xue-nian, a graduate of junior college, is a painter of Tianjin Yan Huang Academy of Caliigraphy and Painting, and Tianjin Yanhuang Culture Research Society's Academy of Calligraphy and Painting. His works have been selected into the National "Light of Hygene" Fine Art Exhibition, and won a first prize in the Tianjin-Hebei Joint Exhibition of Calligraphy and Painting, a bronze prize in the Greeting the World Women's Conference "Hualian Cup" Competition of Calligrapy and Painting, etc. Many of his works have been published and part of the collected by art lovers at home and abroad.

王惠民 《晨露》 国画 69cm × 69cm 1997 年
Wang Hui-min "Morning Dewdrops"
69cm × 69cm Chinese painting 1997

陈学周《春意闹》 70cm × 80cm 国画 1997 年
Chen Xue-zhou "Spring Atmosphere"
70cm × 80cm chinese painting 1997

王惠民，毕业于天津美术学院，职业画家。专攻国画花鸟小写意。作品多次参加市及全国性美展并有获奖。９７年多幅作品在台湾展出。作品入编《海峡两岸书画名家作品集》,《世界当代著名书画家真迹博览大典》。现为天津炎黄画院特聘画师，天津老年大学国画教师。

Wang Hui-min graduated from Tianjin Institute of Fine Art and is now a professional painter. He specializes in flower-and-bird painting with works displayed and awarded in municipal and national exhibitions. He had a number of paintings shown in Taiwan. His works have been edited into the "Collection of Caliigraphic Works and Paintings by Famous Artists on the Two Sides of the Straits" and "Dictionary of Authentic Works by Famous Contemporary Calligrapher and Painters in the World".He is a guest painter of Yan Huang Academy of Paiting in Tianjin and a teacher of Chinese painting in Tianjin Senior Citizens University.

陈学周，职业画家。任天津炎黄文化书画院画师，中外书画家西安联谊画家，北京海天艺术中心特聘画家。作品入选《世界当代著名书画家真迹博览大典》,《海峡两岸名家书画集》等。不少作品被海内外藏家收藏。

Chen Xue-zhou, a professional painter, works in the Tianjin Yan Huang Cultural Academy of Calligraphy and painting and is a painter of the Xi'an Friendship Association of Chinese and Foreign Calligraphists and Painters. His works have been edited into the "Dictionary of Authentic Works by Famous Contemporary Calligraphists and Painters in the World" and the "Collection of Calligraphic Works and Paintings by Famous Artists on the Two Sides of the Straits". Quite a few of his works have been collected by art lovers at home and abroad.

张文君　《翰墨缘》　中国画　121cm × 157cm　1996年
Zhang Wen-jun "Link with Brush and Ink" Chinese Painting　121cm × 157cm　1996

张文君，1956年出生。华南艺大工艺美术系毕业。曾举办个
人展。作品《新课》入选全国美展，获首届红棉奖并刊登在
84年《美术》杂志封面。

zhang Wen-jun,born in 1956, he graduated from the Department of
Industrial Art of South-China Art University. His painting "A New Lesson"
participated in a National Fine Art Exhibition, won the first "Red Kapok
Award" and was selected as a cover picture of the magazine "Fine Art" in
1984.

武剑飞 《纸本山水》 国画 76cm × 51cm
Wu Jian-fei "Moutains and Rivers (Ink on Paper)
Chinese Painting 76cm × 51cm

武剑飞，现任哈尔滨新世纪书画院院长，哈尔滨市当代美术研究所所长，新世纪国际书画交流委员会主席。曾在北京、哈尔滨、广州、上海、俄罗斯、美国举办个展或联展。出版有《武剑飞画集》、《武剑飞山水画集》。

Wu Jian-fei, is president of Ha'erbin New Century Calligraphy and Painting Academy, president of Ha'erbin Contemporary Art Research Institute, and president of New Century International Exchange Committee of Calligraphy and Painting. He has held solo and joint exhibitions in Beijing, Ha'erbin, Guangzhou, Shanghai, Russia, and America. His publications include"Album of Wu Jian-fei's Paintings", and "Collection of Wu Jian- Fei's Landscape Paintings".

龚东庆 《夏日》油画 100cm × 100cm 1997 年
Gong Dong-qing "Summer" Oil Painting
100cm × 100cm 1997

黄克中 《锁》油画 100cmX85cm 1997 年
Huang Ke-zhong "A Lock" Oil Painting
100cm × 85cm 1997

黄克中，毕业于桂林地区教育学院美术系。多次参加全国美展、省美展及海外油画艺展。曾应邀赴马来西亚为最高元首及其夫人绘制巨幅油画肖像。现为职业画家。
电话：（0773）2612922

Huang Ke-zhong graduated from the Department of Fine Art of Guilin District Education Institute, and is now a professional painter. He participated in national, provicial, and overseas oil painting exhibitions for many times. He was invited by Malaysia to draw huge oil painting portraits for the state head and his wife.
Phone:(0773)2612922

龚东庆，毕业于广西艺术学院油画系。现为桂林地区教育学院美术系副主任、副教授，广西美协会员。《阳光下》获93' 博雅全国油画大赛优秀奖。多件作品在国内外展出并被出版和收藏。
电话：（0773）2822672-2131

Gong Dong-qing a graduate of the Department of Oil Painting of Guangxi Institute of Fine Art, Gong is an associate professor and vice dean of the Department of Fine Art in Guilin District Education Institute, and member of Guangxi Artists' Association. His "Under the Sun" won an Excellece prize in the 93' Boya National Oil Painting Competition. Many of his works have been exhibited, published, and collected in andout of China.
Phone:(0773)2822672-2131

叶永青 《溪畔树荫》 水中画 66cm × 66cm 1994 年
Ye Yong-qing "Shade by the brook" Painting in Water 66cm × 66cm 1994

叶永青，擅长山水，独创"水中画"，被刊入《中华之最》大辞典。曾在香港、新加坡、马来西亚等地举办个展。作品在海内外不少报刊发表。

Ye Yong-qing, is good at landscape painting. His special creation of painting in water is recorded in "No. 1 of China". He has held solo exhibitions in Hong Kong, Singapore, and Malaysia. Many of his works have been published by newspapers and journals in and out of China.

杨大生 《春江烟云》 国画 69cm×139cm 作于1997年
Yang Tian-sheng "Mist and Clouds over Spring River" Chinese Painting 69cm×139cm 1997

杨天生，福建美协会员。作品获省职工书画展铜牌、"天马杯"
国际书画大赛三等奖、省纪念毛主席诞辰一百周年美术书法
展三等奖、全国职工美术书法摄影展三等奖。

Yang Tian-sheng a member of Fujian Artists' Association, Yan was
awarded a bronze prize in a provicial workers' exhibition of calligraphic
work and painting, a third prize in the "Tian Ma Cup" International
Competition of Calligraphy and Painting, a third prize in the Provicial
Exhibition of Calligraphy and Painting in Commemeration of the 100
Anniversary of Chairman Mao's Birth, and a third prize in the National
Workers' Exhibition of Calligraphic, Painting, and Photographic Works.

陈春勇　《长城颂》　国画　120cm × 245cm　1997 年
Chen Chun-yong "Ode to the Great Wall"　Chinese Painting 120cm × 245cm　1997

陈春勇，中国书画家协会会员、中国青年美协会员。作品曾
在海内外美术大展中获金奖、一等奖、二等奖、优秀奖、银
奖各一次。
Chen Chun-yong is member of Painters' and Calligraphists' Association
of China, and member of China Young Artists' Association. His works
have won gold, silver, first, second, and excellence prizes in art exhibitions
in and out of China.

刘宗久　《雄风回归九龙还》　中国画　180cm × 96cm　1997 年
Liu Zong-jiu　"Magnificent Return of Nine Dragons"
Chinese Painting　180cm × 96cm　1997

刘宗久，1925年生。作品曾参加国内外大型画展并广被收藏。1996年参加新加坡"腾飞杯中国全国精品创作大赛"获精品金奖，并被授于"当代杰出书画家"荣衔，被国际16家艺术组织联合审定为"世界书画艺术名人"。

Liu Zong-jiu was born in 1925. Many of his works participated large scale exhibitions in and out of China, and were widely collected. In 1996, he won a gold prize in "Teng Fei Cup" National Creative Competition of Excellent Art Works" in Singapore, and was awarded the title of "Outstanding Contemporary Artist". Sixteen art societies in the world have appraised him as a "world famous artist of painting and calligraphy".

刘家振 《一带山河》 国画 180cm × 180cm 1997 年
Liu Jia-zhen "A Ribbon of Rivers and Mountains" Chinese Painting 180cm × 180cm 1997

刘家振，国家高级美术师、广州美术馆常务副馆长、省美协会员、市美协理事、澳门中华文化艺术协会特邀学术顾问。多次举办个展。作品曾参加国内外各类美展，获奖并被收藏。出版有《澳门风光画展图录》、《刘家振画选》。

Liu Jia-zhen is a state senior class artist, vice-president of the Guangzhou Art Gallery, member of the provincial Artists' Association, director of the Municipal Artists' Association, and specially invited academic consultant of Macau Chinese Culture and Art Society. He has held solo exhibitions for many times. His works have participated in exhibitions at home and abroad, being awarded and collected. His publications include "Catalog of Landscape Paintings of Macau", and " Selection of Liu Jia-zhen's Paintings".

乔卫明 《童趣》 中国画 65cm × 65cm 1996 年
Qiao Wei-ming "Children's Fun" Chinese Painting 65cm × 65cm 1996

乔卫明，洛阳铁路书画院院长。一级美术师。河南省美协会员。曾在广州美术学院国画系攻读研究生专业课程。作品入选第八届全国美展。多次参加大型画展并获奖。九五、九六年参加中国艺术博览会。出版有《乔卫明画集》。

Qiao Wei-ming is president of Luoyang Railway Academy of Calligraphy an Painting, a first class artist, and member of Henan Artists' Association. He has had his research courses in the Department of Chinese Painting of Guangzhou Institute of Fine Art. Many of his works have participated in large scale exhibitions such as the Eighth National Art Exhibition, and were rewarded. He took part in the China International Art Fair in 1996.The "Collection of Qiao Wei-ming's Paintings" has been published.

张惠斌 《林逋赏梅图》 中国画 118cm × 68cm
Zhang Hui-bin "Lin Bu Enjoying the Wintersweet" Chinese
Painting 118cm × 68cm

张惠斌，中国美协会员，国家一级美术师，锦州市国画研究会会长。曾在中国美术馆、广州美术馆、香港举办个展。出版有《张惠斌中国画集》、《张惠斌书画集》。作品被中国美术馆、日本前首相中曾根康弘等收藏。

陈炳佳　《离空而悟》　国画　68cm × 136cm　1994年
Chen Bing-jia　"Enlightened"　Chinese Painting
68cm × 136cm　1994

陈炳佳，1963年生于湖南。大学毕业。两次参加中国艺术博览会（广州），三次举办个人画展。作品多有被重要收藏。出版有《陈炳佳画集》。

电话：84219935转8654（办）　84219935转8674（宅）

Chen Bing-jin, born in 1963 in Hunan, a university graduate, Chen twice took part in the Guangzhou International Art Fair and has so far held personal exhibitions for three times. Many of his works are collected. His "Collection of Chen Bing-jia's Painting" has been published.

Tel No.: 84219925-8654 (W) 84219935-8674 (H)

陈炳佳 《景随心起》 国画 68cm × 136cm 1997 年
Chen Bing-jia "Scenes Rise in the Mind" Chinese Painting
68cm × 136cm 1997

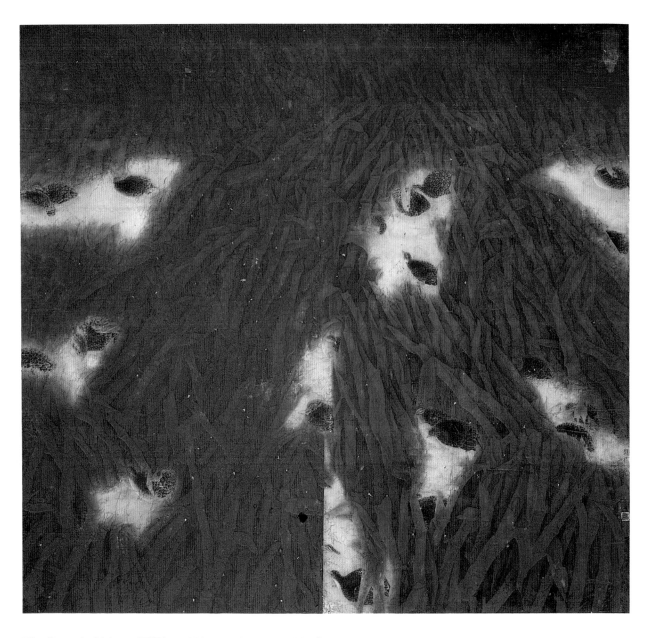

壁 光 《九月九》 国画 200cm × 200cm 1995 年
Bi Guang "Double Ninth Festival" Chinese Painting 200cm × 200cm 1995

壁光，原名陈亮，先后毕业深造于哈尔滨艺术学院、中央美术学院国画系。曾在北京、广州、香港举办壁光画展，作品入选全国第11届花鸟画邀请展。作品《生命》获黑龙江省教师美展一等奖，《天鹅湖》获"金街杯"金奖，《九月九》获"北国杯"美展金奖。

Bi Guang(Chen Liang)a graduate from Ha'erbin Art Institute, furthered his studies in the Department of Chinese Painting in the Centrual Institute of Fine Art, has held Bi Guang exhibitions in Beijing, Guangzhou, and Hongkong. His works participated in the 11th National Invitation Exhibition of Flower and Bird Painting. His "Life" was awarded a first prize in Heilongjiang Exhibition of Teachers' Art Work. and his "Double Ninth Festival" won a gold prize in "Bei Guo Cup" Art Exhibition.

陈英灿 《夏雨》 国画 61cm × 91cm 1984 年
Chen Ying-can "Summer Rain" Chinese Painting 61cm × 91cm

陈英灿，著名书画篆刻家，香港中国美术会会员，美国岭南画会会员。作品多次入选全国书法篆刻大展。97年获香港回归中国书画大展金奖。艺术成就入编多部艺术年鉴、博览会大典、香港名人录。

Chen Ying-can, a famous painter, calligraphist and seal cutter, Chen is member of Hongkong Artists' Association, and member of American Lingnan Painting Society. Many of his works have participated in national exhibitions of calligraphy and seal cutting. He won a gold prize in the Chinese Art Exhibition for the Return of Hongkong. His achievement has been edited in many art dictionaries and handbooks.

杨明（ 石翔 ） 《福》 书法 130cm × 70cm 1996 年
Yang Ming (Shi Xiang) "Happiness" Calligraphy 130cm × 70cm 1996

杨明，世界书画家协会理事。获首届 "淮河杯" 全国书画大赛特等奖、第三届国际书画艺术展评 "国际银奖"。作品被中外十几个国家级博物馆以及最高领导人珍藏，被编入《世界书画家大辞典》、《世界当代著名书画家真迹博览大典》。出版有《石翔现代书法选》。

Yang Ming is a director of the World Painters' and Calligraphists' Association. He won a special-class prize in the first "Huaihe Cup" National Competition of Painting and Calligraphic Works, and an Inational Silver Prize in the third International Exhibition of Calligraphic Works and Paintings. Many of his works have been collected by a dozen of national museums and state leaders of at home and abroad, andcollected in the "Dictionary of Famous Painters and Calligraphists in the World" and "Dictionary of Authenic Works by Famous Contemporary Painters and Calligraphists in the World".Among his publications isthe "Collection of Modern Calligraphic Works by Shi Xiang".

赵永家 《双虎图》 烙印画 150cm × 70cm
zhou Yong-jia "Two Tigers" Branded Painting 150cm × 70cm

赵永家，内蒙包头钢铁公司专职美工、中国美协内蒙分会会
员、包头市美协会员。1994、1995 年曾在包头市、呼和浩特
市举办个人烙画展。有 "烙虎第一人"、"虎威将军" 之称。多
幅作品被美国、台湾、香港等的收藏家收藏。

zhon Yong-jia,being titled the " first man to create branded tigers" and
"General of Fear-Inspiring Prowess", Zhou is a professional art worker
of Baotou Iron and Steel Company of Inner Mongolia, member of Inner
Mongolia Artists' Association, and member of Baotou Artists' Association.
He held personal exhibitions of branded painting in Baotou and Huhehaote
in 1994 and 1995. Many of his works have been collected by collectors
from the US, Taiwan, and Hongkong.

马松林 《天堂之行系列》 油画 50cm × 60cm 1997 年
Ma Song-lin "Travel in Heaven Series" Oil Painting 50cm × 60cm 1997

马松林,1964 年生于南京,1984 年于南京艺术学院进修。现为职业画家。曾多次参加江苏省及南京市举办的大型美展。1996年参加广州国际艺术博览会。作品多被国外收藏家收藏。

Ma Song-lin,born in Nanjing in 1964, Ma studied in the Nanjing Art Institute in 1984, and now is a professional painter. In 1996, he participated in the International Art Fair in Guangzhou. Many of his works are collected by art lovers at home and abroad.

陈 晶 《花鸟》 中国画 68cm × 68cm
Chen Jing "Flowers and Birds" Chinese Painting 68cm × 68cm22

陈晶，现为职业画家。曾进修于中央美院国画研修班。作品多次参加全国性美展并获奖。作品发表在《美术》、《北京日报》等数十家报刊上。曾在北京举办个展。作品入编《当代中国书画名人宝鉴》、《当代中国书画名人图录》。连续五届参加中国艺术博览会、广州国际艺术博览会。

Chen Jing is a professional artist who took refresher courses in the Central Institute of Fine Art. His works have participated in national exhibitions and been awarded. Many of them were published by such journals as "Fine Art" and "Beijing Daily". and collected in the "Dictionary of Contemporary Famous Painters and Calligraphists" and "Catelog of Famous Contemporary Chinese Painters and Calligraphists". He has held a personal exhibition in Beijing. He took part in five China International Expositions and the Guangzhou International Art Fair.

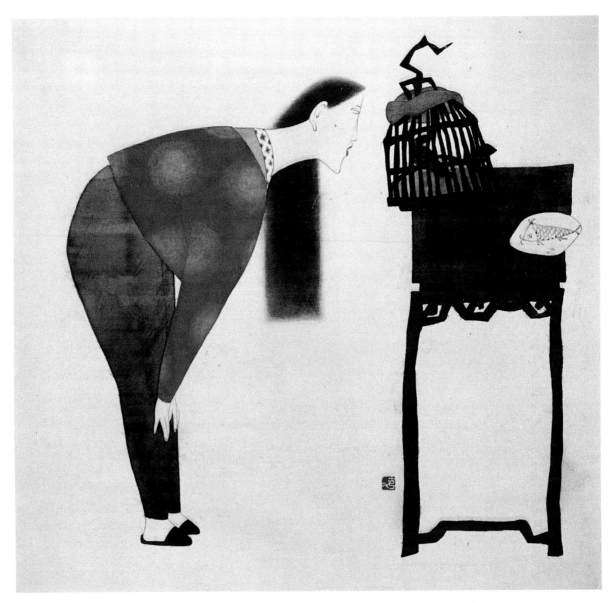

宋克冰 《人之初．性本善》系列之一 中国画 41cm × 43.8cm 1997 年
Song Ke-bin "Man's Nature is Good at Birth" Sery One Chinese
Painting 41cm × 43.8cm 1997

宋克冰，1992 年毕业于鲁迅美术学院中国画系。现执教于北京海淀职工大学美术系。《泉》入选中国当代工笔画二届大展，《秋菊》入选全国第八届美展，《静野》入选首届全国美术院校国画展优秀奖，并有作品入选中国艺术大展等大型展览。

Song Ke-bing graduated from the Department of Chinese Painting in Lu Xun Art Institute in 1992, and now is a teacher of the Art Department of Hai Dian Workers' University in Beijing. "The Spring" joined the Second Exhibition of Contemporary Chinese Gongbi Painting, "Autumn Chrysanthemum" in the Eighth National Fine Art Exhibition, and "TheTranquil Wilderness" won an excellence prize in the First Chinese Pianting Exhibition of National Art Institutes and Schools. Other works were on show in such exhibitions as the Grand Exhibition of Chinese Fine Art.

吴松山 《乡月最温柔》 中国画 64.5cm × 66cm 1997年
Wu Song-shan "Moon of Hometown is the Gentlest" Chinese Painting
64.5cm × 66cm 1997

中国美协黑龙江分会理事。曾在全国各地举办个人画展。作品参加过日本、香港、吉隆坡等地举办的大型国际艺术博览会、展览会。《春雨》在"全国牡丹竞选国花"画展获二等奖，《雪乡图》获省群星作品展金奖，《秋高气朗》获全国《新铸联杯》国画展优秀奖。

Wu Song-shan is director of Heilongjiang Artists' Association, who has held personal exhibitions in many cities of China. He took part in international art exhibitions held in Japan, Hongkong and Kuala Lumpur.His "Spring Rain" won a second prize in the exhibition of "Peonies - -National Flower Competition", "Snowy Country", a gold prize in the "Provincial Stars Exhibition of Art Works", and "Balmy Autumn Day", an excellence prize in the "Xin Zhu Lian Cup" National Chinese Painting Exhibition.

徐勤军 《春泉》 山水画 90cm × 69cm 1996 年
Xu Qin-jun "Spring Fountain" Chinese Painting 90cm × 69cm 1996

徐勤军，毕业于山东艺术学院美术系，后考入中央美院深造。曾应邀在新加坡、加拿大、香港等地举办个展。作品曾获澳大利亚－亚太地区水墨画大赛优秀奖、加拿大枫叶奖等多项国际奖。有不少作品在海内外报刊杂志上发表。出版有《徐勤军山水画集》。

Xu Qin-jin, graduated from the Art Department of Shandong Art Institute, Xu furthered his studies in the Central Institute of Fine Art. He was invited to hold personal exhibitions in Singapore, Canada, and Hongkong. His painting won an excellence prize in the "Australian-Asian-Pacific Area Competition of Chinese Inkwash Painting" and the "Canada Maple-leaf Prize". Many of his works have been published in newspapers and magazines in and out of China. The "Collection of Chinese Painting of Xu Qin-jun" has been published.

陈义水 《鱼乐》 中国画 73cm × 82cm 1996 年
Chen Yi-shui "Pleasure of Fish" Chinese Painting 73cm × 82cm 1996

陈义水,高级美术师,擅画鱼。先后在中国美术馆、香港、新
加坡、美国等地举办个展,并多次在国内国际性大赛中获奖。
作品收入《世界现代美术家辞典》、《世界名人录》等数部辞
书。出版有《陈义水画集》、《陈义水专辑》。

Chen Yi-shui is a senior class artist who is a fish-drawing master. He has
held solo exhibitions in the China National Art Gallery, Hongkong,
Singapore, and America, and won prizes in competitions in and out of
China. His works are collected into such books as the "Dictionary of
Modern Artists in the World", and "Who's Who of the World". His
publications include "Collection of Chen Yi-shui's Paintings", and "Special
Collection of Chen Yi-shui's Works".

祁 峰 《风雪六骆驼》 国画 92cm × 200cm 1996年
Qi Feng "Six Camels in Wind and Snow" Chinese Painting 95cm × 200cm 1996

祁峰，国家高级美术师，职业画家。曾在国内外举办个展，参加第三、四届中国艺术博览会。以画"骆驼"、"毛驴"闻名海内外。其中《八驴图》曾分别获"国际银奖"、"金奖"和"银奖"。作品被人民大会堂等中外博物馆、日中友协会长平山郁夫等收藏。出版有《祁峰书画选》。

Qi Fend is a state senior class artist and professional painter and calligraphist who has held solo exhibitions at home and abroad. He took part in the third and fourth China International Art Expositions. He is famous for his paintings of camels and donkeys. His "Eight Donkeys" has won "international silver", gold, and silver prizes. Hisworks have been collected by such museums as the Great Hall of the People, and by such people as the president of Sino-Japan Friendship Association. His publication is "Selection of Qi Feng's Paintings and Calligraphic Works".

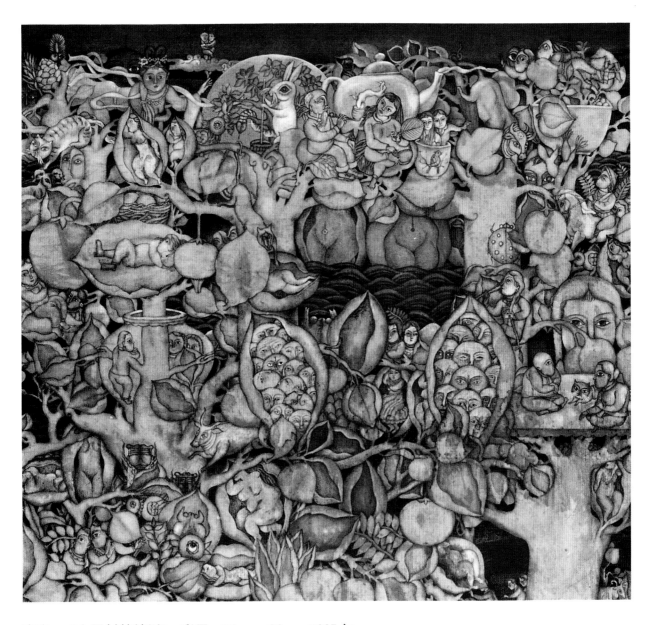

李富　《九凤村的神话》　彩墨　96cm × 96cm　1995 年
Li Fu "A Myth of Nine-Phoenix Village"　Color and Ink　96cm × 96cm　1995

李富，1987年毕业于山东师大美术系，现就职于中国成人教
育杂志社。作品曾参加86年中美艺术交流展，1997年分别在
北京、山东举办个展。作品在《中国教育报》、《人民日报》、
《中国文化报》、《香港大公周刊》等国内外十多种报刊杂志上
介绍发表。

Li Fu,Graduated from the Fine Art Department of Shandong Normal
University in1987. Li is now a member of China Adult Education
Magazine. His works joined a Sino-US Art Exchange Exhibition in
1986. He held solo exhibition in Beijing and Shandong respectively in
1997. His works have been published in a dozen of newspapers and
magazines at home and abroad, including " China Education," "People's
Daily","Chinese Culture" and "HongKong TaiKung Weekly".

陈韵竹　《情系葡萄沟》　国画　68cm × 68cm　1997 年
Chen Yun-zhu "Grape Valley Sentiment"　Chinese Painting　68cm × 68cm　1997

陈韵竹，南昌市八大山人纪念馆专业画家。毕业于广西艺术学院，现居珠海。作品多次入选全国、全省美术作品展。广东美协会员。

chen Yun-zhu a graduate of Guangxi Art Institute, she is a professional painter of Badashanren Memorial Hall in Nanchang City. At present, she resides in Zhuhai. Her works have been selected into national and provincial fine art exhibitions. She is a member of Guangdong Artists' Association.

墨丁　《鲤鱼》　中国画　135cm × 55cm　1996 年
Mo Ding　"Carps"　Chinese Painting
135cm × 55cm　1996

墨丁，1934 年出生。作品先后赴日本、香港、新加坡、欧洲
等地展出获好评。作品曾获 92 年中国画国际大展荣誉奖，93
年《毛泽东诞辰１００周年中华当代文化精粹博览会》佳作
奖，93 年第二届海内外中国书画篆刻大赛优秀奖。

Mo Ding, born in 1934, he has had works exhibited and highly praised in
Japan, Hong Kong, Singapore and Europe. His work won an honored
award in an international exhibition of Chinese paintings in 1992. In an
exposition of the cream of Chinese culture in commemoration of
MaoZedong's 100th birthday, he won an award of good work. In 1993,
he had an excellence award in the second competition of Chinese
calligraphy, painting and seal-cutting works from home and abroad in
1993.

代书斌　《高原的歌》　油画　51cm × 61cm
Dai Shu-bin　"Song of the Highland"　Oil Painting　51cm × 61cm

代书斌，1958年生于四川。四川省美术家协会会员。作品多次参加全国、省、市美展。作品曾在首届四川油画展获奖。1988年作品入选首届中国油画展。此外，作品还在加拿大、日本、香港及东南亚等国家和地区展出，多幅作品被国内外人士收藏。

Dai Shu-bin, born in 1958 in Sichun Province, Dai is member of Sichun Artists' Association. His works have been displayed in national, provincial and municipal fine art exhibitions and won awards in the First Oil Painting Exhibition of Sichuan. In 1988, his painting was selected into the First Chinese Oil Painting Exhibition. His works have been exhibited in Canada, Japan, Hong Kong and Southeast Asian countries. Quite a few of his paintings have been collected by domestic and foreign art lovers.

孟祥顺　《王中王》　中国画　66cm × 67cm　1995年
Meng Xiang-shun　"King of the Kings"　66cm × 67cm　1995

北方画廊　参展画家：孟祥顺、李行简、冯大中。
Bei Fang Gallery Participating Artists : Meng Xing-shun,Li xing-jian,Feng Da-zhong.

孟祥顺，1984年毕业于中央美术学院国画系。中国美协会员。1989年作品《春雪》参加全国美展并获奖。曾在海内外举办个人画展。巨幅作品《归家图》、《群虎图》被中央电视台、香港特别行政区收藏，《山野之魂》、《月下双雄》、《回归》分别被嘉德、荣宝、翰海等拍卖公司拍出高价。

Meng Xiang-shun, a graduate of the Chinese Painting Department of Central Fine Art Institute in 1984, he is a member of China Artists' Association. His "Spring Snow" joined and was awarded in the national fine artexhibition in 1989. He has held personal exhibitions both at home and abroad. His huge paintings "Homecoming" "Two Heroes In Moon" and "Tigers" were collected by CCTV and Hong Kong SAR. "The Spirit of the Wilderness" and "Turnover"were offered high prices by auction companies such as Jiade, Rongbao and Hanhai.

陈建功 《山东岱庙》 中国画 125cm × 125cm 1995年
Chen Jian-gong "Dai Temple in Shandong" Chinese Painting 125cm × 125cm 1995

陈建功，1960 年河北大学毕业后，在中央美院深造。一级美
术师。现任深圳《体育大观》杂志美术顾问。作品被多家出
版社出版挂历、影碟、录像带等。作品多次在国内外比赛中
获奖，并被国内外名家收藏。

Chen Jian-gong, after his graduation from Hebei University in 1960, he
furthered his studies in the Central Institute of Fine Art. He is a first-class
fine artist and art consultant of Shenzhen "Grand Sports" magazine. His
works have been turned into calendars, VCD's and tapes by many
publishers. Many have won prizes in domestic and foreign competitions,
and have been collected by celebrities at home and abroad.

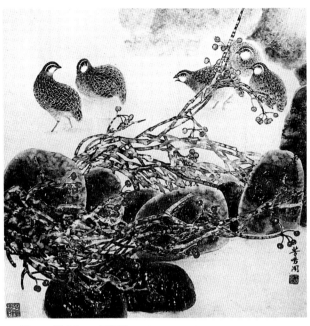

王伟，９６年进修于中央美术学院国画系。作品曾获全国扇面展金奖，入选全国第１２届花鸟展。现为吉林美协会员，四平书画院画家。

Wang Wei had further studies in the Chinese painting Department of the Central Institute of Fine Art, with works awarded a gold prize in the National Fan Painting Exhibition, and shown in the 12th National Flower and Bird Painting Exhibition. He is now a member of Jilin Artists' Association and a painter of Siping Academy of painting.

王伟 《浴雪》 国画 68cm × 68cm
Wang Wei "Snowbath" Chinese Painting
68cm × 68cm

吉林四平书画院
地址：四平市地直街9-1号 （136000）
电话：(0434) 3623410
参展画家：邓子欣，王伟，董才，鲁峰，薛军

Jilin Siping Academy of Painting
Add: 9-1, Dizhi Street, Siping City
Post Code: 136000
Participating Painters: Deng Zi-xin, Wang Wei, Dong Cai, Lu Feng, Xue Jun

邓子欣，中国美协会员，四平市美协主席，四平市书画院院长，一级美术师。多次参加国内外展并获奖。出版《邓子欣画辑》，《邓子欣仙鹤画集》等。

Deng Zi-xin is a member of China Artists' Association, chairman of Siping Academy of Calligraphy and Painting and a first-class artist. He has taken part in many exhibitions at home and abroad and won prizes.His publications include "Selection of Deng Zhi-xin's Paintings", "Collection of Deng Zhi-xin's Paintings of Cranes".

邓子欣 《密林深处》 国画
Deng Zi-xin "Deep in the Forest"
Chinese Painting

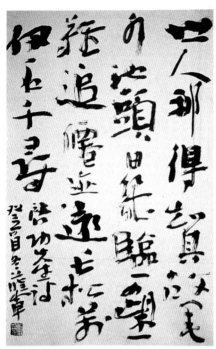

薛军书法
Xue Jun Calligraphy

薛军，现为中国书法家协会会员，四平市书协副主席兼秘书长，四平书画院专业书法家。作品多次参加国内外书法展。作品被中南海，毛主席纪念堂等收藏。

Xue Jun is a member of the China Calligraphists Association, vice-chairman and secretary-general of Siping Calligraphists' Associaiton and a professional calligrapher of Siping Academy of Calligraphy and Painting, with works participating in calligraphy exhibitions at home and abroad, and collected by Zhongnanhai and Chairman Mao's Memorial Hall.

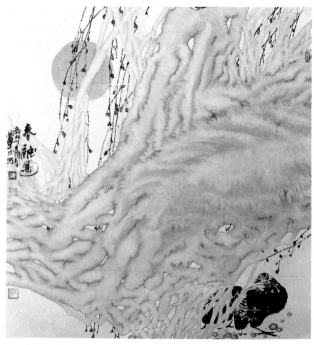

董才 《春融图》 国画 86cm × 98cm
Dong Cai "Snow Melting in Spring"
Chinese Painting 86cm × 98cm

董才，现为吉林美协会员，四平书画院画家。作品曾获国际牡丹杯优秀奖，画院联展一等奖。作品入选全国扇面展，中日友好协会主办的中国名家书画展。９７年在美国举办个展。

Dong Cai is a member of Jilin Artists' Association and a painter of Siping Academy of Calligraphy and Painting. His works won an excellence prize in the "Peony Cup" International Competition, a first prize in the joint exhibition of academies of painting. Besides, he had works selected into the national fan painting exhibition, and an exhibition of calligraphy and painting by famous Chinese painters sponsored by the Sino-Japanese Friendship Association. He held an individual painting exhibition in the US in 1997.

鲁峰 《关东爽秋》 国画 68cm × 68cm
Lu Feng "Crisp Autumn in the Northeast"
Chinese Painting 68cm × 68cm

鲁峰，天津工艺美院毕业。现为吉林美协理事，四平市美协秘书长，四平画院副院长。作品多次参加国内外美展并有获奖和被收藏。

Lu Feng, a graduate of Tianjin Institute of Industrial Fine Art, is a director of Jilin Artists' Association and vice-chairman of Siping Academy of Painting, with many works shown and awarded in domestic and foreign fine art exhibitions.

黄廷海　《沽酒入仙图》　中国画　68cm × 68cm　1994 年
Huang Ting-hai "Join the Fairies When Selling Wine"
Chinese Painting　68cm × 68cm　1994

黄廷海，早年师从傅抱石、亚明。修学于浙江美院。高级美术师。作品入选全国第一届山水画展。作品获"中日国际美术展"、全国"牡丹水墨画大展"金奖。1994年入选英国剑桥《世界名人录》。共九件作品在国内外拍卖成功。出版有《历代名家山水画要析》、《黄廷海中国画集》、《南方山水画派》等。

Huang Ting-hai student of Fu Bao-shi and Ya Ming at his early days, Huang later studied at the Zhejiang Institute of Fine Art, and is now a senior artist. Some of his works were selected into the First National. Exhibition of Landscape Painting, and some awarded gold prizes in "Sino- Japan International Exhibition of Fine Art", and "National Exhibition of `Peonies' Chinese Painting". In 1994, he was listed in the "Who's Who"(Cambridge, Britain).Nine paintings were sold successfully at auctions in and out of China. His publications include "Analysis of Landscape Paintings by Famous Artists Through the Ages", "Collectionof Huang Ting-hai's Chinese Painting", and "South Faction of Landscape Painting".

林玉宇 《大风起号》 中国画 181cm × 98cm 1994 年
Lin Yu-yu "Song of the Rising Wind" 181cm × 98cm 1994

林子宇，1950 年生。1983 年入中央工艺美术学院深造。现为
中国美协福建分会会员。莆田三江画院副秘书长。曾在国内
和香港举办个展。作品多次在国内国际大展中获奖。艺术生
平入编多部大型画集及辞典。

Lin Yu-yu, born in 1950, Lin furthered his studies in the Central Institute
of Industrial Art in 1983. He now is a member of the Fujian Artists'
Association, and the secretary-general of Putian Sanjiang Painting
Acadamy. He used to hold personal exhibitions in mainland and in
Hongkong. Many of his works have won national and international prizes.
His life as an artist has been compiled into many painting collections and
dictionaries.

黄继明　《风月无边》　中国画　98cm × 180cm　　1997 年
Huang Ji-ming "Gentle Breeze and Bright Moonlight" Chinese Painting　98cmX180cm　1997

黄继明，1948 年生于青岛。自幼酷爱绘画，犹擅画虎。作品
多次参加全国各类美展并广被收藏。

Huang Ji-ming born in Qingdao in 1948, Huang became fond of painting
when he was a child. He is especially good at tiger painting. His works
have been displayed in various kinds of fine art exhibitions and collected
by different people.

王靖忠 《花气袭人知画暖》 国画 105cm × 69cm
Wang Jing-Zhong "Flower Fragrance Reveals
the Warmth of Painting"
Chinese Painting 105cm × 69cm

聂振基 《雄踞》 国画 46cm × 42cm
Nie Zhen-ji "Imposing Crouch" Chinese
46cm × 42cm Painting

王靖忠，生于洛阳，洛阳工学院毕业。对牡丹怀有深厚感情。
《经济晚报》曾以《牡丹王》作专题报导。作品多次参加省市
美展并获奖。其作品受美国，日本，东南亚人士欢迎。现为
江西省美协会员，江西老同志大学副教授。

Wang Jing-zhong was born in Luoyang, and graduated from te Luoyang
Industry Institute. He has a deep love for peonies. "Economy Evening"
has given special report of his experience with the title of "King of Peony".
He has taken part in many exhibitions and been awarded. His works
receive warm welcome from people of America, Japan, and South-east
Asia. He is now a member of Jiangxi Artists' Association, and associate
professor of Jiangxi Old Comrades' University.

聂振基，现就职洪都航空工业集团公司工会。从事中国写意
花鸟画创作。作品入选全国首届花鸟画展，中国当代著名花
鸟画家作品展获优秀奖。作品曾在日本，南京等地展出。现
为江西省美协及省书协会员，中国航空美术家协会副主席。
国家二级美术师

Nie Zhen-ji is now working at the Workers' Union of the Hongdu Aviation
Industry Group Ltd. He is engaged in creation of freehand Chinese
flower and bird painting. His works were selected into the first
National Exhibition of Flower and Bird Painting, and the Exhibition ofof
Flower and Bird Paintings by Contemporary Chinese Artists (being
awarded an excellence prize). His works have been shown in Japan,
Nanjing, etc. He is now a member of Jiangxi Artists' Association, and
Calligraphists' Association, and vice president of China Aviation Artists'
Association.

罗锦雯 《归心似箭》 91cm × 61cm 1995 年
Luo Jin-wen "Anxious to Return" 91cm × 61cm 1995

罗锦雯，８９年江西师范大学美术系毕业。作品多次参加全
国展览及出国展，并在省展获奖。现为南昌美协理事，江西
省美协会员，南昌市２７中学教师。
电话：（０７９１）６２１１３３１

Luo Jin-wen is a graduate of the Fine Art Department of the Jiangxi
Normal University. His works have taken part in many exhibitions at
home and abroad, and were awarded in provincial shows. He is now
director of Nanchang Artists' Association, a member of jiangxi Artists'
Association, and a teacher of Nanchang No. 27 Middle School.
Tel:(0791)6211331

李少桦　《雪莲》　油画　108cm × 108cm　1997 年
Li Shao-hua "Snow Lotus"　Oil Painting 108cm × 108cm　1997

李少桦 《礼佛节》 油画 120cm × 120cm 1997 年
Li Shao-hua "Festival of Worshipping Buddha" Oil Painting 120cm × 120cm 1997

李少桦，女，广州美术学院毕业。广东美协会员。油画作品多次参加省市美展，曾获优秀奖，并在各大报刊，《广东画报》，《电视周刊》发表。作品被国内外机构及私人收藏。出版《心源——李少桦油画选》，彩绘中国故事集《狼姑娘》等。

Li Shao-hua, female, a graduate of the Guangzhou Institute of Fine Art, and member of Guangdong Artists' Association. Her oil painting works have taken part in many exhibitions, some of which were awarded excellence prizes, and published by such magazines as "Guangdong Pictorial", and "TV Weekly". Her works are collected by people and organizations at home and abroad. Her publications include "From My Heart -- Selection of Li Shao-hua's Oil Paintings", and "Lady Wolf", a color collection of Chinese stories.

康宏博 《金秋》 国画 97cm × 90cm 1997 年
Kang Hong-bo "Golden Autumn" Chinese Painting 97cm × 900cm 1997

康宏博，辽宁教育学院美术系毕业，后在中央美院深造。现为本溪市第二制药厂美术装潢总设计，辽宁美协会员。作品入选全国首届山水画展，全国第 8 届美展等。多次参加广州，北京的艺术博览会。出版《康宏博山水画集》。大量作品被海内外人士和博物馆收藏。

Kang Hong-bo graduated from the Department of Fine Art, Liaoning Education College, and furthered his studies at the Central Institute of Fine Art. He is now general designer of decoration art in the Second Pharmaceutical Factory in Benxi, and a member of Liaoning Artists' Association. His works have been selected into the first National Exhibition of Landscape Painting, the 8th National Exhibition of Fine Art, etc., and collected by people and museums in and out of China. He has taken part in art expositions held in Guangzhou and Beijing for many times. His publications include "Collection of Kang Hong- bo's Lanscape Painting".

路仁茂　《乳虎》　国画　　68cm × 68cm　　1997 年
Lu Ren-mao "Baby Tigers"　Chinese Painting　68cm × 68cm　1997

路仁茂，５０年生于河北衡水市。现为北京职业画家，以画
动物为主，尤擅画乳虎。作品多次参加国内外画展，曾获９
５ "俊隆杯" 美展铜奖。

Lu Ren-mao was born in Hengshui, Hebei Province in 1950. He is
aprofessional artist in Beijing who is engaged in animal painting,
especially in baby tigers. His works have participated in many exhibitions
held in and out of China, and won a bronze prize in the '95"Junlong Cup"
Exhibition of Fine Art.

韩浪的陶艺　　　　1 9 9 6 年
"Hanlang's Pottery Art"　　1996

千艺的陶艺　　　 **１９９７年**
"Qianyi' Pottery Art"　 1997

千艺美术陶瓷厂，是一间用变革性新概念生产时代风格陶艺
的厂家。它有一批艺术院校的艺术家和陶艺设计师于它共同
成长，愿为人类留下永恒艺术享受。
地址：广东省佛山市五峰路大江同建第二工业区（52800）
电话／传真：（0757）2212486

Qianyi Factory of artistic is a factory making modern potteryworks with
new concepts innovation. It has a lot of artists and potterydesigners from
different art colleges growing with it,and it hopes to bring eternal art
enjoyment to all people.
Add:Second Industrial Zone of Dajiangtongjian, Wufeng Rd., Foshan,
Guangdong
Post Code: 528000
Tel/Fax: (0757)2214486

卢秋 《复苏》 国画 68cm × 68cm 1996年
Lu Qiu "Back to Life" Chinese Painting 68cm × 68cm 1996

卢秋，曾就读于中国美术学院，辽宁美协会员，职业画家。8
8年入编《中国当代美术家名人录》。作品多次参加国内外展
并获奖。作品分别被中国美术学院，浙江省博物馆收藏。9
5，96，97年四次参加北京和广州的艺术博览会。95
年两次在广东举办个展。
地址：辽宁省锦州市广州街四段９７号（１２１０００）
电话：（０４１６）２８２４１２５，２１３８０５５

Lu Qiu, a professional artist, has studied in the China Institute of Fine
Art, and is now a member of Liaoning Artists' Association. His name
was edited into the "Album of Contemporary Famous Chinese Artists".
He has taken part in exhibitions at home and abroad and been awarded
for many times. His works were collected by China Institute of Fine Art,
and Zhejiang Provincial Museum. He has participated into art
expositionsheld in Beijing and Guangzhou for four times from 1995 to
1997, and held solo exhibitions in Guandong twice in 1995.
Add:97, Section 4, Guangzhou St., Jinzhou, Liaoning
Post Code: 121000
Tel: (0416)2824125, 2138055

陈少梅 《山水》 国画 39cm × 66cm 1945 年
Chen Shao-mei "Landscape" Chinese Painting
39cm × 66cm 1945

陈少梅（１９０４．４－１９５４．９），男，湖南衡山人，
自少习画，２１岁时作品获比利时建国百年国际博览会美术
银奖。长期在天津从事书画创作和教学。多次在北京，天津
举办个展。生前为天津市美协主席，天津美术学校校长。不
少作品被中国美术馆和省市博物馆收藏。出版《陈少梅画
集》。

Chen Shao-mei(April 1904--Sept. 1954), male, native Hunan
Hengshan,began to study painting in his childhood. When he was 21, his
works gained a silver art prize in the Belgium International Exposition
Celebrating the 100 Anniversary of the Founding of the Country. He has
been engaged in creation and teaching of painting and calligraphy in
Tianjin, and held solo exhibitions in Beijing and Tianjin for many times.
He was president of Tianjin Artists' Associaition, and Tianjin Art School.
Many of his works have been collected by such museums as the China
National Gallery of Fine Art. His publications include "Collection of
Chen Shao-mei's painting".

周韶华　《八百里洞庭唯此独秀》　国画　66cm × 132cm　　1997 年
Zhou Shao-hua "The Most Beautiful Place in the Eight-Hundred-Li Dongting Lake"
Chinese Painting　66cm × 132cm　　1997

周韶华，华中理工大学，武汉大学兼职教授，７８年任湖北
美术学院长。曾在北京，香港，台湾，广州，深圳，新加坡，
日本，瑞士，泰国等举办个展。出版《大河寻源》，《周韶华
画辑》和多部理论专著。

Zhou Shao-hua, part-time porfessor of Huazhong University of Science
and Engineering, and Wuhan University. He was president of Hubei
Institute of Fine Art in 1978. He held solo exhibitions in Beijing,
Hongkong, Taiwan, Guangzhou, Shenzhen, Singapore, Japan,
Switzerland, and Thailand. His publications include such theoretical
works as "Seeking the Origin of the River" and "Collection of Zhou Shao-
hua's Paintings".

于景才 《初雪》 国画 69cm × 69cm 1997 年
Yu Jing-cai "First Snow" Chinese Painting 69cm × 69cm 1997

于景才，高级美术师，辽宁美协会员，中国书画家协会会员。曾在鲁迅美术学院国画山水班进修。瑞雪山水画多次在全国大赛获奖。个人小传载入《中国当代艺术名人大辞典》等10部辞典。出版《于景才画集》，《中国当代美术精品—于景才专集》。曾获抚顺政府颁发"腾飞奖"。作品被多国人士收藏。

Yu Jing-cai is a senior artist, a member of Liaoning Artists' Association, and of China Artists and Calligraphists' Assocaition. He has further his studies in the Chinese landscape painting class in the Luxun Institute of Fine Art. His snow landscape paintings have been awarded many times in national competitions. His biography was listed in such dictionaries as "Dictionary of Contemporary Chinese Artists". His publications include "Collection of Yu Jing-cai's Painting", and "Contemporary Chinese Refined Art Works--Special Collection of Yu Jing-cai". He was awarded a "Tengfei" prize by the Fushun municipal goverment. His works are collected by people from many countries.

赵净，６６年出生。８６－８９年在南京艺术学院学习。
９２年进修于中国美术学院。作多次参加省市美展。不少作
品被新加坡，台湾，香港人士收藏。现为职业画家。
电话：（025）6420429

Zhao Jing, born in 1966, studied in the Nanjing Art Institute from 1986 to
1989, and furthered his studies in the Central Institute of Fine Art in
1992, with works displayed in provincial and municipal exhibitionsof
fine art; quite a few of his paintings were collected by people from
Singapore, Taiwan and Hong Kong. He is now a professional painter.
Tel:(025) 6420429

赵净　《皖南民居》　油画　60cm × 80cm　1997 年
Zhao Jing　"Houses of the Locals of South Anhui"
Oil Painting　60cm × 80cm　1997

张黎明　《嫁女》　油画　85cm × 60cm　1997 年
Zhang Li-ming "Daughter Being Married Off"
Oil Painting　85cm × 60cm　1997

张黎明，８７年南京艺术学院毕业。作品多次参加全国展览，
曾在《美术》，《画廊》和《江苏画刊》发表。
电话：（020）4511670

Zhang Li-ming graduated fron the Nanjing Institute of Fine Art, with
works participating national exhibitions many times and published in "Fine
Art", "Art Gallery", and "Jiangsu Pictorial".
Tel: (025) 4511670

郭同江　《渔织女》　国画　　80cm × 62cm　　1993 年
Guo Tong-jiang "Fisherwoman Weaver" Chinese Painting
80cm × 62cm　　1993

郭同江，５０年开始习画。获黄新坡，关山月等指导。创作
了大批现代题材作品。《渔女春秋》，《开工之前》，《理发师》
等曾获省和中央鼓励。作品多次参加国内外美展，发表近
2000 件。出版画册 4 本，举办个展 4 次。现为东莞市美协主
席。

Guo Tong-jiang began to study painting in 1950, and was guided by such
famous artists as Huang Xin-bo, and Guan Shan-yue. He created many
works of modern subjects. His "Life of Fisherwomen", "Before Work",
and "A Barber" have been awarded by the provincial and central
governments. His works have participated into many exhibitions at home
and abroad, with nearly 2000 of them published. He has 4 publications of
his won, and has held personal exhibitions 4 times. Now he is president
of Dongguan Municipal Artists' Association.

青岛市雅族陶艺工作室　《附着的生灵》　陶艺　30cm　1995年
Qingdao Yazu Pottery Art Workshop　"Life Attached"
Pottery 30cm　1995

青岛市雅族陶艺工作室

青岛市北区振兴路37号

邮编：266021

电记：3813287，01396427136

参展画家：万里雅，现任职青岛雅族陶艺工作室。88年毕业于青岛远洋学院。作品曾获青岛市10佳美术新人奖，青岛市首届中国雕刻艺术大奖赛大奖。

Qingdao Yazu Pottery Art Workshop
Add: 37 Zhenxing Road, North District, Qingdao
Post Code: 266021
Tel: 3813287, 01396427136
Participating Painter: Wan Li-ya graduated from Qingdao Ocean Collegein 1988. He is now a member of Yazu Pottery Art Workshop. His works wona New Artist Prize in the Qingdao "Ten Best in Fine Art", and a grand award in the first Chinese Carving Competition in Qingdao.

张平树　《虎》　榜书（ 宣纸 ）　　133cm × 66cm　　1996 年
Zhang Ping-shu "Tiger"　Bangshu Calligraphy
133cm × 66cm　1996

张平树，中国书法家协会会员，山东画院画师，擅写榜书。作品入选中国书协举办的新人作品展，中日、中韩书法展。95年在中国美术馆举办个展。96年赴日本举办巡回展。作品被多家国家博物馆，及张学良将军、马哈蒂尔首相等名人收藏。出版《榜书浅说》，《榜书技法》等。

Zhang Ping-shu is a member of the China Calligraphists' Association, and a painter of Shandong Academy of Painting, zhang is good at Bangshu Calligraphy. His works have been selected into the Exhibition of New Works by New Artists, Sino-Japan and Sino-Korean Calligraphy Exhibitions. He held solo exhibitions in the China National Gallery of Fine Art in 1995, and made an exhibition tour in Japan in 1996. Many state museums and such celebrities as General Zhang Xue-liang have collected his works. "Brief Introduction to Bangshu Calligraphy" and "Techniques of Bangshu Calligraphy" are among his publications.

王俊英 《等》 油画 100cm×80cm 1997年
Wang Jun-ying "Waiting" Oil Painting
100cmX80cm 1997

王俊英，女，70年出生。职业画家，辽宁美协会员。曾在
鲁迅美术学院油画系研修。作品多次参加全国及省美展。并
为美国，香港，台湾，马来西亚，新加坡人士收藏。

Wang Jun-ying, female, born in 1970, is a professional painter and a
member of Liaoning Artists Association. She has taken research studies
in the Oil Pianting Department of Lu Xun Institute of Fine Art. Her works
have been on display in national and provincial exhibitions and collected
by people from the U.S., Hong Kong, Taiwan, Malaysia and Singapore.

刘勐 《午后》 油画 55cm×46cm 1996年
Liu Meng "After Noon" Oil Painting
55cm×46cm 1996

刘勐，沈阳教育学院美术系毕业。现为辽宁美协会员。作品
入选全国第8届美展，中国第2届静物油画展，第4届全国
体育美展等。作品还在泰国，新加坡和台湾等地展出。

Liu Meng graduated from the fine art department of the Shenyang
Education College. He is a member of Liaoning Artists Association, with
works selected into the 8th National Exhibition of Fine Art, the 2nd
China Exhibition of Still-life Oil Paintings and the 4th National Exhibition
of Sport Fine Art. He also has works exhibited in Thailand, Singapore
and Taiwan.

亚英 《瓶花》 国画 1995年作
Ya Ying "Flowers in vase" Chinese Painting 1995

亚英，１９５６年生。自幼酷爱绘画。师承花鸟画家陈永锵
先生。曾任南海工艺美术厂美工。

Ya Ying was born in 1956. He has shown great love of painting since he
was a child and studied under the instruction of Mr.Cheng Yong-qiang, a
master of flower-and-bird painting. He used to be a painter in the Nanhai
Industrial Art Factory.

李晓林　《爱尼楼》　油画　　80cm × 60cm　　1997 年
Li Xiao-lin "House of the Ainis"　Oil Painting　80cm × 60cm　1997

李晓林，现为广东佛山《小草屋》成员。８３年毕业于吉林
艺术学院。作品曾参加吉林首届青年美展，星河展并获奖。作
品曾在日本，法国，新加坡和香港等地展出。出版《中外历
史典故》彩色连环画等。

Li Xiao-lin is a member of Foshan "Small Thatched Cottage" society.
Hegraduated from the Jilin Art Institute in 1983, and took part in the first
Jilin Youth's Exhibition of Fine Art, and "Star River" Exhibition and
were awarded. His works have been shown in Japan, France,Singapore,
and Hongkong. His publications include color story book "Historic
Allusions of China and Foreign Countries".

戚大成 《馨春》 国画 187cm × 96cm 1997 年
Qi Da-cheng "Warm Spring" Chinese Painting
187cm × 96cm 1997

戚大成，中国美协辽宁分会会员。多次参加国内外大展并获
奖。先后四次参加广州国际艺术博览会，９４年在日本举行
个展。多幅作品在各种刊物上发表并被国际友人收藏。入编
《中国当代艺术家名人大辞典》等十余部辞书。
电话：0414-4832684

Qi Da-cheng is a member of Liaoning Artists' Association. He took part
in exhibitions at home and abroad and was awarded many times. He has
four times participated in international art fairs, and he held a solo
exhibition in Japan in 1994. Many of his works were published in
journals and collected by people aroud the world. Dictionaries such as
"Dictionary of Famous Contemporary Chinese Artists" have his name.
Tel: 0414-4832684

杜兴久 《故里山花此时开》 国画 180cm × 960cm 1997 年
Du Xing-jiu "Moutain Flowers at Home Blooming" Chinese Painting
180cm × 960cm 1997

杜兴久，著名画家冯大中入室弟子。作品多次参加国内外大
展，多次获奖。多幅作品被中外名人收藏。入编《当代书画
篆刻家》，《当代文艺家》等。现为辽宁美协会员，辽宁国画
研究会会员。

Du Xing-jiu is a student of Feng Da-zhong, a famous painter. His works
have participated in many exhibitions at home and abroad, awarded and
collected. His name has been entered into dictionaries such as
"Contemporary Painters, Calligraphists, and Artists of Seal Cutting", and
"Contemporaries of Literature and Art". He is now a member of Liaoning
Artists' Association, and Liaoning Research Society of Chinese Painting.

陈为中　《雨后》　水彩　80cm×54cm　　1996年
Cheng Wei-zhong "After the Rain"　Water Color 80cm×54cm　　1996

陈为中，中国美术协会会员，安徽省美协会员，高级工艺美术师。曾3次参加全国科普美展。93年获深圳"全国书画印大赛"水彩画金奖。95年在香港举办个人水彩画展。97年参加中国艺术博览会获优秀作品奖。作品在美国等地展出发表并被收藏。

Cheng Wei-zhong, a senior artist, is a member of China Artists' Association, and Anhui Artists' Association. He has taken part in the National Science Art Exhibition for 3 times, and won a gold prize in the '95 National Competition of Painting, Calligraphic, and Seal-cutting Works, and an excellence prize in the '97 China Art Exposition. He held a solo water color exhibition in Hongkong in 1995. His works were published, exhibited, and collected in the U.S..

李跃 《彝族图腾木雕》 木雕 120cm × 80cm 1990 年
Li Yue "Wood Carving of Yi Nationality's Totem" Wood Carving
120cm × 80cm 1990

李跃，中央文化管理干部学院毕业。曾在云南省博物馆，墨西哥驻华大使馆举办个展。作品多次在北京等地展出发表。现为中国美协云南分会会员。９５年被联合国教科文组织和中国文联授予"中国民间工艺美术家"称号。

Li Yue, a graduate of the Central Culture Management Institute for Cardres, is now a member of Yunnan Artists' Association. He has held solo exhibitions in Yunnan Provincial Museum, and Mexico Embassy in China. His works have been exhibited and published in many places. In 1995, he was awarded the title of "Chinese Folk Artist" by UNESCO and the Chinese Writers' Association.

聂天雄 《赤壁赋》 国画 138cm × 68cm 1995 年
Nie Tian-xiong "Versified Prose of Chibi Cliff"
Chinese Painting 138cm × 68cm 1995

聂天雄，自幼酷爱绘画，至今苦学不缀。专攻人物，兼山水
花鸟。作品发表于多家报刊杂志，为国内外友人收藏。《山魂》
获全国冶金系统书画赛一等奖。省级及专业季刊上均有介绍。

Nie Tian-xiong began to love drawing when he was a child and has been
ardently studying painting since now. He specializes in figure painting
and is also good at landscape, flower and bird painting. His works have
been introduced and published by many newspapers and journals, and
collected by people in and out of China. His "Spirit of Mountains"
won a first prize in the National Metallurgical System Competition of
Painting and Calligraphy.

封尘 《立冬》 油画 116cm × 73cm
Feng Chen "The Beginning of Winter"
Oil Painting 116cm × 73cm

封尘，中国美协北京分会会员。曾参加全国第2届青年美展。在国际书画大展中获特别奖。95年在中国美术馆办个展。96年在北京艺术馆举办肖像油画展。96，97年参加北京，广州的艺博会。出版有个人油画集。

Feng Chen is a member of Beijing Artists' Association. He took part in the Second National Youth's Exhibition of Fine Art, and won a Special Prize in the International Exhibition of Painting and Calligraphy. He held a solo exhibition in the China National Gallery of Fine Art in 1995 and an exhibition of oil painting portraits in the Beijing Art Gallery in 1996. He joined in the '96 Beijing and '97 Guangzhou Art Expositions. He has his collection of oil painting published.

王有政　《塔吉克母子图》　国画　145cm × 73.5cm　1985 年
Wang You-zheng "Tajik Mother and Son" Chinese Painting 145cm × 73.5cm 1985

王有政，西安美术学院毕业。国家一级美术师，中国美协会员，陕西美协常务理事。作品曾获第 5 届全国美展银牌奖，第 6 届全国美展铜牌奖。作品在苏联，日本，美国等地展出。现为陕西国画院创作室主任。

Wang You-zheng, a graduate of the Xi'an Institute of Fine Art, is a member of China Artists' Association, a director of Shanxi Artists' Association, and a state first class artist. His works have been shown in Russia, America, and Japan, and won a silver prize in the 5th National Exhibition of Fine Art, and a bronze in the 6th. He is now studio's director of the Shanxi Chinese Painting Academy.

乔玉川 《老志悟道》 国画 138cm × 69cm 1997 年
Qiao Yu-chuan "Laozhi Realizing the Truth"
Chinese Painting   138cm × 69cm   1997

西安秦宝斋画廊参展画家　王有政，乔玉川
Participating Artists of Qing Baozai Art Gallery,
Xi'an
Wang You-zheng, Qiao Yu-chuan

乔玉川，西安美术学院中国画系毕业，高级美术师，中国美
协陕西分会会员，西北书画院研究院院长。上１００件作品
被各家出版社出版发行，在国内外多次画展中获奖。各大报
刊及电影曾作专题报导。

Qiao Yu-chuan graduated from the Chinese Painting Department of Xi'an
Institute of Fine Art, and he is a senior class artist, a member of Shanxi
Artists' Association, and president of the Research Institute of Xibei
Institute of Painting and Calligraphy. Over 100 of his works have been
published and won prizes in many art exhibitions at home and abroad,
with special reports by newspapers and films.

梁根祥 《堤岸清晨》　水彩　110cm X 80cm　　1996年
Liang Gen-xiang "Early Morning on the Embankment"　Water Color　110cmX80cm　1996

梁根祥,广东佛山艺专毕业。87年起先后任佛山雕塑院院长和佛山美协副主席。作品常参加国内外展并获奖。多次在海内外举办个展。出版《梁根祥风景画集》。

Liang Gen-xiang graduated from the Guangdong Foshan Art School. He has become president of Foshan Sculpture Institute, and vice chairman of Foshan Artists' Association successively from 1987. His works were on display and awarded often in exhibitions at home and abroad; and he held solo exhibitions overseas many times. Among his publications is "Collection of Liang Gen-xiang's Landscape Paintings".

罗志奇 《不羁的风》 雕塑 110cm × 60cm × 40cm 1997 年
Luo Zhi-qi "Uninhibited Wind" Sculpture 100cm × 60cm × 40cm 1997

罗志奇，广东省美协会员。作品《李宁盘旋》获１１届亚运会广东省优秀奖。《定海神针》获省二等奖并入选中国体育美展。现任职佛山雕塑院，成立罗志奇雕塑工作室。

Luo Zhi-qi is a member of the Guangdong Artists' Association. His "Li Ning Spiral" won the Guangdong excellence prize in the 11th Asian Sports Meets, and "The Magic Needle Calming the Sea" won a provincial second prize and was selected into the national sports art exhibition. He now works at the Foshan Institute of Sculpture, with his own Luo Zhi-qi Sculpture Studio.

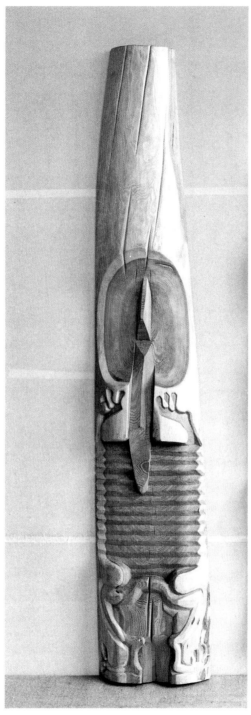

真言雕艺工作室　　红松木雕　　140cm × 26cm　　1997 年
Zhenyan Studio of Sculpture Art　　Woodcut of Red Wood 140cm × 26cm　　1997

真言雕艺工作室，由聋人组成的艺术创作群体。旨在开发聋人的艺术创造潜力。运用聋人独特的造型语言研究创作高品位的艺术作品。97年5月在中国美术馆举办《无言的心声》木雕展。《人民日报》，中央电视台等作了报导。部分作品被中国美术馆收藏，获97中国艺术博览会优秀作品奖。
地址：山东济南市济微路９６号（２５００２２）
电话：（０５３１）７９７３４０２

Zhenyan Studio of Sculpture Art is an art group organized by deaf people in order to bring out their potentials in art creation. The artists study and create high class art works with unique plastic languages of deaf people. In May of 1997, they held a woodcut exhibition named "Wordless Aspirations" in the China National Gallery of Fine Art, which was reported by "People's Daily" and CCTV. Some of their works are collected by the China National Gallery of Fine Art, and won an excellence prize in the '97 China Art Exposition.

朱全增 《情寄潇湘》 国画
Zhu Quan-zeng "Sentiment on Bamboos" Chinese Painting

朱全增，毕业于山东师范大学美术系，现为中国美协山东分会理事、山东画院高级画师。曾在济南、深圳、珠海、杭州、香港等地举办个展，其作品在国内、国际举办的大型美展中获大奖三次，金奖五次、银奖五次、铜奖两次。出版有《中国画集》、《中国朱增全画集》.

Zhu Quan-zeng, a graduate of the Fine Art Department of Shandong Normal University, He is now director of Shandong Artists' Association and senior painter of Shandong Painting Academy. He held solo painting Exhibitions in Jinan, Shenzhen, Zhuhai, Hangzhou and Hong kong so far have won three grand awards, five gold, five silver and two bronze prizes. His publications include "Colledtion of Chinese Paintings" and "Paintings" by Zhu Zeng-quan".

朱全增　《有情牡丹含春泪》　国画
Zhu Quan-zeng "Sentimetal Spring Peony with Tears"
Chinese Painting

柳之雄 《汉作青带山如碧玉簪》 国画 176cm × 90cm
Liu Zhi-xiong "A belt-like River and Jade-Green Hills" Chinese Painting 176cm × 90cm

柳之雄，中国美协广东分会会员，曾任中国美协广西分会理事。作品曾多次获奖。91年在加拿大举办个展，深受赞誉，不少作品被国内外友人珍藏。出版有《柳之雄作品选集》。入刊《中国当代美术家人名大辞典》

Liu Zhi-xiong member of the Guangdong Artists' Association, Liu was a director of Guangxi Artists' Association. Mnay of his works have been awarded and collected by domestic and foreign art lovers. He held in Canada solo exhibitions in 1991, and was highly praised. His publication is "Selection of Liu Zhi-xiong's Works". His name has been edited into "Dictionary of Contemporary Chinese Fine Artists".

克丽丝蒂·特佳 《利贝卡之一》　丙烯　102cm×92cm　1996年
Kirsti Taxgaard "Rebecca 1"　Acrylic on Canvas　102cm×92cm　1996

克丽丝蒂·特佳，挪威艺术学校毕业，曾在丹麦皇家艺术学
院，法国，意大利，希腊等地学习。曾在挪威，丹麦举办个
展和联展。

Kirsti Taxgaard, graduated from a school of art in Norway, studied
at the Gemark Royal Academy of Art, and in such countries as
France, Italy and Greece. He has held exhibitions, both individually
and jointly,　in Norway and Denmark.

戴恩·维拉　《热带花上的青蛙》　丙烯　740cm × 490cm　　1997 年
Dean Vella　"Frog On Tropical Flowers"　Acrylic 740cm × 490cm　　1997

戴恩·维拉的丙烯画色彩明快，以自然景色为主。他在光线交叉运用上具有突破性发展，其独特的技巧使他在艺术世界占有一席地位。他的作品多被机构和私人收藏。

Dean Vella's vibrant impasto acrylic's are characteristic of light and bright colors, often with nature as their themes. His breakthrough in the alternative use of light and unique techique assure him a place in the world of art. Dean Vella's paintings are included in some of the most prestigious collections, both corporate and private.

雷蒙．饶可让 《钢笔画第77号》 淡彩钢笔画 60cm×75cm 1982年
Raymond Georagein "Pen & Ink Drawing No. 77" Ink Drawing with light color
60cm × 75cm 1982

雷蒙．饶可让，法国著名画家。曾在世界各地举办个人画展，中国美术馆举办《绘画回顾展》文化部主办，在西安美术学院讲学并举办行个展。出版有《迷狂的独行者》。

Raymond Georagein, a famous French artist, Georagein has held personal exhibitions around the world, including "Painting Review" in China National Art Gallery (Sponsored by the ministny of Gulture). He also held lectures and a personal exhibition in Xi'an Institute of Fine Art. Among his publications is "A Confused and Feverish Lone Roamer".

帕拉·杰立佛　　《青年》　　油画　　110cm × 75cm　　　1997 年
Palla Jeroff　"Young Man"　　Oil Painting　　110cm × 75cm　　　1997

帕拉·杰立佛获中国水彩画奖。　其油画《青年》极好地揉
合了东西方艺术风格，确为一位前途光明，备受赞誉的国际
性画家。

Palla Jeroff won the Inaugural China National Watercolor Prize. In his
oil painting "Young Man" demonstrats the fusion of eastern and
western art syles. Palla is an international　artist of great merit with a
very promising future.

索文·库玛尔 《文明的融合》 混合材料 40 × 50 × 5cm 1997年
Sovan Kumar, 《Fusion of Culture》 Mixed Media 40 × 50 × 5cm 1997

索文·库玛尔，1969年生于印度浦瓦内瓦尔。根据中印文化
交流协定，目前在北京从事艺术创作。1992年毕业于浦瓦内
斯瓦尔工艺美术学院，1995年获瓦拉纳西视觉艺术系硕士学
位。作品曾多次参加国际、国家级和邦一级画展，并荣获国
家和邦一级奖。1997年在北京保利大厦举办个展。部分作品
被印度主要画廊、博物馆及收藏家收藏。

Sovan Kumar, born in 1969 in Bhubaneswar, India; graduated from
B.K. College of Arts and Crafts, Bhubaneswar in 1992, obtained
master's degree from faculty of visual arts, Varanasi in 1995;
participated in many national and international ex.; held solo ex. in
Poly Plaza Gallery in 1997 (Beijing); awarded in state and national
ex.; works were collected by major Indian art galleries, museums
and private collectors; now working in Bejing.

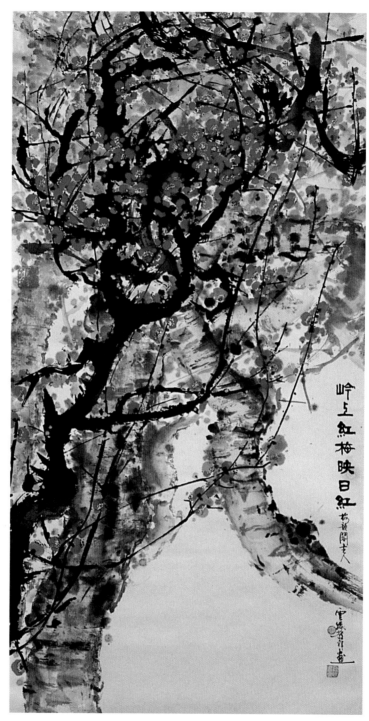

郑发祥 《岭上红梅》 国画 58cm × 118cm 1991 年
Zheng Fa-xiang "Mume Blossoms on the Mountain"
58cm × 118cm Chinese Painting 1991

郑发祥曾深造于中央美术学院。在海内外举办个人书画展十
八次。作品获中国美术馆、军事博物馆等收藏。作品多次在
中央电视台、人民日报等报导和发表。出版有《郑发祥画集》、
《郑发祥梅花书画集》。现任中国人才研究艺术家学部委员会
主任委员．

Zheng Fa-xiang furthered his studies in the Central In Institute of
Fine Art, and held solo exhibitions for eighteen times in and out of
China. His works have been collected by the China National Art
Gallery and the Military Museum, and they have been for many
times introduced by CCTV and published in "People's Daily". He
is now a chief committee member of the Artists Branch Committee
of the China Talent Research Committee. His publications include
"Collection of Zheng Fa-xiang's Paintings" and "Collection of Zheng
Fa-Xiang's Paintings and Calligraphic Works of Wintersweet".

郑发祥 《冰肌玉洁》 国画 68cm × 68cm 1995 年
Zheng Fa-xiang "Purity" Chinese Painting 68cm × 68cm 1995

董俊启 《雪》 国画 68cm × 68cm 1997 年
Dong Jun-qi "Snow" Chinese Painting 68cmX68cm 1997

董俊启，曾于东北美专附中，鲁迅美院附中学习共六年。从事美术事业40春秋。60年代作品曾到越南，阿尔巴尼亚和北京等地展出。80年代经常参加全国，省市书画展，数次获奖。96年在"沈阳风貌"画展中获金奖。作品常被各种报刊发表。

Dong Jun-qi studied at the Middle School Attached to North-East Art School and that to Luzun Institute of Fine Art for 6 years, and he has been engaged in art for 40 years. His works were displayed in Vetnam, Albania as well as Beijing in the 60's. He often took part in national, provincial, and municipal art exhibitions and won prizes in the 80's. He was awarded a gold prize at the "Shenyang Scenery" Painting Exhibition in 1996. His works are often published by different newspapers.

孟庆一 《黄岳烟云》 国画 69cm × 69cm 1996年
Meng Qing-yi "Clouds and Mist Over the Huangshan Mountains"
Chinese Painting 69cm × 69cm 1996

孟庆一，91年毕业于天津美术学院，现为职业画家。90年获天津"弘扬民族文化美术大展"一等奖。91年获天津第2届文艺新人月美展一等奖。同年获天津建党70周年美展三等奖。95年获中国体育美展优秀作品奖。

Meng Qing-yi graduated from the Tianjin Institute of Fine Art in 1991, and is now a professional painter. He won a first prize both in the Tianjin Art Exhibition To Promote National Culture" in 1990, and the second "Tianjin Monthly Art Exhibition of New Artists' Moon" in 1991. He was also awarded a third prize in the "Tianjin Exhibition Celebrating the 70th Anniversary of the Founding of CPC", and an Excellence prize in the "China Sports Fine Art Exhibition" in 1995.

左正尧 《桂子山季节》 国画 90cm×120cm 1990年
Zuo Zheng-yao "Season of the Guizi Mountain" Chinese Painting
90cm×120cm 1990

左正尧，84年广州美术学院国画系毕业。曾任华中师范大学美术系讲师。现在广东美术馆工作。其绘画作品和陶艺作品在国内外多次展出。多家媒体均有介绍发表。

Zuo Zheng-yao graduated from the Chinese Painting Department in the Guangzhou Institute of Fine Art in 1984. He was a lecturer of the Fine Art Department in the Central China Normal University, and is now working at the Guangdong Gallery of Fine Art. His works of painting and pottery have been exhibited at home and abroad for many times, and reported by the media.

莫建文 《高秋图》 国画 66cm × 66.5cm 1990年
Mo Jian-wen "Balmy Autumn Day" Chinese Painting 66cm × 66.5cm 1997

莫建文，广西艺术学院毕业，中央美术学院结业。８２－９３年在广西艺术学院任教。现为深圳新安画院画家。作品入选全国首届书画大赛，９３中国画大展，９７全国首届中国画邀请展。曾在日本，深圳，北京举办展览。出版《莫建文画集》。

Mo Jian-wen graduated form the Guangxi Art Institute and has studied at the Central Institute of Fine Art. He taught at the Guangxi Art Institute from 1982 to 1993, and is now an artist of the Shenzhen Xin'an Painting Academy. His works participated in the first National Competition of Painting and Calligraphy, the '93 Exhibition of Chinese Painting, and the first National Invitational Exhibition of Chinese Painting in 1997. He has held exhibitions in Japan, Shenzhen, and Beijing. His publications include "Painting Collection of Mo Jian-wen".

陈子文，朱海军合作　　《两只牛》　国画　7 7cm × 60cm 1997 年
Chen Zi-wen and Zhu Hai-jun "Two Cows" Chinese Painting
77cm × 60cm　1997

陈子文，湖南美术学院毕业。作品参加全国水彩画大展。在香港回归绘画展上获银奖。作品在十几个国家展出并被收藏。出版《陈子文水彩画集》。

Chen Zi-wen graduated from the Hunan Institute of Fine Art. He has taken part in Grand National Exhibition of Watercolor Paintings, and won a silver prize at the Painting Exhibtion Celebrating the Return of Hongkong. His works are displayed and collected in many countries. His publications include "Collection of Chen Zi-wen's Watercolor Paintings".

朱海军，69 年生。湖北薪春师范艺术班毕业。近年活跃于水彩艺术领域。作品在马来西亚，香港，日本，台湾等地展出，颇受好评。现就职于湖北薪春师范。

Zhu Hai-jum was born in 1969 and graduated from the art class in the Hubei Xinchun Normal School. He has been active in watercolor painting these years, with works praised and displayed in Malaysia, Hongkong, Taiwan, and Japan. He is now working at the Hubei Xinchun Normal School.

王光辉　《杭州大妈》　油画　81cm × 59.5cm　1991 年
Wang Guang-hui　"Aunty From Hangzhou"　Oil Painting
81cm × 59.5cm　1991

乡村画廊
参展画家：王光辉，孙川，韩军，董彦都，肖笑言，江金良，
孙书方，张树贤，张海信
电话：（0398）5894638，5892725
地址：河南义马市朝阳路１５号（472302）

Village Gallery
Participating Painters:Wang Guang-hui, Sun Chuan, Han Jun, Dong Yan-du, Xiao Xiao-yan, Jiang Jin-liang, Sun Shu-fang, Zhang Shu-xian, Zhang Hai-xing
Tel:0398)5894638 5892725
Address:No 15, Chaoyang Road, Yima City, Henan Province
Post Code:472302

陈正清 《墨竹》 国画 137cm × 69cm 1997 年
Chen Zheng-qing "Black Ink Bamboo" Chinese Painting 137cm × 69cm
1997

陈正清 《墨竹》 国画 137cm × 69cm 1997 年
Chen Zheng-qing "Black Ink Bamboo" Chinese Painting 137cm × 69cm
1997

陈宜明　　《夏日》　油画　140cm × 160cm　　1996 年
Chen Yi-ming　"Summer Sun"　Oil Painting 140cm × 160cm　　1996

广东星源经济开发有限公司．艺宝画廊是一家面对国内外市场的专业绘画艺术品经营制作画廊，具有一批艺术造诣高而各具风格的画家。主要经营油画，国画，版画等和仿真国画，油画。

电话：（020）84101041
地址：广州昌岗东路 252 号江南商务中心 408 室（510620）

Yibao Gallery of the Guangdong Xinyuan Economic Development Co.,Ltd. deals with such professional art works as oil painting, Chinese painting and block print as well as imitations in national and international markets. It has a lot of artists with high accademic attainments and unique styles. Tel: (020)84101040

Add: Rm.408, Jiangnan Business Centre, 252, Chengjiang Rd. (E), Guangzhou
Post Code: 510260

杨敬仲 《瑞莲》 国画 65cm × 65cm
Yang Jing-zhong "Lucky Lotus"
Chinese Painting 65cm × 65cm

杨孝军 《百合花》 国画 65cm × 65cm
Yang Xiao-jun "Lilies"
Chinese Painting 65cm × 65cm

杨孝军，徐州汉画像石艺术馆专职画师。曾参加当代第2,3届工笔画展，四季美展并获奖。95年获国际书画展铜奖。部分作品在《美术》,《国画家》等刊物发表并被中国革命博物馆收藏。

Yang Xiao-jun is a profesional painter of Xuzhou Art Museum of Painting and Stone Art of the Han Dynasty. He has participated in the second and third Exhibitions of Gongbi Painting, and the Four Season Art Exhibition, and awarded. He also won a bronze prize in the '95 International Exhibition of Painting and Calligraphy.Some of his works have been published by such journals as "Art" and "Chinese Painters", and collected by the Chinese Revolution Museum.

杨敬仲，徐州国画院高级美术师。南京艺术学院毕业。作品参加中国画大展，国际中国画大展，四季美展，当代第2,3届工笔画展和广州国际艺术博览会并获奖。作品在《美术》,《收藏天地》等刊物发表并被中国革命博物馆收藏。发表论著8篇。

Yang Jing-zhong is a senior class artist of the Xuzhou Institute of Chinese Painting. He graduated from the Nanjin Art Institute and has many works participating and awarded in national and international exhibitions of Chinese painting, the Four Season Art Exhibition, the second and third Exhibitions of Modern Gongbi Painting, and the Guangzhou International Art Exposition. His works have been published by such journals as "Art" and "World of Collection", and collected by the Chinese Revolution Museum. He has 8 thesises pubished.

《太和舞龙》 清朝 1879

《戴安娜世纪婚礼纪念火花》 澳大利亚 1981

《瑞士火花》 5.3cm × 3.2cm
Swiss Sparks 5.3cm × 3.2cm

李伟钦，自幼集藏中外火花，邮票，啤标等。尤以火花为最。藏有100多个国家火花百万枚。现是国际标签协会会员，广州火花协会会长。获"中国民间收藏及工艺品博览会十大优秀收藏家"称号。已发表论文数十篇，出版《中外火花博览》，《世界火花设计精选》。

Li Wei-qing began to collect China and foreign sparks, stamps, and beerbottle labels. He has a collection of one million sparks from over 100 countries. He is now a member opf international labels society, president of Guangzhou Spark Association. He won the tiltle of one of the "Top Ten Collectors of China Folk Collection and Handicraft Works Exposition". He hasd published donzens of papers, and "Chinese and Foreign Sparks", "Selection of the World's Best In Spark Design".

黄向卫　　《雨后》　　水彩　　54cm × 75cm　　1994 年
Huang Xiang-wei　"After the Rain"
Watercolor　54cm × 75cm　1994

黄向阳　　《泊》　　油画　　55cm × 65cm　　1995 年
Huang Xiang-yang　"Anchoring"
Oil Painting　55cm × 65cm　1995

黄向卫，　67 年生。89 年中山大学毕业。90 年广州美术学院夜大学绘画专业毕业，93 年结业于广美水彩画研究生班。

Huang Xiang-wei, born in 1967, graduated from Zhongshan University in 1989. He also studied painting both at the evening uiversity of the Guangzhou Institute of Fine Art in 1990, and the graduate class of water-color in 1993 at the same institute.

黄向阳，　广东工艺美术学校毕业。多次参加省市和全国专题性展览并发表于国内外多种报刊。《画廊》曾作专题介绍。油画《小湖边》获全国奖专题展三等奖。现为广东美协会员，深圳美协会员。

Huang Xiang-yang graduated from the Guangdong Industrial Fine Art School. He has taken part in national, provincial, and municipal exhibitions for many times, and has his works published in such journals as "Art Gallery" at home and abroad. His oil painting "Beside the Lake" won a third prize in the national Special Subject Exhibition. He is now a memeber of both the Guangdong and Shenzhen Artists' Associations.

李连信　《渔舟唱晚》　　国画　46cm×51cm　　1997年
Li lian-xin　"Fishermen's Song Meeting the　Coming of Night"
Chinese Painting　46cm×51cm　1997

李连信，中央工艺美院毕业。现为天津工艺美院教授，中国工艺美术家协会会员，中国科技协会会员。不少作品发表于天津及国内各种报刊。曾获 "天津市弘扬民族文化优秀作品" 三等奖。多幅作品赴澳大利亚，新西兰，美国参加大展，被当地收藏。

Li lian-xin graduated from the Central Institute of Industrial Art. He s a member of China Industrial Artists' Association, and China Sciece and Technology Association, and a professor of Tianjin Institute of Industrial Art. Many of his works have been published by newspapers in the country. He participated in exhibitions held in Australia, New Zealand, and Amercia, with works collected by local art lovers. He was awarded a third prize in the Tianjin Outstanding Works Exhibition to Promote National Culture".

黄诗筠　《古风》　　油画　　80cm × 80cm　　1996 年
Huang Shi-yun　　"Antiquities"
Oil Painting　　80cm × 80cm　　1996

黄诗筠，广州美术学院毕业。参加第7届全国水彩画大展，中国艺术博览会，并获全省美展优秀奖。部分作品发表并被国内外收藏家收藏。现为佛山美协会员。

Huang Shi-yun graduated from the Guangzhou Institute of Fine Art. She took part in the 7th National Exhibtional of Watercolor Paintings, the China Art Exposition, and won an excellence prize in the national fine art exhibition. Some of her works were published and collected in and out of China. She is now a member of the Fushan Artists' Association.

刘穗艳　《宁静》　　油画　　54cm × 45cm　　1997 年
Liu Sui-yan　"Peacefulness"
Oil Painting　　54cm × 45cm　　1997

刘穗艳，广州美术学院学士毕业。现任教于华南文艺成人学院。出版《刘穗艳水彩画集》。

Liu Sui-yan graduated from the Guangzhou Institute of Fine Art with an B A degree, and is now teaching at the South China Culture and Art Institute for Adults. Her publications include "Collection of Liu Sui-yan's Watercolor Paintings".

梁明明　《非花》　油画　60cm × 80cm
Liang Ming-ming　"Nonflower"　Oil Painting　60cm × 80cm

梁明明，广州美术学院毕业。作品入选全国和省美展。96年举办个展并参加广州国际艺术博览会。出版《梁明明油画辑》。部分作品发表并被海内外私人收藏。现为广东美协会员，省青年美协会员。

Liang Ming-ming graduated from the Guangzhou Institute of Fine Art. His works were selected into national and provincial art exhibitions. In 1996, he held solo exhibitions and took part in the Guangzhou International Art Exposition. His publications include "Collection of Liang Ming-ming's Oil Painting". Some of his works were published and collected at home and abroad. He is now a member of the Guangdong Artists' Association, and of the provincial Young Artists' Association.

刘学峰　《千古江山》　国画　150cm × 75cm　1997 年
Liu Xue-feng　"Eternal Moutains and Rivers"　Chinese Painting　150cm × 75cm　1997

刘学峰，辽宁美协会员。进修毕业于鲁迅美术学院。获日本国际画展银奖，中国青年画展一等奖。合作的国画作品被张学良旧居博物馆收藏。名字收录在《当代书画篆刻家辞典》。

Liu Xue-feng, a member of the Liaoning Artists' Association, graduated from the Luxun Institute of Fine Art. He won a silver prize at the Japan International Art Exhibition, and a first prize at the China Youth's Art Exhibition. His Chinese painting (co-painter) was collected by the Zhang Xue-liang's Former Residence Museum. His name was edited into the "Dictionary of Contemporary Painters, Calligraphists, and Seal Cutting Artists".

广州金夫人婚纱影楼
Guangzhou Madame Jin's Wedding-Dress Studio

广州金夫人婚纱影楼，以"实实在在做人，认认真真服务"为宗旨，不断倾注智慧，情感为每对新人留下一生中珍贵瞬间。以锐意进取之气势不断推动婚纱摄影艺术的发展。
电话：83186715
地址：广州越秀区小北路232号

Guangzhou Madame Jin's Wedding-Dress Studio,with its principle of "Honesty and Ernest" and with wit and emotions, tries its best to keep the most valuable moment of the newly-weds, and promotes the art of wedding-dress photography.
Tel:83186715
Add: 232, Xiaobei Rd. Guangzhou

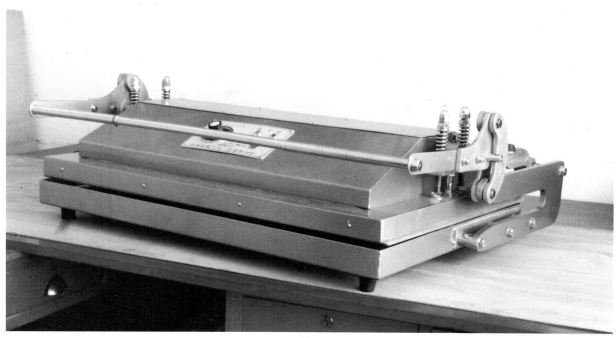

AA 书画装裱机展示
AA Mounting Machine shows

AA型书画装裱机由天一庄文化艺术有限公司研究出品。最大装裱可达6尺整宣。操作简单快捷，耗电量少，连续开机12小时只需5度电。单幅作品装裱2小时。装裱后作品平整不变形。

电话：（024）2821704

地址：沈阳大东区小什字街87号楼（110042）

AA Mounting Machine produced by Tianyi zhuang Cultural & Art Company Ltd can mount 6 chi whole piece xuan paper at maxinum. It is easy to operate, and electricity-saving (It needs 5 kwh for 12 hours running). A single work can be done within 2 hours and it remains smooth forever.

Tel : (024)2821704

Add: Building 87, Xiao-Shizi St., Dadong District, Shenyang City

Post Code:110042

羊羔 《子淑》 油画 73cm × 61cm   1997 年
Yang Gao "Zi Shu" Oil Painting 73cm × 61cm 1997

羊羔毕业于哈尔滨建筑大学,职业画家。作品多次参加市,全
国美展并获奖。"立体堆积画"画种发明人。多幅作品被美国,
荷兰,奥地利和台湾友人收藏,并在《天津日报》,《书画苑》
等报刊发表介绍。参加'97中国艺术博览会。

Yang Gao, a professional painter, graduated from the Ha'erbin Architecture University.
He has participated in many municipal,and national exhibitions and won prizes. He, the
creator of 3D Heap Painting, has many of his works collected by people from America,
Holland, Austria, and Taiwan, and reported by such journals as "Tianjin Daily", and
"Garden of Painting and Calligraphy". He took part in the China Art Exposition in
1997.

张广志　《岁岁年年》　　油画　　117cm × 117cm　　1997 年
Zhang Guang-zhi "Year after Year"　　Oil Painting　　117cm × 117cm　　1997

张广志，鲁迅美术学院毕业。本溪艺术馆副教授，中国美协
会员，中国油画学会会员。参加第 7,8 届八国美展，庆祝建
军 70 周年全国美展，水粉画获全国展一等奖并编入《中国现
代美术全传》。曾在日本，中国美术馆举办画展。出版《张广
志油画作品选集》，《张广志油画精品集》。

Zhang Guang-zhi, a graduate from the Luxun Institute of Fine Art, is an associate
professor of the Benxi Art Museum, a member both of the China Artists' Association
and the China Oil Painting Society. He took part in the 7th, 8th Eight-Country Art
Exhibitions, the National Fine Art Exhibition Celebrating the 70 Anniversary of the
Founding of the Army.   His famille rose painting won a first prize in national exhibition
and was edited into the "General Biography of Morden Chinese Art". He held exhibitions
in Japan and the China National Gallery of Fine Art. His publications include "Zhang
Guang-zhi's Selection of Oil Painting", and "Zhang Guang-zhi's Refined Work Collection
of Oil Painting".

曾道宗　《春山雪峰》　　国画　　68cm × 68cm　　1997 年
Zeng Dao-zong　"Snowy Peaks of Spring Mountains"　Chinese Painting　68cm × 68cm　1997

广东艺术师范学校
电话：87706737
地址：广州沙河燕岭路（510507）
参展画家：曾道宗，黄兵，郑丽美，姚亮，李润，潘岚，李
跃，邓启龙，黄荣赤，陈怡宁，何翔，张学君

Guangdong Normal Art School
Tel: 87706737
Add: Yanling Road, Shahe, Guangzhou
Post Code: 510507
Participating Painters: Zeng Dao-zong, Huang Bing, Zheng Li-mei, Yao Liang, Li Run,
Pan Lan, Li Yue, Deng Qi-long, Huang Rong-chi, Chen Yi-ning, He Xiang, Zhang
Xue-jun.

曾道宗，广州美术学院毕业。擅长人物山水画。作品多次参
加全国美展，在多个国家，地区展出并获奖。现为中国美协
理事，特级教师，广东艺术师范学校副校长。

Zeng Dao-zong, a graduate from the Guangzhou Institute of Fine Art, is good at portrait
and landscape painting. His works have participated in national exhibitions for many
times and have been displayed and awarded in many countries and areas. He is now a
director of the China Artists's Association, a teacher of a special class, and vice president
of the Guangdong Normal Art School.

黄兵　《屋》　水彩　　55cm × 72cm
Huang Bing　"House"　Watercolor　55cm × 72cm

黄兵，65年生于湖南。89年广州美术学院毕业。现为广东艺
术师范学校讲师。擅长水彩画，油画。
电话：87716575

Huang Bing, born in Hunan in 1965, graduated from the Guangzhou Institute of Fine
Art in 1989. He is now a lecturer good at watercolor and oil painting of the Guangdong
Normal Art School.
Tel: 87716575

《七星名砚工艺厂之 1200 平方米端砚奇石展示厅》
The 1200 square meter show-room

七星名砚工艺厂是肇庆（端州）生产端砚规模最大的企业。端砚有 1300 年历史。本厂生产的端砚采自各坑（老坑，坑仔岩，麻子坑，宋坑，梅花坑等），精雕而成。销往全国各地和日本，韩国，台湾，东南亚。受到海内外书画家，收藏家青睐。

电话：(0758) 2717899
地址：广东肇庆端州黄岗（526060）
手机：2717232
厂长：李自强

Seven-Star Inkslab Factory is the largest enterprise producing inkslabs in Shaoqing (Duanzhou). Duanzhou inkslabs have a history of 1500 years. The inkslabs are made with stone from stone pits (Laokeng, Kengzaiyan, Mazikeng, Songkeng, Meihua keng, etc.)They are sold all over the country and in Japan, Korea, Taiwan, and Southeast Asia. They are warmly received by painters, calligraphers and collectors at home and abroad.

Tel: (0758) 2717899
Add: Huanggang, Duanzhou, Zhaoqing
Post Code: 2717232
Portable Phone No.: 2717232
Director: Li Zi-qiang

叶秀炯　《细语》　国画　33.5cm × 91.5cm　80年代
Ye Xiu-jiong　"Whisper"
Chinese Painting　33.5cm × 91.5cm　1980'S

叶秀炯，广东美协会员，广州书画学院国画系主任，教授。以山水画为主，擅长金鱼。作品多次在国内外参展，并在北京，哈尔滨，香港等10多个城市举办个展。作品获国家新时代杯优秀奖，日本国际文化交流特等奖。出版《叶秀炯中国画选集》，《叶秀炯作品选集》。作品和简介入编多部辞书。

Ye Xiu-jiong, a member of the Guangdong Artists' Association, is a professor and dean of the Chinese Painting Department in Guangzhou Institute of Painting and Calligraphy. He took part in many exhibitions in and out of China, and held solo exhibitions in such cities as Beijing, Ha'erbin, and Hongkong. He won an excellence prize in the National "New Times" Cup Exhibition, and a Special Class prize in Japan International Culture Exchange Exhibition. His publications include "Selection of Ye Xiu-jiong's Chinese Paintings", and "Selection of Ye Xiu-jiong's Works". His works and experience were edited into many dictionaries.

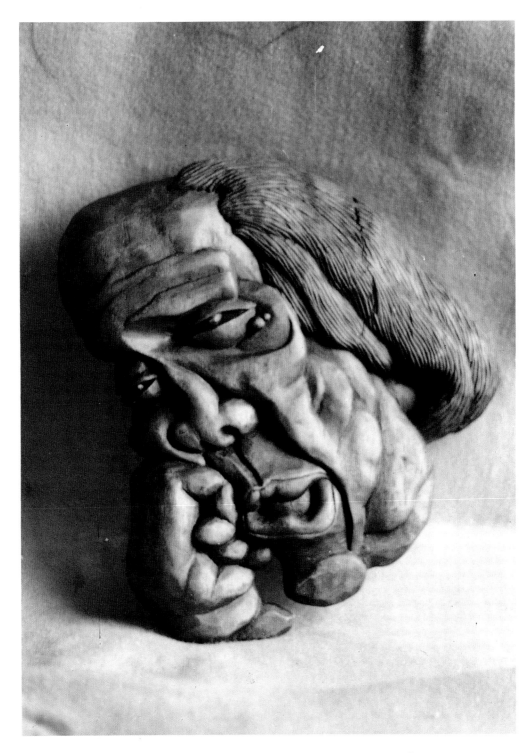

韦正彬 《飘逝的彩云》之二 浮雕 40cm × 32cm 1989年
Wei Zheng-bin "Wandering Colorful Clouds"
Relief Sculpture 40cm × 32cm 1989

韦正彬，作品参加全国第6届美展，省美展及版画大展。部分作品在有关刊物发表并被广西电视台，《广西日报》等新闻机构报导。近年创作了近百件木质艺术品，受到传媒和收藏者好评。

Wei Zheng-bin has had his works taking part in the 6th National Exhibition of Fine Art, provincial exhibitions, and exhibitions of block print. Some of his works were published and reported by such journals as the Guangxi TV and Guangxi Daily. In recent years, he has created nearly 100 pieces of wood art works which are highly praised by the media and collectors.

黄宾虹　《黄山图》　国画　　96cm × 55.5cm
Huang Bing-hong　"The Huangshan Mountains"
Chinese Painting　　96cm × 55.5cm

范京生　《吉日》　　油画　　40cm × 30cm　　1997 年
Fan Jing-sheng　"Lucky Day"　Oil Painting　40cm × 30cm　　1997

范京生，石家庄魔林研究所高级工艺美术师，河北工艺美术
学会会员，中国发明协会会员。参加'95,'97 中国艺术博览
会（广州），'96 广州国际艺术博览会，'96 欧洲共同体世界
艺术博览会并荣获骑士勋章。部分作品被法国，比利时，德
国，美国，新加坡及香港人士收藏。出版《魔林想象画》。

Fan Jing-sheng, a senior class industrial artist of the Shijiazhuang Molin Research
Institute, is a member both of the Hebei Industrial Artists' Association, and the China
Invention Society. He took part in the '95, and '97 China Art Expositions(Guangzhou),
'96 Guangzhou International Art Exposition, and the '96 EEC World Art Exposition,
in which he was awarded a Knight Medal. Parts of his works were collected by
people from France, Belgum, Germany, America, Singarpore, and Hongkong. His
publications include "Molin's Paintings of Imagination"

黄树德　《西沙的海》　　水彩　　54cm × 75cm　　1996 年
Guang Shu-de "Sea of Xisha"　Watercolor　54cm × 75cm　1996

黄树德，中国美协和版协会员，广州水彩画研究会副会长。作品多次参加全国展览和选送出国展。出版《黄树德版画集》，《黄树德水彩画选辑》，《海之歌水彩画选集》等。

Huang Shu-de, vice president of the Guangzhou Watercolor Research Society, is a member of the China Artists' Association and of the Block Print Artists' Association. He has participated in national and international exhibitions for many times. His publications include "Huang Shu-de's Collection of Block Prints", "Huang Shu-de's Selection of Watercolor Paintings", and "Songs of the Sea--Selection of Watercolor Paintings"

程辉　《山村叠翠》　　国画　34cm × 34cm　　1991 年
Cheng Hui　　"Green Village"　　Chinese Painting　34cm × 34cm　　1991

程辉，东南大学毕业。曾举办 3 次个展，88 年获广州美术大赛金牌奖。89 年获广州美展建国 40 周年优秀奖和文艺奖第三名。出版《程辉山水画集》，《程辉写生画集》，《程辉山水精粹》。现为广州美术馆特聘画家，广州市美协会员。

Cheng Hui, a graduate from the South-east University, has held solo exhibitions 3 times. He won a silver prize in the Guangzhou Competition of Fine Art in 1988, and was given an excellence prize and a third of Culture and Art Prize in the Guangzhou Art Exhibition Celebrating the 40th Anniversary of the Founding of the PRC. His publicatrions include "Collection of Cheng Hui's Landscape Paintings", "Collection of Chen Hui's Sketches", and "Refined Works of Cheng Hui" He is now a guess painter of Guangzhou Art Gallery and a member of Guangzhou Artists' Association.

董毓明 《榜书中堂》 书法 134cm × 67cm 1996年
Dong Yu-ming "Zhongtang Scroll" Bangshu Calligraphy
134cm × 67cm 1996

董毓明，中国书法家协会会员。曾在深圳，石家庄举办个展
7次。作品多次参加国内外大展并获各种奖项。作品编入《现
代书法界人名辞典》等20多部辞书，被全国多个碑林和博物
馆收藏。
电话（0319）5223365

Dong Yu-ming, a member of the China Calligraphists' Association, has held solo exhibitions in Shenzhen, and Shijiazhuang for 7 times. He has participated and been awarded in many exhibitions at home and abroad. His works were edited into over 20 dictionaries, including "Dictionary of Modern Calligraphists", and collected by gardens of forest of steles and museums in the country.
Tel: (0319)5223365

牛亚平　《地灵》　宣纸彩墨　150cm × 180cm　1996 年
Niu Ya-ping　"Glorious Place"　Color Ink on Paper
150cm × 180cm　1996

牛亚平，北京职业技术师院毕业。参加第 7 届全国美展，亚洲妇画展获一等奖，世妇会美术家作品展被中国美术馆收藏。第 3,4 届全国体育美展和全国群星美展获优秀奖。
地址：河北衡水市人民中路 44 号市群艺馆（053000）
电话：（0318）2057748，（010）62019298

Niu Ya-ping, a graduate from the Beijing Normal Institute of Technology , took part in the 7th national exhibition, the 3rd, 4th National Sports Fine Art Exhibition, and won a first prize in the Asian Women's Art Exhibition, and an excellence prize at the National Stars Exhibition of Fine Art. The China National Gallery of Fine Art collected her work which had participated the Art Exhibition of the World Women's Confrence.
Add:Mass Art Museum, No 44, Renmin Road (C), Hengshui City, Hebei Province
Post Code:053000
Tel:(0138) 2057748, (010) 62019298

李东伟　　《静观．斜阳旧梦》　　国画　　68cm × 68cm　　1996 年
Li Dong-wei　"Quiet Observation, Old Dreams in the Setting Sun"　　Chinese Painting
68cm × 68cm　　1996

李东伟，广州美术学院毕业，国家一级画家，广州画院专业
画家。作品入选第 7,8 届全国美展，亚细亚国际美术展览会，
中央美术学院和中国画研究院主办的"当代山水印象"展。
中国美术馆，中国画研究院，广东美术馆，泰国国皇钦赐淡
浮院曾收藏其作品。出版《李东伟作品集》，《李东伟－－静
观·夕阳旧梦 96 专集》，《李东伟－－静观·古典 95 作品集》，
《李东伟艺术和生活 97 档案》。

Li Dong Wei, a graduate from the Guangzhou Institute of Fine Art, and a professional
artist,is a first class artist. His works were selected into the 7th, 8th National Exhibition
of Fine Art, Asia International Art Show, and the "Contemporary Image of Landscape"
Exhibition sponsored by the Central Institute of Fine Art and Chinese Painting Research
Institute. Museums, such as the National Gallery of Fine Art and Chinese Painting
Research Institute, have had his works collected. His publications include "Li Dong-
wei's Work Collection", "Li Dong-wei--Quiet Observation, '96 Special of Old Dreams
in the Setting Sun", "Li Dong-wei---Quiet Observation, '95 Classic", and " '97 File of
Art and Life of Li Dong-wei".

李东伟　《静观．斜阳旧梦》　国画　68cm × 68cm　1996 年
Li Dong-wei　"Quiet Observation, Old Dreams in the Setting Sun"　Chinese Painting
68cm × 68cm　1996

李东伟　《静观．岁月》系列之一　　国画　　240cm × 120cm　　1997 年
Li Dong-wei "Quiet Observation" Series 1   Chinese Painting
240cm × 120cm   1997

李东伟 《静观．岁月》系列之一 国画 240cm × 120cm 1997 年
Li Dong-wei "Quiet Observation" Series 1 Chinese Painting
240cm × 120cm 1997

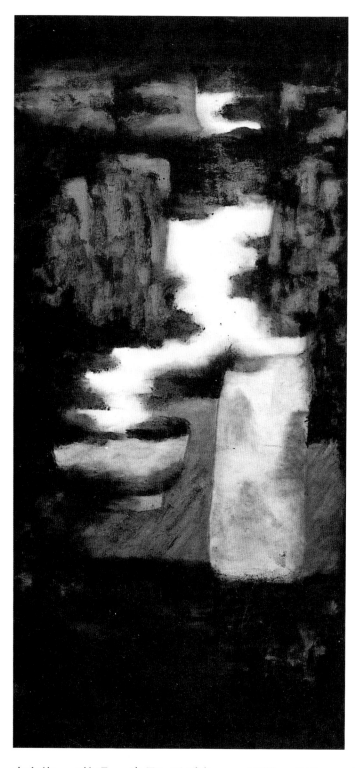

李东伟　《静观．岁月》系列之一　　国画　　240cm×120cm　　1997年
Li Dong-wei "Quiet Observation" Series 1　Chinese Painting
240cm×120cm　　1997

《峰山》　直纹石
"Peak"　Straight Veining Stone

花都市福星工艺有限公司是目前国内最大的专业生产"天王牌"遥控式多功能云雾山水盆景厂。"天王牌"是国家传统工艺和现代科技相结合的结晶。93年获国家专利号ZL92242900.6。该产品能产生大量空气负离子，清新空气，排除气体中的杂质异味，令你健康愉快，制造自己的"世外桃源"。
地址：广东花都市新华镇九塘部队房管处内（510800）
电话：86863025
传真：86863592

Guangzhou Fu Star Craft Factory is at present the largest factory in the country which produces remote-control cloud and mist potted miniature landscapes. Its Tianwang Brand product is a combination of traditional art and modern technology, and has received national patent (number ZL92242900.6)in 1993; it can produce a lot of anions to purify air, and make you feel pleased and healthy.
Add:Jiutang, Huadu City, Guangdong Province
Post Code:510800
Tel:86863025
Fax:86863592

《峰山》 花石
"Peak" Tissue Color Stone

陈永锵　《葵花》　国画　180cm × 140cm　1995 年

Chen Yong-qiang　"Sunflower"　Chinese Painting　180cm × 140cm　1995

陈永锵，毕业于广州美术学院中国画系，获硕士学位。作品
多次入选全国美展，为国家部门收藏。曾在广州，新加坡，美
国，马来西亚，香港，台湾，澳门等地举办个展。出版个人
画集 3 本。现为广州市文学艺术界联合会常务副主席，中国
美协理事，广东美协副主席，广州画院名誉院长。

Chen Yong-qiang is a master of Chinese Painting from the Guangzhou Institute of
Fine Art. His works were selected into national art exhibitions and collected by state
departments. He has held solo exhibitions in Guangzhou, Singarpore, America,
Malaysia, Hongkong, Taiwan and Macau, and has 3 personal art books published. He
is now standing vice president of Guangzhou Culture and Art Federation, director of
China Artists' Association, vice president of Guangdong Artists' Association, and
honorary president of Guangzhou Art Academy.

陈永锵　《藤》　国画　180cm × 140cm　1995 年
Chen Yong-qiang　"Vines"　Chinese Painting　180cm × 140cm　1995

陈永锵 《花鸟组画》　国画　3 × 136cm × 22cm　1996 年
Chen Yong-qiang　"Flower and Bird"　Chinese Painting
3 × 136cm × 22cm　1996

谭伟成 《秋山图》 国画 68cm × 68cm 1996年
Tan Wei-cheng "Autumn Mountains" Chinese painting 68cm × 68cm 1996

谭伟成,广东美协会员,广东年画艺委会会员。作品多次入
选省市美展和国外展出。并由广东岭南美术出版社出版多幅
作品。多次为国内外各大报刊介绍刊登。传记载入《中国当
代文艺名人辞典》,《中国人物志》。

Tan Wei-cheng, member of both Guangdong Artists' Association, and Guangdong
New Year Picture Art Committee, has participated in national, provincial exhibitions.
Guangdong Lingnan Art Publishing House has published many of his paintings. His experience
was edited into "Dictionary of Contemporary Famous Chinese of Culture and Art",
and "Annual of Chinese People".

赖建成 《听泉》 国画 136cm × 68cm
Lai Jian-cheng "Listening to the Spring" Chinese Painting 136cm × 68cm

赖建成，作品多次参加省市以上美展，获奖，被收藏。代表作《灵通山烟云图》被漳州市人民政府作为礼物送给日本。《人民日报》海外版，《福建日报》，《厦门日报》，《海峡之声》等报刊和电台相继报导其艺术业绩。传略载入《中国当代名人录》，《中国当代书画家名典》。现为北京艺术交流中心聘任山水创作画家。

Tai Jian-cheng has many of his works selected into exhibitions, awarded , and collected. His representative work "Clouds and Mist of Nintong Mountain" was given to the Japanese Government by the Zhangzhou People's Goverment. His achievement was reported by such journals and radio station as "People's Daily" (overseas edition), "Fujian Daily", "Xiamen Daily", and the "Sound of the Straights". His experience was edited into "Record of Contemporary Famous Chinese People", and "Dictionary of Contemporary Chinese Artists and Calligraphists". He is now creation artist of landscape engaged by the Beijing Art Exchange Center.

范贯忠　《吹箫引凤》　油画　180cm × 150.4cm　1997 年
Fan Guan-zhong　"Playing the Fife, Calling for the Phonex"　Oil Painting
180cm × 150.5cm　1997

范贯忠，哈尔滨师范大学美术系毕业。曾任黑龙江省鹤岗市教育学院美术系讲师。现为专业画家。作品多次参加省市、国外私人联展，并广为收藏。

Fan Guan-zhong, a graduate of the Fine Art Department from the Har'erbin Normal University, used to be a lecturer of the Fine Art Department of the Hegang Normal Institute, Heilongjiang Province. He is now a professional artist. His works have taken part in many exhibitions and been collected by different people.

蔡超 《面壁图》 国画 68cm × 68cm 1996年
Cai Chao "Meditation" Chinese Painting
68cm × 68cm 1996

蔡超，南昌市文联主席，南昌画院院长兼南昌美术馆馆长，
国家一级美术师，获国务院优秀专家政府特殊津贴，文化部
先进工作者称号，中国美协会员，南昌美协主席，香港海外
文艺家协会名誉主席，江西艺术系列高级职称评委。
地址：江西南昌市南湖路51号（330008）
电话：（0791）6781457,8333128,6770190

Cai Chao is president of Nanchang Culture Federation, president of Nanchang Art
Academy and Nanchang Gallery of Fine Art, state first class artist. He is given outstanding
specialist subsidy by the State Council, and awarded the title of "Advanced Worker" by
the Culture Ministry. He is now a member of the China Artists' Association, president
of Nanchang Artists' Association, honorary president of Hongkong Overseas Writers
and Artists' Association, and judge for High-Class Professional Titles in Art of Jiangxi.
Add: 51, Nanhu Rd., Nanchang, Jiangxi
Post Code: 330008
Tel: (0791) 6781457, 8333128, 6770190

叶泉　《朝颜》　国画　68cm × 68cm　1997 年
Ye Quan　"Morning Glory"　Chinese Painting　68cm × 68cm　1997

叶泉，加拿大卑斯大学客座教授，曾在加拿大亚洲中心，新加坡乌节坊，法国巴黎，中国苏州举办个展。参加 95，96，97 广州国际艺术博览会。出版《叶泉菊花集》（澳洲市政厅出版），《叶泉美加之旅》（加拿大出版），70×70cm原大限量印刷品 12 款（加拿大出版）。获第 8 届全澳冠军。

Ye Quan is a exchange professor to Canada. He has held solo exhibitions in Canada, Singapore, France, and Suzhou of China. He took part in the Guangzhou International Art Exposition from 1995 to 1997. His publications include " Ye Quan's Chrysanthemum Painting Collection" (published by the Municipal Government in Australia), " Ye Quan's Journey in America and Canada" (published in Canada), and twelve sets of 70cmX70cm original size publications (published in Canada).

叶泉 《鱼乐图》 国画 122cm × 122cm 1997 年
Ye Quan "Happy Fish" Chinese Painting 122cm × 122cm 1997

叶泉 《绿云》 国画 68cm × 138cm 1997 年
Ye Quan "Green Clouds"
Chinese Painting 68cm × 138cm 1997

叶泉　《珍珠球》　国画　68cm × 100cm　1997 年
Ye Quan　"Pearl Ball"　Chinese Painting　68cm × 100cm　1997

叶泉　《花潮》　国画　488cm × 244cm　1997 年
Ye Quan　　"Sea of Flowers"　　Chinese Painting　　488cm × 244cm　　1997

叶泉 《金秋》 国画 122cm × 122cm 1997 年
Ye Quan "Golden Autumn" Chinese Painting 122cm × 122cm 19997

叶泉　《悠游图》　国画　122cm × 122cm　1997 年
Ye Quan　"Leisurely Wondering"　Chinese painting　122cm × 122cm　1997

叶泉　　《傲霜枝》　　国画　　122cm × 122cm　　1997 年
Ye Quan　"Proud Branches in the Cold"　Chinese Painting　122cm × 122cm　1997

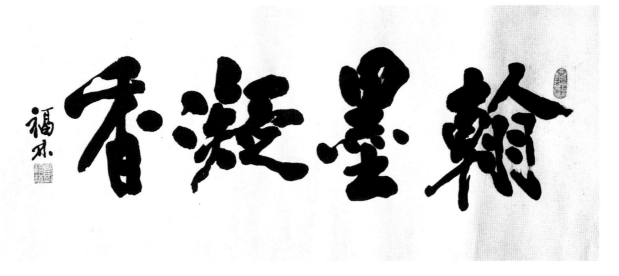

邓福林   书法   1997 年
Deng Fu-lin   Calligraphy   1997

邓福林，北京师范学院毕业。57年起在西南师范大学美术学院教学，任国画书法教研室主任。现为副教授，四川美协会员。作品多次参加国内外展出并被收藏。小传载入《世界当代书画篆刻家大辞典》，《现代中日美术通鉴》等。

Deng Fu-lin is a graduate from the Beijing Normal Institute. He began to teach in the Fine Art Institute of the Southwest Normal University in 1957 as dean of teaching and research section of Chinese Painting and Calligrapy. He is now an associate professor, and a member of the Sichuan Artists' Association. His works took part in many exhibitions and were collected at home and abroad. His biography is edited into "Dictionary of Contemporary Painters, Calligraphists and Seal Cutting Artists in the World", and "General Introduction of Modern Sino -Japanese Art".

黎雄才　《幽谷图》　水墨　83.5cm × 30.5cm　1961年
Li Xiong-cai　"A Quiet Velley" Water and Ink　83.5cm × 30.5cm　1961

文联庄

书画笔墨文房四宝总汇

地址：香港中环永吉街29-35号恒丰大厦2字楼

电话：254430515,25446965

传真：（852）15459750

联 系 人：李望达

参展画家：赵少昂，黎雄才，关山月，杨善深，
　　　　　欧豪年，倪冰等。

经营项目：国内外书画名笔，金笺宣纸，端溪
　　　　　名砚，国画颜料，画绢绫锦，美浓
　　　　　麻纸，画集碑帖，高级印材，徽墨
　　　　　墨汁，磁质色碟，装裱字画，酸枝
　　　　　镜架，零售批发，邮寄服务，名家
　　　　　书画仲介买卖。

Man Luen Choon

Chinese Cultural and Artist Supplies

Add:29-35 Wing Kut Street, 2/F Harvest Bldg., Central Hongkong

Tel:254430515,25446965

Fax:(852)25459750

Contact:Lee Mon Tat

Particpating Artists: Zhou Shao-ang, Li Xiong-cai, Guan Shan-yue,Yang Shan-shen,
　　　　　　　　　　Ou Hao-nian, Ni Bing, Etc.

Businesses: Chinese brushes, paper, ink, inkstone, inkstick, color, art books of Chinese
　　　　　　paintings and Calligraphies; traditional oriental mounting of paintings;
　　　　　　Seal Carving; custom framing; conservation framing;retail and wholesale;
　　　　　　mailorder service;Chinese art's and callegraphies; consutltant, etc.

佟雨　《伫望》　摄影　1994 年
Tong Yu　"To Stand Watching"　Photography　1994

佟雨，名曾彤宇，68 年生。自由摄影者。部分作品多次见诸
报刊。作品优美清寂，平实无华，富个人品性。

Tong Yu (Zeng Tong-yu), born in 1968, is a freelance photographer. Many of his works, plain but lovely and full of personality, were published by journals and newspapers.

江云龙 《静物》 油画 50cmX60cm
Jiang Yun-long "Still Life" Oil Painting 50cmX60cm

江云龙,中国艺术研究院书画师,无锡市书法家协会会员,工艺美协会员。作品在全国各类大赛中多次获奖并广泛发表于各类报刊。入编《中国现代艺术家》等辞典。现为无锡市横云书画艺术院副院长、专业画家。

Jiang Yun-long, a professional painter, Jiang is a painter and calligraphist of the China Art Research Institute, vice president of Wuxi Hengyun Art Institute of Painting and Calligraphy, member of Wuxi Calligraphists' Association, and of Industrial Artists' Association. His works have been awarded in many national competitions and published by various kinds of newspapers and magazines. His name has been entered into "Modern Chinese Artists" and other dictionaries.

许荣　　《朱竹寿石图》　　国画
Xu Rong　"Bamboos and Rocks"　Chinese Painting

许荣，广州美院毕业。受教于名家黎雄才等。作品先后在新
加坡，西德，台湾等地举办个展和联展。出版《许荣画集》。

Xu rong, a graduate of the Guangzhou Institue of Fine Art, has been a student of many
famous artists such as Li Xiong-cai. He has held solo exhibitions in Singapore, West
Germany, and Taiwan succesively. His publications include "Xu Rong's Painting
Collection".

张石培 《人欢鱼跃》 68cm × 48cm 国画 1992 年
Zhang Shi-pei "Happy People and Lively Fishes" Chinese Painting 68cm × 48cm 1992

张石培，42 年生。68 年毕业于广州美术学院。职业画家。

Zhang Shi-pei, born in 1942, graduated from the Guangzhou Institute of Fine Art in
1968, and is now a professional painter.

许喜裕　《云松伴天都》　国画　120cm × 60cm　1997 年
Xu Xi-yu　"Clouds and Pinetrees of Tiandu Moutain"　Chinese Painting
120xm × 60cm　1997

许喜裕，广州美术学院毕业。广东美协会员，广州环境设计
协会会员，中国对外贸易中心（集团）美术工艺师。作品参
加全国，省美展并获奖。作品《喜看香港回归》参加 '97 全
国外经贸系统美展获三等奖。

Xu Xi-yu, a member of the Guangdong Artists' Association, and of the Guangzhou
Environmental Designers' Association, graduated from the Guangzhou Institute of
Fine Art. He is now an industrial fine artist of the China Foreign Trade Center (Guoup).
Many of his works, such as the "Welcoming the Return of Hongkong with Joy", took
part in exhibitions and were awarded.

倪秋汉　《云漫群山》　电脑绘画　44cm×33cm　1997年
Ni Qiu-han　"Clouds around the Mountains"　Computer Painting　44cm×33cm　1997

倪秋汉，广州美术学院毕业。广州环境装饰设计会会员。现任中国对外贸易中心（集团）展览公司设计部经理。作品多次发表于报刊，杂志。热衷电脑绘画。自辟蹊径。作品光色皆丽，别有新意。

Ni Qiu-han, a graduate from the Guangzhou Institute of Fine Art, is now a member of the Guangzhou Environmental Designers' Association, and manager of the Design Department in the China Foreign Trade Center (Gruop)'s Exhibition Company. His works have been published in many newspapers and journals. He is keen on computer painting, which is colorful and unique.

李金明　《晨起》　油画　93cm×66cm　1992年
Li Jin-ming　"Rising in the Morning"　Oil Painting　93cm×66cm　1992

李金明，广州美术学院毕业。任职于中国出口商品交易会，高级美术师，中国美协会员。出版《李金明油画选集》，《李金明访欧作品》，《李金明－－广东美术家丛书》。

Li Jin-ming, a graduate of the Guangzhou Institute of Fine Art and a member of the China Artists' Association, is now working at the China Export Commodities Fair as a senior class artist. His publications include "Li Jin-ming's Collection of Oil Paintings", "Li Jin-ming's Works During His Visit in Europe", and "Li Jin-ming--Series of Guangdong Artists".

李正天　《千年沉睡》　油画　240cm × 120cm
Li Zheng-tian　"Thousand Years of Sleep"　Oil Painting　240cm × 120cm

李正天，哲学家，艺术家。42年生于恩施，山东临沂人。现任教于广州美术学院。出版哲学专著《超越理性，广义本体论》。创作油画《生命九章》。擅长书法，任"中国当代书法大展"评委。

Li Zheng-tian, philosopher and artist, born in Ensi in 1942, is a native of Linyi, Shandong Province. He is now teaching at the Guangzhou Institute of Fine Art. His publications include a philosophical treatise "Surpass Rationality--General Moumenon". "Nine Chapters of Life" is his oil painting creation. Also good at calligraphy, he used to be a judge of the "Contemporary Chinese Calligraphy Exhibition".

李正天 《苏醒》 油画 240cm × 120cm
Li Zheng-tian "Consciousness" Oil Painting
240cm × 120cm

艾欣　《花魂》　油画　75cm × 95cm　　1997 年
Ai Xin　"Spirit of Flowers"　Oil Painting　75cm × 95cm
1997

艾欣，女，68年生，专业艺术家，擅长油画，书法。95年举
办"艾欣书法展"，97年参加48回广东星河展"花魂－－艾
欣油画展"。

Ai Xin, female, born in 1968, is a professional artist good at oil painting and
calligraphy. She held "Ai Xin's Exhibition of Calligraphy" in 1995, and took part in
the 48th Guangdong Star River Exhibition with her "Spirit of Flowers--Ai Xin's Oil
Painting Exhibition".

艾欣　《月光奏鸣曲》　油画　　60cm × 75cm　　1997 年
Ai Xin　"Moonlight Sonata"　Oil Painting　60cm × 75cm　　1997

艾欣　《呵护》　80cm × 60cm
Ai Xin　"Blessing"　80cm × 60cm

艾欣　《庄严弥撒》　80cm × 60cm
Ai Xin　"Noble Missa"　80cm × 60cm

艾欣　《花蚀》　80cm × 60cm
Ai Xin　"Flower Eclipse"　80cm × 60cm

艾欣　《孕》　95cm × 75cm
Ai Xin　"Pregnance"　95cm × 75cm

新麗墙畫系列产品簡介

豪美墙画彩印有限公司，是一家中外合作企业。主要生产各种墙画，复制画，海报和布画。引进先进德国海德堡罗兰印刷机。产品以独特个性让商店，营业场所，居家更加出色。

电话：（020）8485828，83338848

地址：广东番禺石基镇新桥村（511450）

Haomei Wall-painting and Color Printing Co. Ltd. is a joint venture mainly producing different kinds of wall-paintings, reproductions, posters, and cloth paintings with advanced printing machines inported from Germany. Its unique products add good looks to shops, malls and homes.

Tel:(020)8485828, 83338848

Address: Xinqiao Village, Shiji Town, Panyu, Guangdong Province

Post Code:511450

地丁 《月是故乡明》　　国画　　68cm × 68cm　　1995 年
Di Ding　"The Moon of Hometown is the Brightest"　Chinese Painting
68cm × 68cm　　1995

地丁，多次获省一，二，三等奖（书画）。95 年参加中国艺
术博览会（广州）；96 年参加广州国际艺术博览会。曾获国
家级，国际书展优秀奖。

Di Ding has been provincial prizes (firat-, second- and third-class) and excellence prizes
at national and international levels for his painting calligraphic works. He took part
in the '95 China Art Exposition(Guangzhou), and '96 Guangzhou International Art Fair.

杨伟 《人物肖像》 国画 65cm × 39cm 1994 年
Yang Wei "Portrait" Chinese Painting 65cm × 39cm 1994

杨伟，中国书法家协会会员，辽宁美协会员，辽宁铁岭市书协主席。多次参加国内外书画展，获奖30余次。曾在东京第51回国际书道展中获金牌并被东京美术馆收藏。手指画在97香港回归全国书画展中获铜牌。曾两次赴日办展。出版《三友书画集》，《一墨指画集》。

Yang Wei is a member of the China Calligraphists' Association, and Liaoning Artists' Association. He has taken part in art exhibitions in and out of China many times, and won prizes for over 30 times. His works won a gold medal in the 51st Tokyo International Exhibition of Calligraphic Works, and were collected by Tokyo National Gallery of Fine Art. His finger-painting also won a bronze medal in '97 National Painting and Calligraphic Works Exhibition for Hongkong's Return". He has held solo exhibitions twice in Japan. "Painting and Calligraphic Works Collection of Three Friends" and "Collection of Yi Mo's Finger-Paintings" are among his publications.

深圳市怡家饰品有限公司室内装饰品，陶瓷工艺品，树脂工
艺品，西班牙工艺品。
地址：深圳市华侨城湖滨花园潋芳阁6楼D座
邮编：518053
电话：（0755）6602657

Shenzhen IGA Household Decoration , LTD.
Products include interior decoration articles, resin handicrafts, ceramics handiwork,
Spanish handicrafts,etc.
ADD:Unit D, 6th Floor, Lianfang Building, Lakeshore, Overseas Chinese City,
Shenzhen, China.
P.O.:518053
TEL:(0755)6602657

孔凡超　《静物》　油画
Kong Fan-chao　"Still Life"　Oil Painting

孔凡超，87年毕业于广州美术学院工艺系。87-89年任中山市职业中学美术教师。89-91年中山市煜昌金属工艺厂美术师。91年至今任中山大明红木家具厂设计员。

Kong Fan-chao graduated from the Industrial Art Department of the Guangzhou Institute of Fine Art in 1987. He was an art teacher in the Zhongshan Vocational Middle School from 1987 to 1989, and an art worker in Zhongshan Da Yu Chang Metal Industrial Art Factory from 1989 to 1991. Now he is a designer of the Zhongshan Da-ming Red Wood Furniture Factory.

石里溪　《风雨撼黄山》　中国画　　48cm × 46cm　1997 年
Shi Li-xi　"Storm Shaking the Huangshan Mountain"　Chinese Painting　48cm × 46cm　1997

石里溪，合肥师范学院艺术系毕业。作品参加德国举办的
"安徽中国现代画展"，在日本举办的"黄山画近作联展"，
"第2届中韩书画交流展"，"中国青年国画大展"，"第9届当
代中国花鸟画邀请展"等。传略入编《当代美术家人名录》等
多部辞典。出版《石里溪画集》。

Shi Li-xi graduated from the Fine Art Department of Hefei Normal College. His works
have participated in the China Modern Art Exhibition of Anhui Province held in
Germany, the Joint Exhibition of Current Works on Huangshan Painting (Japan), the
second Sino-Korean Exchange Exhibition of Painting and Calligraphy, the Exhibition
of Chinese Youth's Traditonal Chinese Paintings", and the 9th Contemporary
Invitational Exhibition of Chinese Flower and Bird Paintings, etc. His experience has
been edited into many dictionaries such as the "Album of Modern Artists". "Painting
collection of Shi Li-xi" is his publication.

孙成斌 《金秋行舟图》 国画 137cm × 70cm 1992 年
Sun Cheng-bin "Boat Trip in Golden Autumn" Chinese Painting 137cm × 70cm 1992

孙成斌，西安教育学院毕业，从事绘画创作 20 多年，中国美术家协会陕西分会会员。作品多次参加省市级画展并获各种奖。84年入选全国第6届美展。作品在各类报纸杂志多有发表。

Sun Cheng-bin, a graduate of the Xi'an Normal College, has been engaged in painting for over 20 years. He is a member of the Shanxi Artists' Association, and has participated in many art exhibtions such as the 6th National Exhibition of Fine Art in 1984, and been awarded. His works are published in many newspapers and journals.

袁学君 《三峡烟云》 中国画 97cm × 176cm 1997 年
Yuan Xue-jun "Clouds and Mist over the Changjiang Gorges" Chinese Painting
97cm × 176cm 1997

袁学君，92年广州美术学院毕业。作品入选首届中国青年国
画大展，广东省第 8 届美展，广东文联采风成果展等。作品
在《中国青年国画家》，《92-93中国艺术收藏年鉴》，《中国
文化报》等各种报刊发表。不少作品被法国，丹麦，新加坡，
日本等政府机构和私人收藏。出版《袁学君山水画集》。

Yuan Xue-jun graduated from the Guangzhou Institute of Fine Art in 1992. He has
taken part in the first Exhibition of Chinese Youth's Traditional Chinese Paintings,
the 8th Guangdong Exhibition of Fine Art, and Guangdong Writers' Association's
Exhibition of Achievements in the Collection of Folk Art. Many of his works were
published by such journals as "China's Young Painters of Traditional Chinese Painting
of Chinese Painting", "Introduction to Chinese Art Collections(92-93)", and "Chinese
Culture", and some were collected by people and organizations from France, Danmark,
Singapore, and Japan. His publications include "Yuan Xue-jun's Collection of Landscape
Painting".

田婕 《李清照》 国画 136cm × 68cm 1993 年
Tian Jie "Li Qing-zhao" Chinese Painting
136cm × 68cm 1993

田婕，西安美院毕业。中国艺术协会（台）作品决审委员，陕
西美协会员，陕西省妇女书画协会副主席。作品多次参加国
内外美术大展。91年赴日办个展。出版《田婕仕女画选》。艺
术简历刊入《陕西地方志》,《中国文艺家传集》等多部辞典。

Tian Jie graduated from the Xi'an Institute of Fine Art, and is a work evaluation member of China Art Association(Taiwan), a member of Shanxi Artists' Association, and vice chairman of Shanxi Women's Association of Painting and Calligraphy. Her works have taken part in many large scale exhibitions. In 1991, she held a solo exhibition in Japan. Her experience has been edited into such dictionaries as "Annals of Shanxi", and "Biography of Chinese Writers and Artists". Her publications include "Tian Jie's Collection of Beauty Painting".

张向军　《菡萏图》　中国画　200cm×60cm　中国画　1996年
Zhang Xiang-jun　"Lotus"　Chinese Painting　200cm×60cm　1996

张向军，93年毕业于北京解放军艺术学院美术系。作品入选全国第8届美展，纪念抗日战争和世界反法西斯战争胜利50周年美展，军队10位名家作邀请展，建军65周年美展，巴黎中国书画展，多次获奖。出版有《诸子百家－－孔子》，《唐诗书画艺术集》。

Zhang Xiang-jun graduated from the Fine Art Department of Beijing PLA Art Institute. His works were selected into the 8th National Exhibition of Fine Art, the National Exhibition in Commemoration of 50 Anniversary of the Victory of Anti-Japanese and Anti-Fascist War,the Invitational Exhibition of Ten Famous Army Artists, the Art Exhibition in Commenoration of 65 Anniversary of Army Founding, and the Paris Exhibition of Chinese Painting and Calligraphic Works. His publications include "Confusius", and "Art Collection of Painting and Calligraphic Works on Tang Poems".

南岭梅 《红梅一笑天下春》 中国画 1996年
Nan Ling-mei "The Blooming of Red Wintersweet
Anouncing the Coming of Spring" Chinese Painting
1996

南岭梅（王春华），山西美术家协会会员，中国书画专业委员
会常务副会长，太原金龙画廊艺术总监。 曾先后在太原，广
州，梅州等市举办个展。书画作品多次参展获奖。出版《王
春华南岭书画集》。

Nan Ling-mei (Wang Chun-hua) is a member of Shanxi Artists' Association, vice
president of the standing committee of China Professional Art Commitee, and art
supervisor of Taiyuan Jinglong Gallery. He has held solo exhibitions in cities such as
Taiyuan, Guangzhou, and Meizhou. Many of his works were awarded. His publication
is "Wang Chun-hua's Nan Ling Collection of Painting and Calligraphic Works".

杜浩 《东北虎系列之八—雄风》 油画 145.5cm×112.1cm 1997年
Du Hao "Dongbei Tigers Series 8 — Mighty Tiger" Oil Painting
145.5cm×112.1cm 1997

杜浩，59年生于辽宁锦州。84年鲁迅美术学院毕业。作品多次参加全国及省市美展并获奖。辽宁省美协会员，任职于锦州市群众艺术馆。

Du Hao was born in Jinzhou, Liaoning Povince in 1959. He graduated from the Luxun Institute of Fine Art in 1984. Many of his works have participated in national and provincial art exhibitions and been awarded. He is now a member of Liaoning Artists' Association, working at the Jinzhou People's Art Museum.

张桥 《牧羊女》 油画 80cm × 65cm 1997 年
Zhang Qiao "Shepherdess" Oil Painting 80cm × 65cm 1997

张桥，87年加入中国美术家协会广西分会。88-89年在广州
美术学院油画系学习。

Zhang Qiao has been a member of Guangxi Artists' Association since 1987. He studied
in the Oil Painting Department of Guangzhou Institue of Fine Art from 1988 to 1989.

孙黎　《桐树花》　油画　120cm×100cm　1990 年
Sun Li "Flowers of Phoenix Trees"　Oil Painting　120cm×100cm　1990

广东教育学院

地址：广州市新港中路 351 号（510303）
电话：84218877
参展画家：胡钜湛，孙黎，张洪亮，司徒锦鹰，石萍，程耀，
曹伟业，王豫湘，冯艺，何汉求，陈中科，刘立民

Guangdong Education College
Addrss: No. 351, Xing Gang Zhong Road, Guangzhou
Post Code: 510303
Tel: 84328877
Participating Painters: Hu Ju-zhan, Sun Li, Zhang Hong-liang, Si Tu Jing-ying, Shi Ping, Cheng Yao, Cao Wei-ye, Wang Yu-xiang, Feng Yi, He Han-qiu, Chen Zhong-ke, and Liu Li-ming.

胡钜湛，广州美院、广东教育学院教授，系主任，著名水彩
画家、油画家。作品多次参加全国美展。出版《胡钜湛水彩
画选》，《静物临本》等专集。

Hu Ju-zhan, dean of Guangzhou Institute of Fine Art, and Guangdong Education College, is a famous artist of water color and oil painting. His works have taken part in many national art exhibitions. His publications include "Selection of Hu Ju-zhan's Water Color Paintings",and "Copies of Still Life".

孙黎，广州美院毕业，中国美协会员，副教授，系副主任。多
次参加全国性美展，并获奖。作品被中国美术馆收藏（5 件）
及国外人士收藏。

Sun Li, a graduate of the Guangzhou Institute of Fine Art, is a member of China Artists' Association, associate professor, and vice-dean of the department. He took part in many national art exhibitions and was awarded. His works have been collected by the China National Gallery of Fine Art (5 pieces) and by foreign art lovers.

冯艺，87 年广州美术学院毕业。89 年作品《黎族少女》编入
《中国高等美术学院作品全集》。

Feng Yi graduated from the Guangzhou Institute of Fine Art.In 1989, his "Lady of Li Nationality" is edited into the "General Collection of Works from Chinese Art Institutes of Higher learning".

王豫湘 《毛毛雨》 国画 97cm×82cm 1996年
Wang Yu-xiang "Drizzles" Chinese Painting 97cm×82cm 1996

司徒锦鹰，78年毕业于台湾艺术雕塑系。95年广州美院硕士研究生毕业。现为台湾桃园美术教育学会会员，日本正锋书道会一级会员，台湾东方画廊经理。

Si Tu Jing-ying, a graduate of Sculpture Department in Taiwan in 1978, is an MA of the Guangzhou Institute of Fine Art in 1995. He is a member of Taiwan Taoyuan Art Education Society, first class member of Japan Zhengfeng Calligraphy Society, and manager of Taiwan Dongfang Gallery.

曹伟业，83年西安美院毕业。作品入选全国第6届美展，全国首届当代中国画山水画邀请展。

Cao Wei-ye is a '83 graduate of the Xi'an Institute of Fine Art. His works have been selected into the 6th National Exhibition of Fine Art, and the first National Invitational Exhibition of Modern Chinese Landscape Paintings.

王豫湘，82年湖南师范大学美术系毕业。88年毕业于湖北美术学院研究生班。中国画，连环画作品入选第6届全国美展。89年《夏河响浪》入选第7届全国美展。

Wang Yu-xiang graduated from the Fine Art Department of the Hunan Normal University in 1982, and finished his graduate courses in the Hubei Institute of Fine Art. His Chinese paintings and story books have been selected into the 6th National Exhibition of Fine Art. In 1989, his "Waves of Xiahe River" took part in the 7th National Exhibition of Fine Art.

张洪亮　　《保姆肖像》　　油画　　146cm × 114cm　　1994 年
Zhang Hong-liang　"Portrait of a Babysitter"　Oil painting
146cm × 114cm　　1994

陈中科，89 年广州美术学院毕业。89 年水彩画《正月》参加广东省美展，96 年多幅作品在《南方日报》发表。

Chen Zhong-ke is a graduate of the Guangzhou Institute of Fine Art in1989. His water color painting "The First Moon" took part in the Guangdong Provincial Exhibition of Fine Art in 1989, and many of his other works are published by the "Nanfang Daily" in 1996.

张洪亮，92 年广州美术学院毕业，硕士学位。广东美协会员。作品入选第 8 届全国美展，第 4 届全国体育美展（获省展优秀奖），首届中国水彩画艺术展。多次入选省展。

Zhang Hong-liang, an MA of the Guangzhou Institute of Fine Art in 1992, is a member of Guangdong Artists' Association. His works have been selected into the 8th National Exhibition of Fine Art, the 4th National Sport Fine Art Exhibition (being awarded a provincial excellence prize), and the first Chinese Art Exhibition of Water Color Painting.

刘立民，广州美术学院毕业，在该院油画系进修研究生课程。水彩画作品 2 幅参加省美展，中国首届水彩艺术展，第 7 届中国水彩画大展。多件作品，论文在报刊发表。

Liu Li-min, a graduate of the Guangzhou Institute of Fine Art, has further his studies in the Department of Oil Painting at the same institute. Two pieces of his water color paintings took part in the provincial exhibition, the first Chinese art exhibition of water color Paintings, and the 7th China Exhibition of Water Color Paintings. Many of his works and papers are published in newspapers and magazines.

石萍　《曼陀罗的空间之一》　漆画　60cm × 60cm
Shi Ping　"The Space of Datura" Serial 1　Lacquer Painting　60cm × 60cm

石萍，湖北工学院工业美术系毕业。结业于广州美院研修班。现为美术系讲师，工艺教研室主任。设计作品曾获"鲁艺杯"优秀奖，首届华人平面设计大赛铜奖。

Shi Ping is a graduate of the Industrial Fine Art Department of the Hubei Industry Institute. She furthered her studies in the Guangzhou Institute of Fine Art. Now she is a lecturer in the Fine Art Department, and dean of the industrial art studio. Her works were awarded the "Lu Yi Cup" excellence prize, and a bronze prize in the first plane design competition for Chinese original.

何汉求，广州美术学院毕业。87-96年任教于广州市工艺美术职业学校。现为广东教育学院美术系教师。96年参加北京首届美术博览会。

He Han-qiu is a graduate of the Guangzhou Institute of Fine Art. He has been a teacher in the Guangzhou Art Vocational School from 1987 to 1996. Now he is teaching in the Fine Art Department of Guangdong Normal Institute. He took part in the first Fine Art Exposition in Beijing in 1996.

程耀，中央工艺美院毕业，结业于广州美院研修班。中国工艺美术协会会员，中国工艺设计协会会员，中国展示协会会员。美术讲师。

Cheng Yao, a graduate of the Central Institute of Industrial Art, has furthered his studies in the Guangzhou Institute of Fine Art. He is a member of the China Industrial Artists' Association, China Industrial Art Designers' Association, etc. He is an art lecturer.

庄小尖　《山水》　　国画　　70cm × 70cm　1997 年
Zhuang Xiao-jian　"Landscape"　Chinese Painting　70cm × 70cm　1997

庄小尖，广州美院毕业。广东省美术家协会会员，广东省书
法家协会会员，广东省装帧艺术研究会会员，中国装帧艺术
研究会会员。现为广东旅游出版社美术副编审。出版《庄小
尖书画集》。

Zhuang Xiao-jian, a graduate from the Guangzhou Institute of Fine Art, is a member
of the Guangdong Artists' Association, the Guangdong Calligraphists' Association,
the Guangdong Committee of Mounting Art, the China Research Society of Mounting
Art. He is now associate copy editor of art in the Guangdong Tourist Publishing House.
Among his publications is "Collection of Zhuang Xiao-jian's Calligrahic and Painting
Works".

庄小尖 《山水》 国画 70cm×70cm 1997年
Zhuang Xiao-jian "Landscape" Chinese Painting 70cm×70cm 1997

庄小尖 《山水》 国画 70cm × 70cm 1997 年
Zhuang Xiao-jian "Landscape" Chinese Painting 70cm × 70cm 1997

邓崇龙 《夏日》 油画 46cm × 54cm 1997 年作
Deng Chong-long "Summer Sun" Oil Painting 46cm × 54cm 1997

邓崇龙，出版《邓崇龙人体油画选》。曾参加香港《中国美术家十老联展》。作品发表于国内外报纸刊物，参加广东历史画集第二批作品展。94,95 年参加中国艺术博览会（广州），96,97 年参加广州国际艺术博览会。

Deng Chong-long took part in the Joint Exhibition of Ten Old Chinese Artists in Hong Kong, the Second Exhibition of Painting Collection of Guangdong History , the '94 and '95 China International Art Exposition(Guangzhou, the '96 and '97 Guangzhou International Art Fair. His works have been published in newspapers and journals in and out of China. His publication is "Deng Cong-long's Oil Painting Collection of Human Body".

邓崇龙 《闲情》 油画 100cm × 130cm 1997 年作
Deng Chong-long "Pleasure of Leisure" Oil Painting
100cm × 130cm 1997

张秋华　《盼归》　国画　80cm × 80cm　1997 年
Zhang Qiu-hua "Longing for Returning"　Chinese Painting　80cm × 80cm　1997

张秋华，沈阳鲁迅美院毕业。中国美协辽宁分会会员。现任
职辽宁营口市群众艺术馆。20多件作品在省以上大型美展中
展出并获奖。出版《辽宁民间舞蹈集成》。
电话：(0417) 2834899

Zhang Qiu-hua, a member of the Liaoning Artitsts' Association, graduated from the
Shenyang Luxun Institute of Fine Art, and is now working at the People's Art Museum
in Yingkou of Liaoning Province. Over twenty of his works have been displayed in
provincial and national exhibitions and awarded. His "Collection of Liaoning Folk
Dances" is among his publications.
Tel: (0417) 2834899

王盛　《宏途》　国画　200cm × 100cm　1997 年
Wang Sheng　"Great Road"　Chinese Painting　200cm × 100cm　1997

王盛，1941 年生。
作品多次参加国内外美术大展和艺术博览会。
地址：辽宁营口市鲅鱼圈北国艺术公司
电话：(0417) 6256607

Wang Sheng was born in 1941. His works have taken part in many large scale exhibtions
and art fairs at home and abroad.
Address: Beiguo Art Company, Bayuquan, Yingkou, Liaoning Province
Tel:(0417)6256607

王首麟　《壮别图》　　国画　　138cm × 68cm　　1996 年
Wang Shou-lin　"A Lofty Parting"　Chinese Painting　138cm × 68cm　1996

王首麟，北京画院研修班毕业。作品《雅士图》参加第 8 届
全国美展，《文姬归汉》获首届扇面大展优秀奖，《战地黄花》
参加全国纪念抗战胜利 50 周年展，《对弈图》参加全国体育
美展。出版《中国画精品集－－王首麟专集》。

Wang Shou-lin took research courses in Beijing Art Academy. His "Refined Scholars"
participated in the 8th National Exhibition of Fine Art, "A Game of Chess" in the
National Sports Art Exhibition, "Warfield Chrysamthemums" in the National Exhibition
in Commemoration of the 50th Anniversary of Anti-Japanese War Victory, and his
"Lady Wen Ji Returning to Han Government" won an excellence prize in the First Fan
Design Exhibition. His " Collection of Chinese Refined Art--Collection of Wang Shou-
ling's Works" is his publication.

耿郁文 《翠竹四喜图》 工笔画 66cm × 115cm 1989 年
Geng Yu-wen "Green Bamboos and the `Four Happiness'" Gongbi Painting
66cm × 15cm 1989

耿郁文，58 年于中央工艺美院进修。作品参加全国盟员美展，第 5,9,11,12 届当代中国花鸟邀请展，并被出版收藏。现为辽宁美协会员，工艺美术大师，营口市美协副主席，市国画研究会会长。

Geng Yu-wen is member of Liaoning Artists' Association, a master of industrial art, vice-chairman of Yingkou Artists' Association, and president of the municipal Chinese Painting Research Society. He took refresher courses in the Central Industrial Art Institute in 1958. His works have participated in the National Alliance Members' Exhibition of Fine Art, the 5th,9th,11th, and 12th Invitational Exhibition of Contemporary Chinese Flower-and-Bird Painting, and were published and collected.

刘增孝　《鹰》　国画　132cm × 66cm　1997 年
Liu Zeng-xiao "Eagle" Chinese Painting
132cm × 66cm 1997

刘增孝，毕业于内蒙师大美术系。中国美协内蒙分会会员。
被列入《中国当代美术家名人录》一书。作品在《中日现代
美术通鉴》有介绍。曾多次参加省以上美展，部分获奖，并
被国内外收藏家收藏。

Liu Zeng-xiao, a graduate of the Fine Art Dapartment of the Inner Mongolia Normal
University, is a member of Inner Mongolia Artists' Association. His name has been
listed in the "Dictionary of Famous Contemporary Chinese Artists", and his works
have been intruduced in the "General Introduction to Sino-Japanese Modern Art". He
participated in provincial and national art exhibtions for many times and was awarded.
His works have also been collected by people in and out of China.

苟正翔　《一天云海隔尘寰》　　国画　　176cm×95cm　　　1996年
Gou Zheng-xiang　"A Sea of Cloud　Separating the Earth From Heaven"
Chinese Painting　176cm×95cm　　1996

苟正翔，中国人才研究会艺术委员，省美协会员，省国画家
学会会员，陇中画院荣誉画师。91年在北京举办个展。中央
电台及《人民日报》均报导。参加首届国际绘画书法艺术大
展获优秀奖。出版有《苟正翔山水画集》。
电话：（0932）6624555

Gou Zheng-xiang, an honored painter of Longzhong Art Academy, an art member of
the art committee of China Talent Research Society member of the provincial Artists'
Association, and the porvincial Chinese Painting Artists Society. He held solo exhibition
in Beijing in 1991, which was reported by the Central People's Broadcast Station, and
"People's Daily". His work won an excellence prize in the first National Art Exhibition
of Painting and Calligraphic Works. "Gou Zheng-xiang's Collection of Landscape
Painting" is among his publications.
Tel: (0932) 6624555

傅文刚　《长恨歌》　　250cm × 160cm　　1997 年
Fu Wen-gang　"Sorrow of Seperation"　　250cm × 160cm　　1997

傅文刚，深造于西安美院，为盛唐佛院设计了一尊48米高的四面大佛。作品曾在法国，美国，澳大利亚，日本，新加坡等国展出，并被巴黎国际艺博会收藏。多次入选全国体育美展，纪念鲁迅诞辰120周年美展，全国扇面美展，全国八届美展，获金，银，铜奖，并被收藏。现任宝鸡炎黄画院院长。
电话：（0917）3246398

Fu Wen-gang, president of Baoji Yanhuang Art Academy, had furthered his studies in the Xi'an Institute of Fine Art, and designed a 48-meter-high statue of four-face-buddha for the Flourishing Tang Monastery. His works have been exhibited in France, America, Australia, Japan and Singapore, and collected by the Paris International Art Fair. He took part in many of the exhibitions such as the national art of sports exhibition, Art Exhibition in Commemoration of Luxun's 100 Birthday" ,the National Fan Design Art Exhibition, and the 8th National Exhibition of Fine Art. His works also won gold, silver, and bronze prizes in them and were collected.
Tel:(0917) 3246398

王长明　《景观系列：No.1》　布面油彩　63cm × 70cm　1997 年
Wang Chang-ming　"Serial Views: No. 1" Oil on Canvas　63cm × 70cm　1997

王长明毕业于上海美院（分部），致力于实验性写实绘画创
作。其作品广为港台及东南亚地区收藏家青睐，现已引起欧
美收藏家的注目。95、96、97 年参加广州国际艺术博览会。
现为浙江画院画廊画家。
电话：0510-5757178（工作室）

Wang Chang-ming A graduate of Shanghai Institute of Fine Art (Branch), he devotes
himself to experimental realistic painting creation. His works have been an attraction to
collectors in Hong Kong, Taiwan and Southeast-Asian countries, and now aroused the
attention of European and American collectors. He participated in the '95, '96 and '97
Guangzhou International Art Expositions in succession. He is now an artist of Zhejiang
Painting Academy's gallery.
Tel: 0510-5757178 (Studio)

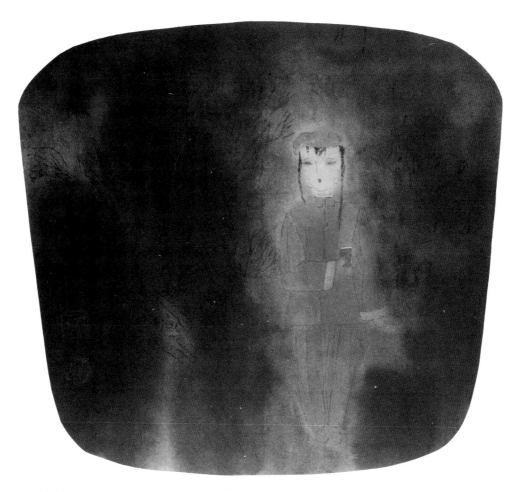

刘老五　《火红的年代系列之五》　　国画　　34cm × 32cm　　1997 年
Liu Lao-wu "The Flaming Years Series No. 5" Chinese Painting
34cm × 32cm　　1997

刘老五　1965 年生。1987 年就读于东北师范大学美术系版画
专业，1992 年于中央美术学院进修。1997 于中国美术馆举办
《刘老五水墨人物展》。

Liu Lao-wu born in 1965, he entered the Fine Art Department of North-East Normal
University in 1987, and furthered his studies in the Central Institue of Fine Art in 1992.
He held the "Exhibition of Inkwashed Figures by Liu Lao-wu" in the China Fine Art
Gallery in 1997.

季智俞 　《溪山会友》 　中国画 　138cm × 68cm 　1997 年
Ji Zhi-yu 　"Meeting Friends at Xishan Hill" 　Chinese Painting 　138cm × 68cm 　1997

季智俞 1959 年生于江苏南京。南京市美协会员，江都画院
特聘画师。

Ji Zhi-yu, born in Nanjing, Jiangsu Province in 1959, is member of Nanjing Artists'
Association and guest painter of Jiangdu Painting Academy.

田应福 《正午云当头》 国画 50cm × 50cm 1994年
"Clouds Overhead at Noon" Chinese Painting 50cm × 50cm 1994

程其德 《寒夜》 国画 50cm × 50cm 1994年
"A Cold Night" Chinese Painting 50cm × 50cm 1994

田应福，现为中国历史文化名城书画研究会理事，遵义市美协理事，贵州黔北画院副院长。作品多次参展，发表，获奖。不少作品被美国，瑞典，新加坡，日本等国人士收藏。

Tian Ying-fu, vice president of Guizhou Qianbei Academy of Painting, is a director of the Research Society of Chinese Painting and Calligraphy in China's Historical and Cultrual Cities, and of Zunyi Artists' Association. His works have been selected into exhibtions, published, awarded, and collected by people from America, Sweden, Singapore, and Japan.

程其德，贵州省美协会员，遵义市美协理事，贵州黔北画院副院长。专攻花鸟。不少作品参加各美展并被发表。多件作品被海内外人士收藏。

Cheng Qi-de is a member of Guizhou Artists' Association, a director of Zunyi Artists' Association, and vice president of Guizhou Qianbei Academy of Painting. He specializes in flower and bird painting. Many of his works have participated in exhibitios, quite a few have been published and collected by people at home and abroad.

陈艳梅　《雪艳》　国画　100cm × 100cm　1997 年
Chen Yan-mei　"The Charm of Snow"　Chinese Painting　100cm × 100cm　1997

陈艳梅先后学习于中央美院徐悲鸿画室，北京画院。曾在北京、深圳等地举办个展，并两次出画集。连续三次参加广州、北京艺博会，作品多次在国内外获奖，并收入《世界华人艺术家大辞典》、《中国当代名人录》等。作品被中南海、徐悲鸿纪念馆、深圳博物馆等收藏。

Chen Yan-mei studied at the Xu Bei-hong Studio of the Central Institute of Fine Art and then the Beijing Painting Academy. And she has held personal painting exhbitions in such places as Beijing and Shenzhen, and had two painting collections published. She took part in the International Art Expositions in Beijing and Guangzhou three times in succession. Many of her works have been awarded and collectd in "Dictionary of Artists of Chinese Origin in the World" and "Who's Who, Contemporary Chinese", and some collected by Zhongnanhai, Xu Bei-hong Memorial Halland the Shenzhen Museum as well.

深圳市福传工艺制作有限公司　《鹏程万里》　木雕工艺　630cm × 1200cm　1997
Shenzhen Fuchuan　Industrial Manufacture Company, Limited
"A Roc That Makes a Flight of a Thousnd Li"　Woodcarving
630cm × 1200cm　1997

深圳市福传工艺制作有限公司设备先进，技艺精湛，能适应
现代化新潮装饰欣赏水平的挑战。主要生产仿古木雕和现代
玻璃彩绘工艺品两大类。
电话：(0755) 7909945，7909917，7904930

Shenzhen Fuchuan Industrial Manufacture Company, Limited, with advanced equipment
and excellent techniques, can meetthe challenge of the new level of appreciation of
modern decoration. Its main products include imitated ancient woodcarving and modern
painted glass handcrafts.
Tel: (0755)7909945, 7909917, 7904930

纪淑文 《花卉》 工笔国画　82cm × 82cm　1997 年
Ji Shu-wen "Flowers" Gongbi Painting　82cm × 82cm　1997

纪淑文，锦州市美协常务理事，锦州画院特聘画家，辽宁美
协会员。作品多次参加市省级画展并获奖。《清香拂醉》收入
《全国首届花鸟画展》并编入画集第244页。该作品随后于96
年参加世界妇女大会画展。

Ji Shu-wen Standing director of Jinzhou Artists' Association and member of Liaoning Artists' Association, Ji is a guest painter of Jinzhou Painting Academy with works displayed in provincial and municipal painting exhibitions. "Drunk in Fragrance" was collected in the catalog(p.244)of "The First National Flower-and-Bird Painting Exhibition", and it was on later shown in the Painting Exhibition of the '96 World Women's Conference.

纪淑文 《罗汉图》 工笔国画 656cm × 220cm 1997 年
Ji Shu-wen "Arhats" Gongbi Painting 656cm × 220cm 1997

王锦清 《蟹》 油画 60cm × 50cm 1996年
Wang Jin-qing "Crabs" Oil Painting 60cm × 50cm 1996

王锦清，湛江画院画家。作品多次入选省及全国性美展，曾在湛江、深圳等地举行个展。多幅作品在各种报刊上发表，并被编入《'93博雅油画大赛获奖作品集》和《中国风景油画》等画册。

Wang Jin-qing, painter of the Zhanjiang Painting Academy, Wang has had works shown in a lot of provincial and national fine art exhitions, many of which have been published by newspapers and magazines. He has held solo exhibitions in Zhanjiang, and Shenzhen. Many of his works have been published in newspapers and magazines, and selected into such publications as "Collection of Awarded Works of the `93 Boya Oil Painting Competition" and "Oil Paintings of Chinese Landscape".

陈 圻 《油瓶与马铃薯》 油画 70cm×60cm 1997年
Chen Qi "An Oil Bottle and Potatos" Oil Painting 70cm×60cm 1997

陈圻，湛江画院画家。毕业于广州美术学院油画系。油画《山村》入选95年全国风景画展，《万年青》入选97年全国第二届油画静物展。

Chen Qi, a graduate of the Department of Oil Painting of Guangzhou Institute of Fine Art, Chen is now an artist of Zhanjiang Painting Academy. His "Mountain Village" was selected into the `95 National Exhibition of Landscape Painting, and "Japanese Rohdea" selected into the second National Exhibition of Still-life Oil Painting.

许如秀　《奇石巧龟》—刻有孙子兵法13篇，共7000多字
Xu Ru-xiu　"Peculiar Rocks and Wonderful Tortoise"—with 13 peices of Master Sun's Art
of War　(over 7000 characters)　carved on them

许如秀，中国书画研究会会员。从事微雕艺术四十多年。多次参加省、市、全国展览并多次获奖。其作品入选'97北京国际艺术精品博览会并获优秀奖。作品多被美国、日本、香港及东南亚地区收藏。

Xu Ru-xiu is member of the China Research Society of Painting and Calligraphy. He has been engaged in mini-carving for over forty years. Many of his works have taken part in municipal, provincial, and nationalexhibitions such as the 97' Beijing International Exposition of Outstanding Art Work, and been awarded. His works have also been collected by people from America, Japan, Hongkong, and South-east Asia.

张红曼 《香远莲塘》 国画 63cm × 63cm 1996 年
Zhang Hong-man "Fr agrance of a Lotus Pool" Chinese Painting 63cm × 63cm 1996

张红曼 ,1962 年生。1986 年毕业于浙江美术学院，1991 年入
读广州美院国画研修班。现任教浙江温州师范学院美术系。
浙江美术家协会会员。出版有《张红曼作品选》。

Zhang Hong-man, born in 1962, graduated from the Zhejiang Institute of Fine Art in1986.
In 1991, she took research courses of Chinese painting in the Guangzhou Institute of
Fine Art. She now is a teacher of the Departmentof Fine Art of Wenzhou Normal Institute,
Zhejiang Province and member of Zhejiang Artists' Association. Her "Selection of Zhang
Hong-man's Works" has been published.

梁少兴 《山中月色》 国画 68cm × 68cm 1988年
Liang Shao-xing "Moonlit Valley" Chinese Painting 68cm × 68cm 1988

梁少兴,1954年生。1988年毕业于广州美术学院,1991年入
读广州美院国画研修班。曾在广东画院举办三人联展。现任
广州师范美术讲师,广州山水画研究学会秘书长,广州美协
会员。

Liang Shao-xing born in 1954, is a graduate of Class 88 of the Guangzhou Institute of
Fine Art, and took research courses in 1991 at the same institute. He has held joint
exhibitions with other two people in the Guangdong Painting Academy. He is now a
lecturer of Fine Art in the Guangzhou Normal Institute, secretary-general of the
Guangzhou Landscape Painting Research Society, and member of the Guangzhou Artists'
Association.

吴荣文　《长汀云霭》　国画　90cm × 97cm　1997
Wu Rong-wen　"Sea of Cloud at Changting"　Chinese Painting　90cm × 97cm
1997

吴荣文，潮州画院院长，潮州市美协主席，中国版画家协会会员。作品先后赴日本、西德、泰国、新加坡等地展览。曾在北京、香港、广州等地举办个展。作品《千里韩江》为天安门城楼收藏、陈列，多件作品发表于《人民日报》、《中国文化报》、《大公报》、《文汇报》等海内外报刊。出版有《吴荣文山水画集》、《吴荣文版画选集》。

Wu Rong-wen is president of Chaozhou Painting Academy,chairman of Chaozhou Artists' Association, and member of China Engraving Painting Artists' Association. His works have been exhibited in Japan, Germany, Thailand, and Singapore. He has held solo exhibitions in Beijing, Hongkong and Guangzhou. His "The Thousand li Hanjiang River" is collected by the Tian'an Men Rostrum. Many of his works were published by "People's Daily", "China Culture", "Taikung Bao", "Wenhui Bao" and others.His publications include "Collection of Wu Rong-wen's Landscape Paintings", and "Selection of Wu Rong-wen's Engraving Paintings".

王衡鉴　《荣华富贵》　中国画　四堂屏　　1995年
Wang Heng-jian "Peonies" Chinese Painting　Hanging Srolls　1995

王衡鉴，中国书画家协会会员，中国人才研究会艺术家学部委员，云南民族画院顾问。擅长写意花鸟画，尤以牡丹画独树一帜。作品多次参加国内外展览、刊登、获奖、珍藏。出版有《王衡鉴书画集》、《王衡鉴的牡丹世界》。

Wang Heng-jian is member of China Painters' and Calligraphiests' Association, member of the Artist Branch of China Talent Research Committee, and a consultant of Yunnan Nationality Painting Academy. He is good at drawing flowers and birds freehand, expecially in peonies. many of his works have been exhibited, awarded, published and collected. His publications include "Collection of Wang Heng-jian's Calligraphic Works and Paintings" ,"Wang Heng-jian's World of Peonies".

陈 恺　《夏月》　工笔重彩　　34cm × 34cm　　1996
Chen Kai　"Summer Moon"　Gongbi Painting with Colors　34cm × 34cm　1996

陈恺，中国美协北京分会会员．现任教于北京轻工职工大学设计艺术系。《暴风雨》、《山地》等作品被刊于《美术》等杂志。《雨山》入选首届中国山水画展并被评为优秀作品。作品两次入选加拿大"枫叶杯"展。95、96连续参加中国艺术博览会。出版有连环画册近二十部。

Chen Kai, a member of Beijing Artists' Association, Chen is now a teacher of the Department of Art Design of Beijing Light Industry Workers' University. His "Storm" and "Moutains" were published in such magazines as "Fine Art".His "Moutains in Rain" was awarded an excellence prize in the first China Landscape Painting Exhibition. His works took part in Canada's "Maple-leaf Cup" Exhibition twice. He participated in the 95'and 96' China International Art Exposition, and had almost 20 sets of picture-story books published.

吴贤淳　　《牡丹》　　国画　　60cm × 50cm
Wu Xian-chun　　"Peonies"　　Chinese Painting　　60cm × 50cm

吴贤淳，中国美协会员，中国书画函授大学教授，高级美术
设计师。毕业于中央美院。曾主持人民大会堂陕西厅装饰美
术设计。作品多次获全国丝绸、纺织美术设计一等奖。编著
有《图案艺术》、《美术字》等图书。

Wu Xian-chun, is member of China Artists' Association, professor of China
Correspondence University of Painting and Calligraphy, and a senior class fine art
designer. He graduated from the Central Institute of Fine Art, and took charge of the
design and decoration of the Shanxi Hall in the People's Great Hall. His works have
won first prizes innational silk and textile design competitions. Among his publications
are "The Art of Patterns"and"Art Lettering".

吴强，81年毕业于西安美院，作品入选第六届全国美展。广
东美协会员。

Wu Qiang, graduated from the Xi'an Institute of Fine Art in 1981, Wu is member of
Guangdong Artists' Association. His works have been selected into the 6th National
Exhibition of Fine Art.

刘秦生 《太白山乡鸭常鸣》 国画 68cm × 136cm 1997 年
Liu Qin-sheng "Ducks Quacking in a Taibai Mountain Village" Chinese Painting
68cm × 136cm 1997

刘秦生，西安美院毕业，曾参加93首届中国山水画展，并被中南海紫光阁收藏，出版。作品被《中国现代山水画库》出版。

Liu Qin-sheng is a graduate of Xi'an Institue of Fine Art. His painting joined the First Chinese Landscape Painting Exhibition in 1993, was colected in Ziguangge of Zhongnanhai, and published. His works have been put into "Collection of Modern Chinese Landscape Painting".

邹莉　《水觞》　国画　150cm × 180cm
Zhou Li　"Mourning Water"　Chinese Painting　150cm × 180cm

邹莉，广州美术学院国画系硕士研修班毕业。现为广东美协
理事。作品曾参加全国、省、市美展并多次获奖。出版《中
国一百后妃图》，《邹莉画选》等。曾在日本、香港、广州、佛
山、中山举办个展。94 年赴美国进行学术交流考察。现受
聘为南海画院、广州美术馆画家。

Zhou Li graduated with an MA degree from Chinese painting Department of the
Guangzhou Institute of Fine Art. She is now director of Guangdong Artists' Association,
and an artist of the Nanhai Academy of Painting, and Guangzhou Gallery of Fine Art.
Her works have taken part in national, provincial, and municipal exhibitions, and been
awarded. Her publications include "Paintings of 100 Queens and Imperial Concubines
of China", and "Selection of Zhou Li's Painting". She held solo exhibitions in Japan,
Hongkong, Guangzhou, Foshan, and Zhongshan, and went to America in 1994 for
academic exchange.

黎明晖 《南天丽日系列》 国画 200cm × 240cm
Li Ming-hui "Blue Sky and Bright sun Series" Chinese Painting 200cm × 240cm

黎明晖，南海画院院长，广东美协会员，佛山画院特聘画家。广州美术学院国画系研究生进修班毕业。作品多次入选各级美展并在国内外报刊杂志发表。曾在广州，佛山，深圳举办个展。

地址：广东南海市盐步区南井村 169 号 （528247）

电话：(0757) 5773870

Li Ming-hui is president of the Nanhai Academy of Painting, a member of Guangdong Artists' Association, and guest artist of the Foshan Academ of Painting. He furthered his studies in Chinese Painting Guangzhou Institute of Fine Art. His works have been selected into many exhibitions and published by newspapers and magazines at home and abroad. He has held solo exhibitions in Guangzhou, Foshan and Shenzhen.

Add: 169, Nanjing Village, Yanbu District, Nanhai City, Guangdong

Post Code: 528247

Tel: (0757)5773870

谢桂森　《水乡清晨》　　国画
Xie Gui-sen　"Morning of a Water Village"

Chinese Painting

谢桂森，88年华南文艺业余大学中国画系毕业。94年广州美
院国画系硕士研究生班进修山水画课程。现为南海画院副院
长，广东美协会员，佛山市美协常务理事，南海市美协副秘
书长。

地址：南海市小塘永安路鸿运楼702号（528222）

电话：（0757）6663032

Xie Gui-sen is a graduate of Chinese Painting Department of the South China Amateur
University of Literayure and Art in 1988. He furthered his studies in landscape painting
courses in the Chinese Painting Department of the Guangzhou Institute of Fine Art in
1994. He is now vice president of the Nanhai Academy of Painting, a member of
Guangdong Artists' Association, managing director of Foshan Artists' Association, and
vice secretory-general of Nanhai Artists' Association Address:No.702, Hongyun
Building, Yongan Road, Xiaotang, Nanhai
Post Code: 528222
Tel:(0757)6663032

梁国荣 《近水山庄》 国画 135cm × 110cm
Liang Guo-rong "Waterside Villa" Chinese Painting 135cm ×
110cm

梁国荣，广东美协会员，南海画院画家，中国画专业毕业。作品参加全国，省，市大型展览。国画《绿云》获省颂南粤锦秀画展一等奖。曾举办个展和联展。作品和艺术传略编入《中国书画家大辞典》等书。
电话：（0757）2240219

Liang Guo-rong, a graduate of Chinese Painting Speciality, is a member of Guangdong Artists' Association, and an artist of the Nanhai Academy of Painting. He took part in large scale exhibitions and won a first prize in the provincial Art Exhibition "Praise of the Beautiful Guangdong" with his "Green Clouds". He has held solo and joint exhibitions, and his experience and works are edited into such dictionaries as "Dictionary of Chinese Painters and Calligraphists".
Tel:(0757)2240219

高伟彬 《春梦》 国画
Gao Wei-bin "Spring Dreams" Chinese Painting

高伟彬，自少喜爱绘画，几十年从未间断，以研究中国画工
笔鸟为主。作品参加各级展览。现为广东美协会员，南海画
院院士。
地址：广东南海市大沥镇振兴路2号（528231）
电话：（0757）5554623,5554211

Gao Wei-bin loved to draw when his was still a child, and has been studying painting
for all these years. He is engaged in the study of bird painting, and has participated in
many exhibitions. He is now a member of Guangdong Artists' Association. and an
academician of the Nanhai Academy of Painting.
Address:No 2, Zhenxing Road, Dali county, Nahai, Guangdong Province
Post Code:528231
Tel:(0757)5554623, 5554211

林子超　《祈》(局部)　　油画　　167cm × 85cm　　1995 年
Lin Zi-chao　　"Praying" (local)　　Oil Painting　　167cm × 85cm　　1995

林子超，南海画院画家，广东美协会员。油画作品分别入选
文化部主办的中国艺术大展，主题创作展，丁绍光奖全国美
展，和当代油画艺术展。并获 96 年省展一等奖。参加 96 广
州国际艺术博览会。作品被海内外有关机构和人士收藏。
地址：广东省佛山市建设路 13 号 507 室（528000）
电话：（0757）6323283

Lin Zi-chao is an artist of the Nanhai Academy of Painting, and a member of Guangdong
Artists' Association. His oil paintings were selected into the China Art Exhibition held
by the Ministry of Culture, the Subject-Creation Exhibition, "Ding Shao-guang" Award
National Exhibition, and the Art Exhibition of Contemporary Oil Painting. He won a
first prize in the '96 provincial exhibition, and took part in the '96 Guangzhou International
Art Exposition. His works are collected by organizations and people at home and abroad.
Address: Room 507, No.13, Jianshe Road, Foshan, Guangdong Province
Post Cod: 528000
Tel:(0757)6323283

李任孚 《都市之夜》
Li Ren-fu "The Night of a Metropolis"

李任孚，广东美协会员，佛山市美协副秘书长，南海画院画
家。广西艺术学院美术系毕业。作品多次参加省、市、全国
性美展并获奖。作品参加新西兰首届中国书画名家作品展。
传略和作品编入《中国当代艺术界名人录》。
地址：广东省南海市桂城区南新一路文化公园南海画院
（528200）
电话：（0757）6225314，6223494

Li Ren-fu is a member of Guangdong Artists' Association, vice secretary-general of Foshan Artists' Association, and an artist of the Nanhai Academy of Painting. He graduated from the Fine Art Department of Guangxi Art Institute. Many of his works took part in exhibitions and were awarded. He participated in the first Work Exhibition of Famous Chinese Painters and Calligraphists held in New Zealand. His experience and works are edited into the "Album of Modern Chinese Artists".

杜炜　《雪野 幽禽》　国画
Du Wei　"Animal in snow"　Chinese Painting

杜炜，66年广州美术学院毕业。现为佛山大学副教授，中国
美协会员，南海画院画家。作品入选第5,6,7届全国美展，获
第2届连环画评奖二等奖。中国美术馆收藏其作品12幅。
地址：佛山市佛山大学南区15座602室（528000）
电话：(0757) 2268656

Du Wei is a graduate of the Guangzhou Institute of Fine Art in 1966. He is now an
associate professor of the Foshan University, a member of China Artists' Association,
and an artist of the Nanhai Academy of Painting. His works were selected into the 5th,
6th, and 7th National Exhibition of Fine Art, and awarded a second prize in the second
Story Book Competition. Twelve of his works are collected by the China National
Gallery of Fine Art.
Address:Room 602, Building 15, South District, Foshan University, Foshan
Post Code: 528000
Tel: (0757)2268656

广东省丝绸进出口（集团）公司具有40多年历史，年出口4亿多美元，贸易遍及50多个国家和地区。国家级大型外贸企业。

地址：中国广州市东风西路198号（510180）

电话：（020）83337448

传真：（020）83187339

电子信箱：http://www.tradcchanncl.com/db/08966.ad.html

Guangdong Silk Imp.& Exp. Corp.(Group) is a large national exportenterprise with 40 years in business. It has an annual export up to US $400 million, trading with 50 countries and regions.

Address:198 Dongfeng Road West, Guangdong, China

Tel : (020)83337448

Fax : (020)83187339

Email£¡http://www.tradcchanncl.com/db/08966.ad.html

广东省丝绸进出口（集团）公司具有40多年历史，年出口4亿多美元，
贸易遍及50多个国家和地区。国家级大型外贸企业。
地址：中国广州市东风西路198号（510180）
电话：（020）83337448
传真：（020）83187339
电子信箱：http://www.tradcchanncl.com/db/08966.ad.html

Guangdong Silk Imp.& Exp. Corp.(Group) is a large national exportenterprise with 40
years in business. It has an annual export up to US $400 million, trading with 50 countries
and regions.
Address:198 Dongfeng Road West, Guangdong, China
Tel ：(020)83337448
Fax : (020)83187339
Email£ºhttp://www.tradcchanncl.com/db/08966.ad.html

黄乘黄　　《春韵》　　国画　　78cm × 78cm　　1996 年
Huang Cheng-huang　　"Charm of Spring "　　Chinese Painting　　78cm × 78cm　　1996

黄乘黄（黄慧玲），省美协会员，中国工艺美术家学会会员。曾任陕西人民美术出版社美编。现为广东南海画院画家。作品入选全国，省市美展，获省一等，二等奖。作品被澳大利亚博物馆，新加坡，台湾，香港，澳门等地收藏。小传入编多部专业辞书。

Huang Cheng-huang (Huang Hui-ling) is a member of provincial Artists' Association, and China Industrial Artists' Society. She used to be art editor of Shanxi People's Art Publishing House. Now she is an artist of the Nanhai Academy of Painting, Guangdong Province. Her works were selected into national, provincial and municipal art exhibitions and awarded first and second prizes. Many of her paintings are collected by museums and people of Australia, Singapore, Taiwan, Hongkong, and Macau. Her biography was edited into many dictionaries.

逯树林　《跳涧虎》　　国画　101cm × 65cm　　1988 年
Lu Shu-lin　"Tiger Jumping Across A Stream"　Chinese Painting　101cm × 65cm　　1988

逯树林。92年三幅作品入选文化部批准举办的国际中国画展，
入编20世纪中华画苑掇英大画册续集。93年入选海内外河南
省籍著名书画家作品邀请展。　93,95年参加中国艺术博览会
（广州）并获荣誉证书；96年参加广州国际艺术博览会。

Lu Shu-lin had three works selected into the international exhibition of Chinese
Paintings Approved by the Ministry of Culture in '92, and they were edited into the
second volume of a grand album of the Selection of the 20th Century Outstanding
Paintings of China. He took part in the Invitation Exhibition of Works by Famous
Calligraphists and Painters of Henan Origin in 1993, joined the '93 and '95 China Art
Expositions(Guangzhou)respectively and had honor certificates. In 1996, he participated
in the Guangzhou International Art Exposition.

符超军　《居民构图三号》　　油画　　60cm × 60cm　　1996 年
Fu Chao-jun　"Residence No.3"　　Oil Painting　　60cm × 60cm　　1996

符超军 ,1962 年生于广州市，1987 年毕业于广州美术学院。
现为《南方日报》社美术编辑。

Fu Chao-jun, born in Guangzhou in 1962, graduated from the Guangzhou Institute of
Fine Art in 1987. He is now a fine art editor of Nanfang Daily.

甘迎祥 《南岛绿韵》 国画 150cm × 60cm 1996 年
Gan Ying-xiang "Green on Nandao Land" Chinese Painting 150cm × 60cm 1996

甘迎祥，1965 年毕业于广州美术学院。历任南方日报美编室主任，编辑。现为南方书画院院长。作品参加过全国省市画展，有的被中国美术馆收藏。1996 年参加广州国际艺术博览会，1997 年在广州举办个展。历年来出版、发表作品 500 多件。

Gan Ying-xiang graduated from the Guangzhou Institute of Fine Art. He was director of the fine art editing unit of Nanfang Daily,director-editor. He is now head of Nanfang Calligraphy and Painting Society. His works have been on show in national, provincial and municipal exhibitions and part of them collected by the China Art Gallery. He joined the Guangzhou International Art Exposition in 1996 and held solo exhibitions in 1997 in Guangzhou. He has so far published over 500 works.

黄战生　《金色的池塘》　　油画　　60cm×50cm　　1996年
Huang zhan-sheng　"Golden Pond"　Oil Painting　60cm×50cm　1996.

黄战生，1962年生。现任职于《广东画报》杂志社。
Huang zhan-sheng, born in 1962 is a member of "Guangdong Pictorial".

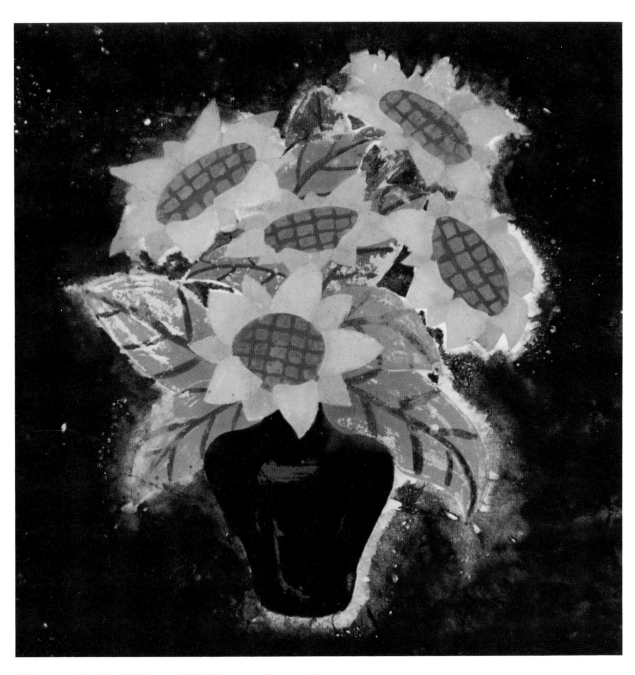

甘丹　《金色向阳花》　装饰画　　45cm × 45cm
Gan Dan　"Golden Sunflowers"　Decoration Picture　45cm × 45cm

甘丹，女，1995年毕业于广州美术学院附中，后就读于广州
美术学院。曾任《炎黄世界》和《南方周末》美编。现为《南
方都市报》美术编辑。从事装饰画创作。

Gan Dan, female, studied at the Guangzhou Institut of Fine Art after she graduated from
its Middle School. She was art editor of "The World of Yandi and Huang Di" and
"Nanfang Weekend". She is now art editor of "Nanfang Metropolis", engaged in
decoration painting.

胡锦雄　　《自在飞蝶轻似梦》　　彩墨画　　68cm × 68cm　　1997 年
Hu Jin-xiong　　"Carefree Butterflies, Like Dreams"　　Ink & Color
68cm × 68cm　　1997

胡锦雄，广州画院、广州美术馆特聘画家，广东青年美协展
览部副部长，广州美协会员。作品曾入选省市、海外等大型
美展及获奖，并发表于各专业刊物与多种报刊杂志之上。出
版有《胡锦雄作品选》，《胡锦雄国画集》。
地址：广州市洪德路聚龙大街 15 号 103 室
电话：020-84493547
手机：1392295475

Hu Jin-xiong, specially engaged paintor of the Guangzhou Academy of Painting and
the Guangzhou Art Gallery, deputy director of the exhibition department of the
Guangdong Youths' Association of Fine Art, and member of the Guangzhou Artists .
His works have been selected into Association. His works have been selected into
provincial,municipal and overseas large-scale exhibitions and awarded,and published
in jounals of many kinds. He has published four painting collections, among which are
"Selected Paintings by Hu Jin-xiong" and "Hu Jin-xiong's Chinese Paintings".
Add: Rm. 103, Julong St. Hongde Rd., Guangzhou
Tel: 020-84493547
Portable Phone: 1392295475

《晶彩陶瓷．汴绣五牛图》　　38.5cm × 263cm　　1997 年

"Crystal-color Ceramics : Kaifeng Embroidery - Five Oxen"　　38.5cm × 263cm　　1997

广东粤广工艺彩瓷公司，是广东省陶瓷公司的直属分公司，经营全国各地陶瓷精品及工艺品，是目前广州市最具规模的陶瓷工艺总汇。

地址：广州市环市中路 268 号陶瓷大厦 1-2 楼

电话：83366154，83369737

传真：83366153

联系人：周圆

Guangdong Yueguang Artistic Colored Ceramics Company is a banch office directly under the Provincial Pottery & Ceramics Company, dealing incramic works and artifacts from all over the country. It is the largest enterprise of this kind in Guangzhou.

Add: Fls 1-2, the Pottery & Ceramics Building, 268 Huanshi Rd.(C), Guangzhou

Tel: 83366154, 83369737

Fax: 83366153

Contact: Zhou Yuan

蒋媛　《黄山晴烟》　　国画　　65cm × 126cm
Jiang Yuan　"Mist over Huangshan Mountains"　Chinese Painting　65cm × 126cm

蒋媛，成都市美协会员，峨眉山画院理事、副秘书长。毕业于成都社会大学绘画专业。作品入选成都市美展、成都兴龙杯画展、成都市女画家展。《蜀山云起》入选成都画派首届现代山水画展。

Jiang Yuan, a graduate of the Painting Speciality of Chengdu Social University member of Chengdu Artists Associaiton, director and vice-secretary-general of Er Mei Mountain Academy of Painting with works selected into the Chengdu Exhibition of Fine Art, the Chengdu Xinglong Cup Painting Exhibition, and the Chengdu Exhibition of Women Painters' Works. "Clouds over Sichuan Mountains" participated in the First Modern Landscape Paintings of the Chengdu School.

博雅画艺饰品中心
主营：英国锡箔画，画框饰条，各类相架，装饰画，工艺品
地址：广州市解放南路"大都市精品广场" 34 号
电话：83344633

Boya Oainting and Decoration Items Centre
Businesses: English tinfoil pictures, frames deorations, photo frames, decoration pictures and handicrafts.
Add: No 34 of Metrpolis Plaza of Refined Artifacts, Jiefangnan Rd. Guangzhou
Tel: 83344633

于文江　《旧梦系列之－－西厢入梦》　彩墨　68cm×68cm　1996年
Yu Wen-jiang　"Old Dreams Series──Dreams in the Western Chamber"　Colour and Ink
68cm×68cm　1996

于文江，山东画院高级美术师，中国美协会员，中国工笔画学会理事。作品曾获第六届全国美展优秀作品奖，全国首届工笔山水画展一等奖，纪念毛泽东《在延安文艺座谈会上的讲话》发表50周年全国美展银奖，全国首届中国画大展铜奖，第三届中国工笔画大展金奖。其作品被中国美术馆、中南海、各地博物馆及香港、东南亚、日本、美国等收藏家所收藏。

宜雅斋艺术画廊
地址：广州市环市东路淘金坑66号侨福苑1座607
邮编：510095
电话：020-833507997
BP：84321888-5689

Yu Wen-jiang, senior painter of Shandong Academy of Painting, member of China Artists Associaiton, and director of China Gongbi Painting Society. His works won an excellence prize in the 6th National Exhibition of Fine Art, a first prize in the Fisrt National Gongbi Landscape Painting Exhibition, a silver prize in the National Fine Art Exhibition in Commemoration of the 50th Anniversary of the Publication of Mao Zedong's Talks at the Yan'an Forum of Art nad Literature, a bronze prize in the First National Chinese Painting Grand Exhibition and a gold prize in the 3rd National Gongbi Painting Grand Exhibition Part of his works have been collected by the China Art Gallery. Zhongnanhai, museums at home and art lovers in Hong Kong, Southeast, Asia, Japan, the U.S.

Yi Ya Zhai Art Gallery
Add: Qiaofuyuan 1-607, No.66 Taojinkeng, Huanshi Rd. (E), Guangzhou
Post Code: 510095
Tel: 020-83507997
BP: 84321888-5689

柳月良 《月夜牡丹》 国画 400cm × 900cm 1997年
Liu Yue-liang "Peonies in the Moonlight" Chinese Painting
400cm × 900cm 1997

柳月良，中国牡丹花画研究会会长，作品被世界五十多个国家和地区的爱好者收藏。多次在国内外举办个展。其中一部分作品备国内外博物馆和美术馆收藏。

Liu Yue-liang, chairman of the China Peony Paintings Research Society, with works collected by art lovers in more than fifty countries and regions in the world. He has held many individual exhibitions at home and abroad. Part of his works have been collectced by domestic and foreign museums or art galleries.

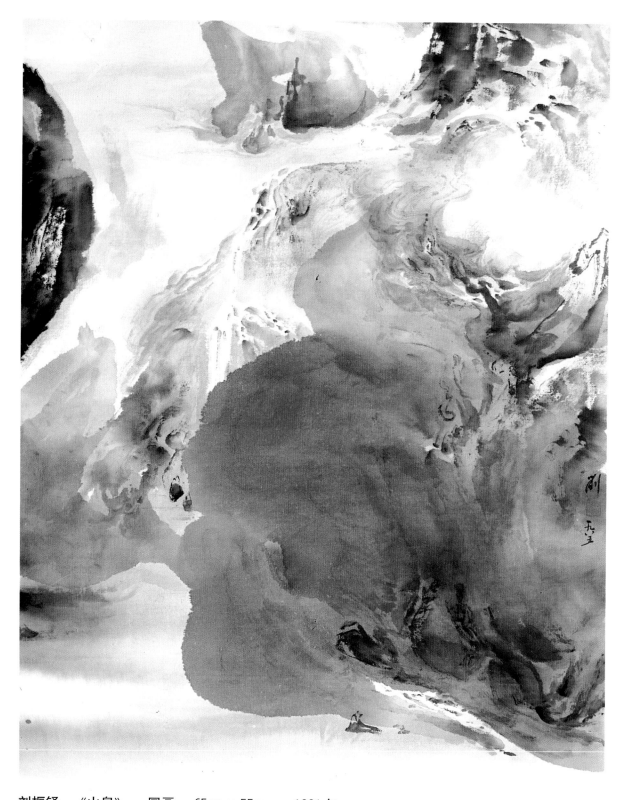

刘振铎　《山泉》　国画　65cm × 55cm　1991 年
Liu Zhen-duo　"Mountain Stream"　Chinese painting　65cm × 55cm　1991

刘振铎，黑龙江美术家协会常务理事、创作室主任，一级画师。作品参加历届全国大展，有的获奖，有的被收藏。作品曾在日本、新加坡、俄罗斯、朝鲜、香港等国家和地区展出。

Liu Zhen-duo is standing director of Heilongjiang Artists Association, head of the creation unit, and first-class painter. His works have been on display in the past national grand exhibitions. Some of them have been awarded, and some collected, and some exhibited in such places as Japan, Singapore, Russia, Korea, and Hong Kong.

白靖夫　《暖冬》　　国画　　66cm × 66cm　　1996 年
Bai Jing Fu "A Warm Winter"　Chinese Painting　66cm × 66cm　1996

白靖夫，一级美术师。曾参加首届中国百家大展，在巴黎、日本、毛里求斯、新加坡等地举办画展。出版有《白靖夫画集》。

Bai Jing-fu, first-class artist, has participated in the First Chinese painting Exhibition of Works by 100 Painters and held painting exhibitions in Paris, Japan, Mauritius and Singapore. Among his publications is "Collection of Bai Jing-fu's Paintings".

刘诗东　　《南方的风》　　国画　　145cm × 145cm
Liu Shi-dong　　"Wind From The South"　　Chinese painting　　145cm × 145cm

刘诗东，广州美术学院学士毕业。曾进修于广州美术学院国
画系山水研究生主要课程班。现为广东美协会员，广东青年
美术家协会理事，广州师范学校美术讲师。作品多次入选全
国美展和国内外大型美展并获奖。出版《刘诗东作品集》。

Liu Shi-dong graduated from the Guangzhou Institute of Fine Art with BA degree. He
had postgraduate courses in the Chinese Painting Deaprtment of the same institute. He
is now member of Guangdong Artists Association, director of Guangdong Young Artists
Association and lecturer of Guangzhou Normal School. He has many works selected
into national and overseas exhibitions and awarded. "Works by Liu Shi-dong"is his
publication.

曾嵘 　《飞越黄河》 　国画 　145cm × 145cm
Zeng Rong　"Flying Across the Yellow River"　Chinese Painting　145cm × 145cm

曾嵘，广东美协会员，广州现代书画艺术研究会会长，广州
美术馆特聘画家。93年获全国自学成材勋章。作品入选国内
外大型展览，中国当代名家邀请展，并多次获奖。先后在中
国，美国，澳大利亚举办个展。出版《曾嵘作品选》，《曾嵘
山水画集》，《曾嵘画集》。
电话：（020）83184135

Zeng Rong, member of Guangdong Artists Association, chairman of the Guangzhou
Research Society of Contemporary Calligraphy and painting, specially engaged painter
of the Guangzhou Art Gallery. He won a state medal for self-taught talents in 1993. His
works have been selected into large-scale exhibitions at home and abroad, the Invitation
Exhibition of Works by Famous Contemporary Artists and have won prizes many times.
He has held solo exhibitions in China, the U.S. and Australia respectively. His
publications include "Selected Works by Zeng Rong", "Collection of Zeng Rong's
Landscape Paintings" and "Collection of Zeng Rong's Paintings".
Tel:(020)83184135

邓铭　　《早上八、九点钟的太阳》　　油画　　100cm × 80cm
Deng Ming　"The Sun at about 8 or 9 in the Morning"　　Oil Painting　　100cm × 80cm

邓铭，中国美协会员。多次参加全国，省市画展。作品《夏》
获全国美术大展油画作品一等奖。93年参加首届中国艺术博
览会。作品被美国，新加坡，台湾友人收藏。

Deng Ming, member of the China Artists Association, has taken part many national,
provincial and municipal painting exhibitions. His "Summer" won a first class prize
for oil paintings inthe Grand National Exhibition of Fine Art. He partcipated in the first
China Art Exposition in 1993. And part of his works have been collected by friend from
the U.S., Singapore and Taiwan.

《文帝行玺》　金印　（广州西汉南越王墓出土，复制）　3.1cm × 3cm × 1.8cm
"The Seal of King Wendi"　Gold Seal　(Duplicate of the one unearthed in the
Tomb of King of Nanyue, West Han Dynasty)　3.1cm × 3cm × 1.8cm

广州新星投资顾问工程公司是一间极具投资策划和有着广泛
联系的机构。成立半年已经成功引进外商在穗投资逾亿港币。
广州是一座迅速崛起的国际化大都市，孕育着巨大的发展机
会。我们将竭力为希望在广州拓展业务的海内外投资者提供
成功的机遇。
地址：广州市府前路一号，市府大院综合楼
电话：（8620）83330360-6833，6834
传真：（8620）83385333
邮编：510032

Newstar Investments and Projects Consultant Co. is an organization specializes in
investment consultation with wide connections. Since ts establishment half a year ago,
it has successfully introduced foreign investment in Guangzhou totalling HK$100 million.
Guangzhou is a rising international metropolis with great opportunities of development.
We will do our utmost to provide chances of success for investors at home and abroad
who hope to expand their businesses in Guangzhou.
Add: The Municipal Government Complex, No.1, Fuqian Rd., Guangzhou
Post Code: 510032
Tel: (0862)83330360-6833, 6834
Fax: (0860)83385333

96-33　萧荣　　黄河石（河南）　　27 × 15 × 33cm
96-33　Yellow River Stone　(Henan)　　27 × 15 × 33cm

萧荣,1953 年生于湛江，自小酷爱艺术，尤其对奇石别有一番特殊感情。近几年萧荣走遍天涯海角，用独特的视野寻觅石的踪迹。愿天下人领略石性人情，以石养性，石道人道，以石悟道的真谛而共勉。

Xiao Rong born in Zhanjiang in 1953, he had a deep love for fine art when he was a child. He has a special feeling for peculiar stones. In recent years, Xiao has been to many places, looking for stones according to his unique point of view. He hopes that people all over the world can understand stone's character and human feelings, cultivate their own characters by appreciating stones. Study the ways of stones and human beings, and find truth through stones.

94-52　萧荣　嫦娥石（广西）　　19 × 19 × 52cm
94-52　Yellow River Stone　(Guang Xi)　　19 × 19 × 52cm

萧　荣　藏　石　记
林　　墉
石不言，人有心，石不动，人有情。
人有情，石有性，性寄情，石亦言。
是故石中看人，人中看石，皆有情乎！

Xiao Rong's Stone Collection
Lin Yong
Stones are speechless; human beings have a heart.
Stones are motionless; human beings have feelings.
Human beings have feelings while stones have character.
Character shows feelings, so stones also speak.
Hence, we can see human in stones and see stones in human beings because of feelings.

97-29　萧荣　古铜石（广西）　30 × 29 × 44cm
97-29　Bronze-colored Stone　(Guang Xi)　30 × 29 × 44cm

藏石玩石者，莫非情也。观石者，亦宜有情。盖人之所以有
人味，其实正是人情。藏石玩石之所以有味，莫非人味欤！

It is with feelings that people collect and appreciate stones. And it is necessary to
appreciate stones with feelings. Huamn beings are human because they have feelings.
To collect and appreciate stones is interesting because of feelings!

96-16-1217　萧荣　红水河石（广西）　22 × 12 × 20cm
96-16-1217　Hong shui Stone （Guang Xi）　22 × 12 × 20cm

观石一瞬有所悟，喜怒哀乐，咸甜酸辣，说不出，道不清，细流过心间，不须尽倾诉，波澜过后，平熨舒然，石在心间动矣！

One is enlightened the moment onesees a stone;but the mixed feelings cannot be told. Like a stream, they run through one's heart. When the feelings subside, one has thestone in one's mind!

96-26   萧荣   彩陶石（广西）   33 × 18 × 26cm
96-26   Color-ceramic Stone   (Guang Xi)   33 × 18 × 26cm

余看石，爱其浑然，赏其大器。即就形象，也不求周全逼真。
仿佛为佳，光泽可鉴，随其自然，无须油腊。石如人，情趣
皆在自然处。

I appreciate a stone for its harmonious whole. As for its shape, likeness is better than
realness. Smooth and bright, it should retainits original state without alterations. Stones
are like human beings;their interest lies in naturalness.

97-44-01　　萧荣　　盘江石（贵州）　　28 × 14 × 44cm
96-44-01　　Pan jiang River Stone　　(Guang Xi)　　28 × 14 × 44cm

萧荣藏石，在在入余眼，式式通余心，抚摸再三，怦然心动。
呜呼，魄然之物竟有此温柔乡，是亦人间奇趣，旷世奇遇也！
　　　　　　　　　　　1997年五羊三牛一马堂记

Xiao Rong's stones are quite to my taste. I can't help falling in love with them when I stroke them. Alas, the tough stones should be so gentle. It is so fascinating, and so rare in this world!

Written in Five-Sheep-Three-Oxen-One-Horse Hall 1997

国祥了静　《居士》　禅油画　30cm × 43cm
GuoxiangLiaojing　"Devotee"　The oils ofs Zen　30cm × 43cm

国祥了静，58年中央戏剧学院舞台美术系毕业。高级美术设
计师，禅油画研究会副会长。多年来以油画修，名为"禅油
画"。多家刊物发表其作品和评论。出版《禅和国祥油画集》。
现居广州。
电话：（020）81360845
电传：（020）86366831

Devotee Guoxiang Liaojing, graduated from rhe Stage Art Department in the Central
Institute of Oils of Zen Research Society.For many years he studies Zen in the way of
oil painting,which is called "Oils of Zen",His works and comments were published by
many journals,His publications inculude" Zwn and Collection of Guoxiang's Oil
Paintings".He is now living in Guangzhou.
Tel:(020)81360845
Fax:(020)86366831

国祥了静　　《人世间》　　禅油画　　120cm × 120cm
GuoxiangLiaojing　"This World"　The oils of Zen　120cm × 120cm

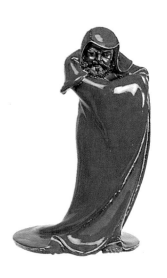

石湾美术陶瓷厂专业生产美术陶瓷和建筑装饰陶瓷的现代化大型企业。广东省先进企业和国家二级计量企业。全国工艺行业十强。生产品种有：美术陶瓷、古建园林陶瓷、日本瓦、西班牙瓦、釉面马赛克等。

地址：广东佛山市东风路17号（邮编：528301）
电话：0757-2715039，2272516
联系人：徐志伟

Shiwan Fine Art Ceramics Factory, a large modern enterprise that specialises in the production of fine art ceramics and that for construction and decoration, is an advanced enterprise ranking among the top ten in the line of industeial art in the country. Products include fine art ceramics, ceramics for ancient- style gardens, Japanese tiles, Spanish tiles, glazed mosaic.
Add : 17, Dongfeng Rd., Foshan City
Post Code : (528301)
Tel : 0757-2715039, 2272516
Contact : Xu Zhi-wei

张玉茂 《不尽清泉落天来》 国画 88.5cm × 67.5cm 1992 年
Zhang Yu-mao "An Inexhaustible Clear Spring from Heaven"
Chinese Painting 88.5cm × 67.5cm 1992

张玉茂,中国美协会员,沈阳市美协理事。从师著名画家宋
雨桂先生。作品多次参加国内外画展并获奖。多幅作品被中
国美术馆,辽宁省美术馆及博物馆收藏。出版《张玉茂画集》。

Zhang Yu-mao is a member of China Artists' Association, and a director of Shenyang
Artists' Association. He is a student of Mr Song Yu-gui, a famous painter. His works
have taken part in many art exhibitions and won prizes. Many of them are collected by
museums such as the China National Gallery of Fine Art, and the Liaoning Provincial
Gallery of Fine Art. His publications include "Collection of Zhang Yu- mao's Painting".

深圳寄梅堂画廊参展画家:张玉茂,王义胜

Paticipated Artists from ji Mei Tang
Art Gallery, Shenzhen : Zhang Yu-mao, Wang
Yi-sheng

王义胜　《仕女图》　　国画　　136cm × 67cm　　1997 年
Wang Yi-sheng　"Beautiful Ladis"
Chinese Painting　　136cm × 67cm　　1997

王义胜，现为中国美协会员，鲁迅美术学院国画系教授．多次参加全国美展并获奖。多幅作品被中国美术馆，中国画研究院等单位收藏。出版《王义胜工笔人物画教程》，《写意仕女画法》

Wang Yi-sheng is a member of the China Artists' Association, and a Chinese Painting Department professor of Luxun Institute of Fine Art. Many of his works have been awarded in national art exhibitions, and collected by organizations such as the China National Gallery of Fine Art, and the Research Institute of Chinese Painting. His publications include "Wang Yi-sheng's Courses of Gongbi Figure Painting", and "Methods to Paint Beauties Freehand".

张智量　《蕉荫》　国画　55cm × 110cm
Zhang Zhi-liang　"Shade of Plantains"
Chinese Painting　55cm × 110cm

张智量，中国书协会员，深圳美学会理事，师承钱君陶先生。
电话：（0755）5800930

Zhang Zhi-liang, student of Mr. Qian Jun-tao, is member of the China Calligraphists
Association, director of the Shenzhen Society of Aesthetics.
Tel: 0755-5800930

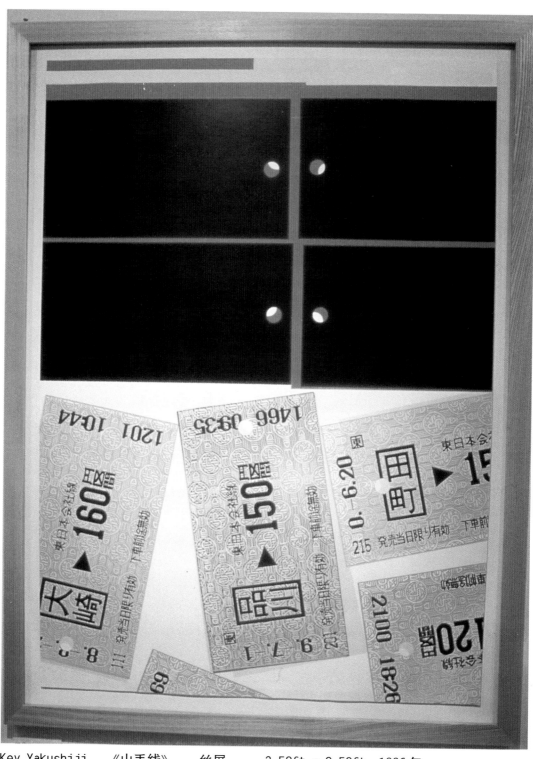

Key Yakushiji　《山手线》　丝屏　3.58ft × 2.58ft　1996年
Key Yakushiji　"Yamatesem"　Silkscreen　3.58ft × 2.58ft　1996

Key Yakushiji，日本画家，1962年生。任职于 K 工作室。1992
年参加 "0" 艺术馆联展，93、94、96年分别有作品在京都市
艺术馆、町田市画廊及 "0" 画廊展出。

Key Yakushiji, born in 1962, is a Japanese Painter. He now works at Studio K. He
joined a group show in the "O" Art Museum in 1992, and took part in exhibitions in
Kyoto City Art Museum(1993), Machida City Gallery(1994) and "O" Gallery (1996).

刘长福　　《风》　　木画　　100cm × 800cm　　1997 年
Liu Chang-fu　　"Wind"　　Wood Picture　　100cm × 800cm　　1997

刘长福，毕业于鲁迅美术学院，获学士学位。首创木画艺术，
曾获首届香港大陆画展一等奖，全国首届风俗画展特别奖。
作品多次参加海内外画展并获奖。作品多被马来西亚，加拿
大，澳大利亚，香港等国家地区收藏。现任沈阳福田木艺总
经理。

Liu Chang-fu graduated from the Luxun Art Institute with a BA and is the first to
create the art of wood-picture. He has won a first prize in the Firsr Hong Kong-
Mainland Exhibition of Painting, and a special prize in the First National Genre
Exhibition. Besides, his works have been exhibited at home and abroad, awarded, and
many collected by collectors from Malysia, Canada, Auistralia, Hong Kong, etc. He is
now general manager of the Shenyang Futian Wood Art.

叶志华　《默耘心田》　　油画　　100cm × 75cm　　1994 年
Ye Zhi-hua　　"Quiet Cultivation of the Mind"
Oil Painting　　100cm × 75cm　　1994

叶志华，作品多次在全国，省市美展获奖，并在美术馆，展览馆举行多次画展。作品获韩国文化体育部，韩国现代美术人协会颁发 "97 国际美术大展东洋画类特选赏"。参加 97 中国艺术博览会（北京），96，97 广州国际艺术博览会。作品被欧洲，澳洲，南韩，菲律宾等港澳同胞收藏。出版《叶志华油画集》，《叶志华画选》。

Ye Zhi-hua has won many prizes in national, provincial and municipal exhibitions and held painting shows in museums and exhibition halls.He won a special prize of East-Asian Paintings in the '97 International Fine Art Exhibition issued by the Ministry of Sports and Culture and the Modern Fine Artists Society of South Korea. He took part in the '97 China Art Exposition (Beijing), '96 and '97 Guangzhou International Art Fair. His works have been collected by art lovers from Europe, Australia, South Korea, the Philipines and compatriots from Hong Kong and Macau as well. His publications include "Collection of Ye Zhi-hua's Oil Paintings", "Selection of Ye Zhi-hua's Paintings".

柳根青　《进港》　　油画　　132cm × 113cm　　1973 年
Liu Gen-qing　"Entering Port"　　Oil Painting　132cm × 113cm　　1973

柳根青，44年生。62年在上海东方画室拜吴爱华，任微音老
师学画。66年开始在浙江渔村生活8年。81年拜浙江书画大
师谭建丞为先生。作品多次参加国内外展览。现为广州东南
亚画室画师。

Liu Gen-qing, born in 1944, learned painting from Wu Ai-hua and Ren Wei -yin in the
Shanghai East Studio in 1962. He spent eight years in fishing villages in Zhejiang
beginning from 1966. He became a student of master calligraphist and painter Tan
Jian-cheng of Huzhou, Zhejiang   in 1981. His works have been on show in many
exhibitions at home and abroad. He is a painter of Guangzhou South-east Asia Studio.

肖广成 《音乐女神》 雕塑 145cm × 63cm 1994年
Xiao Guang-cheng "Godess of Music"
Sculture 145cm × 63cm 1994

肖广成，广州美术学院雕塑系毕业。现任职广东亨泰环境艺
术有限公司。

Xiao Guang-cheng, a graduate of the Sculture Department of the Guangzhou Institute
of Fine Art, is a member of the Guangdong Hengtai Environmental Art Company,
Ltd.

马艺星 《耽迷其身》 油画 122cm × 46cm
Ma Yi-xing "Self-Indulgence"
Oil Painting 122cm × 46cm

马艺星，中国美术学院油画系毕业。现任职于杭州文联。期间同郑胜天先生创办杭州"国际艺术村"，同肖峰先生创办"西湖美术馆"。曾在上海举办个展。作品发表于香港《明报月刊》，新加坡《亚洲艺术家》。其传记小说《爱河》由新华出版社出版。

地址：杭州翠苑新村二区 30-1-10（310012）

电话：8062100

Ma Yi-xing, a graduate of China Institute of Fine art, is a member of the Hangzhou Federation of Culture. He has, together with Mr. Zheng Tian-shen, set up the Hangzhou "International Art Village"; and the "West Lake gallery" with Mr. Xiao Feng. He has once held an Solo exhibition in Shanghai and had works published in Hong Kong and Singapore. His biographical novel "River of Love" was published by the Xinhua Publishing House.

Add: 30-1-10, Zone 2, Cuiyuan Xincun, Hangzhou

Post Code: 310012

Tel: 8062100

广州星月木雕工艺美术品有限公司
该公司工艺品既有强烈生活气息，又有传统艺术风格和现代
文化艺术特色。作品生动形象，丰富多姿，具有较高艺术魅
力。
地址：广州黄埔大道 159 号富星商贸大厦西塔 14 楼 E 座
（510620）
电话：87590292，1382905008
传真：87590292

Guangzhou Star- Moon Wood- Carving Industrial Handicraft Corporation Ltd.
The works of this corporation have a combination of the   rich   flavor   of life,
traditional artistic   style and the characteristics of modern culture and art. And
they have great artistic charm with their vivid images and variety.
Add : 14 fl. E, West Tower of Fuxing Commerce & Trade Building, No. 159,
Huangpudadao Rd., Guangzhou
Post Code : 510620
Tel : 87590292, 1382905008
Fax : 87590292

张燕根 《生灵系列之十一》
木雕 60cm × 55cm 1997 年
Zhang Yan-gen "People Series 11"
Wood-Carving 60cm × 55cm 1997

张燕根 《渡－－之二》
木雕 50cm × 50cm 1996 年
Zhang Yan-gen "Ferry 2"
Wood-Carving 50cm × 50cm 1996

张燕根 《生灵系列之四》
木雕 65cm × 55cm 1996 年
Zhang Yan-gen "People Series 4"
Wood-Carving 65cm × 55cm 1996

张燕根，解放军艺术学院美术系毕业，广西美协会员，现任
教于广西艺术学校。多次在国内外举办个展，作品被德，美，
新加坡等收藏家收藏。先后为广西南宁国际机场等大型建筑
设计制作壁画多件。97年参与设计制作完成广西省府赠送香
港特区政府礼品。中央电视台等新闻媒介均作报道。传略载
入《世界名人录》。

Zhang Yan-gen graduated from the Fine Art Department of the PLA Art Institute. He is
member of Guangxi Artists Association and teacher of the Guangxi Art School. He has
held many times solo exhibitions at home and abroadwith works collectd by collectors
from Germany, the U. S. , Singapore, etc. He has designed murals for such huge
complexes as the Naning International Airport of Guangxi.He was one of those who
designed and produced Guangxi Government's present for Hong Kong SAR, which was
reported by CCTV and other agencies. His art history is listed in the "Who's Who of
the World".

陈可之　《东方情圣之六 －－ 世纪之恋》　油画　140cm × 100cm　1995 年
Chen Ke-zhi　"Great Lovers of the East 6 -- Love of the Century"
Oil Painting　140cm × 100cm　1995

陈可之，毕业于四川美院。中国美协会员，国家高级美术师。曾入编《中国当代名人录》、英国剑桥《世界名人录》。作品《历史》被中国美术馆、林肯艺术中心收藏。87年获首届全国油画展览优等奖，90年《东方之子》由国际奥委会总部（瑞士）收藏。曾赴日本、新加坡、东欧、香港等举办画展。作品被广为收藏。

Chen Ke-zhi graduated from the Sichuan Institute of Fine Art. He is member of the China Artists Associaiton and state senior-class artist. His name was listed in the Who's Who of Contemporary Chinese", and "Who's Who of the World" of Cambridge. His painting, "History" was collected by the China Art Gallery and the Lincoln Art Center. He won an excellence prize in the First National Oil painting Exhibition in 1987. And in 1990, his "Sun of the East" was collected in the Headquarters of Olympic Games Committee. He has held exhibitions in Japan, Singapore, East Europe and Hong Kong. His works are widely collected.

蔡圣委 《女人一号》 油画 73cm × 61cm 1996年
Cai Sheng-wei "Female, No.1" Oil painting 73cm × 61cm 1996

蔡圣委，毕业于厦门大学美术系，后到中央美术学院油画系进修。作品《梁祝》获好评并留于中央美院。多件作品参加各大美展。

Cai Sheng- wei graduated from the Fine Art Department of Xiamen Uiversity and had further studies in the Oil painting Departmenet of the Central Institute of Fine Art. His "Liang Shan- bo and XZhu Ying -tai" was warmly received and is kept in CIFA. Quite a few of his works have been shown in grand exhibitions of fine art.

梁业鸿　　《赏夏》　　国画　　68cm × 68cm
Liang Ye-hong　"Enjoying the Summer Days"
Chinese Painting　　68cm × 68cm

梁业鸿　　《映日》
Liang Ye-hong　"Reflection of the Sun"

梁业鸿，广州美协副主席，高级美术师，广州香雪书画社社长。作品多次获奖并被一些艺术机构及个人收藏。在北京，广州，台湾，香港等地举办个展，并应邀赴美国，日本，马来西亚，马尔他等国进行艺术交流。个人传略入编多种美术辞典。出版《梁业鸿画集》，《梁业鸿作品选》。

Liang Ye-hong is vice-chairman of the Guangzhou Artists Association, senior class artist and head of the Guangzhou Xiangxue Painting and Calligraphy Society. He has works awarded and collected by artistic units and art lovers. He has held solo exhibitions in Beijing, Guangzhou, Taiwan and Hong Kong and has been on invitation to the U.S., Japan, Malysia and Malta for art exchanges. His biography is listed in several dictionaries. Among his works are "Liang Ye-hong's Paintings" and "Selection of Liang Ye-hong's Works".

梁业鸿 《洁灵天地》 国画 138cm × 68cm

Liang Ye-hong "The Sky, Fair and Clear" Chinese Painting 136cm × 68cm

古原　《民居》之一　彩绘　90cm × 90cm　1997 年
Gu Yuan "Residence" 1 Color Painting 90cm × 90cm

古原，1967年生。1989年在中国美术学院学习，1991年在北京画院研修。1991年在北京举办个展。曾参加全国画展。1995、1995、1996年参加中国艺术博览会；1996年参加广州国际艺术博览会。1997年4月参加新加坡国际艺术博览会。出版《古原画集》。

Gu Yuan, born in 1967, studied in the China Institute of Fine Art in 1989 and had research in the Beijing Academy of painting in 1991. The same year, he held a solo exhibition in Beijing. He has participated in national exhibitions and the China International Art Exposition in 1994, 1995 and 1996. Also in 1996 he was among the artists who joined the Guangzhou International Art Exposition and in April 1997, he joined the Singapore International Art Exposition. "Collection of Gu Yuan's Paintings" is his publication.

古原　《民居》之二　　彩绘　　90cm × 90cm　　1997 年
Gu Yuan "Residence" 1　　Color Painting　90cm × 90cm　1997

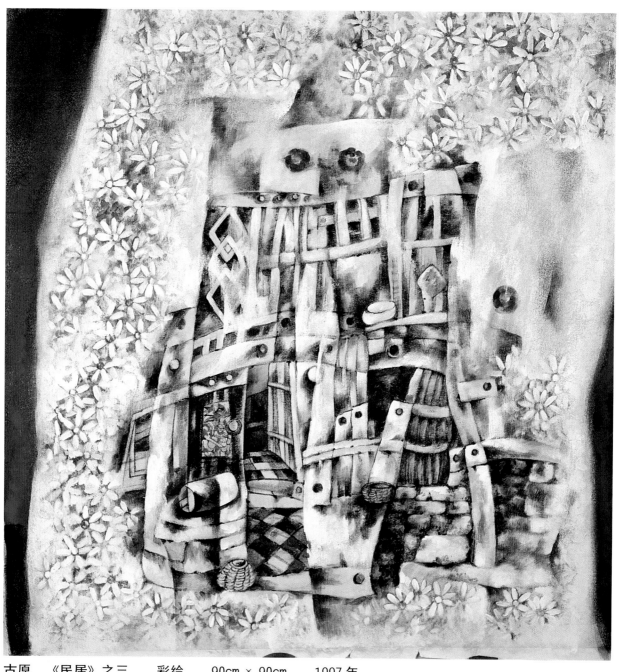

古原 《民居》之三 彩绘 90cm×90cm 1997年
Gu Yuan "Residence" 1 Color Painting 90cm×90cm 1997

古原 《花卉》之一 彩绘 70cm×70cm 1997年
Gu Yuan "Flowers" 1 Color Painting 70cm×70cm 1997

古原　《花卉》之二　　彩绘　　70cm×70cm　　1997年
Gu Yuan "Flowers" 2　　Color Painting　70cm×70cm　　1997

宝兰釉大碗　　　年代 － 清乾隆
Baolan Glazed Bowel
(Qianlong's Reign, Qing Dynasty)

粉彩瓷瓶　　　年代 － 清乾隆
Famille Rose Enamel Vase
(Qianlong's Reign, Qing Dynasty)

贵州省人民政府驻湛江办事处

贵州古称"夜都"，是一个风光秀丽、历史悠久、民族众多的
省份。本单位汇集了贵州丰富的民间珍藏的历代瓷器、铜器，
名人字画及少数民族工艺品。欢迎业务联系。
地址：广东湛江市霞山解放西路 17 号之一
邮编：524013
电话：(0759) 2169087
联系人：吴先生，李小姐

zhangjiang Agency of the Guizhou Provincial People's Government
Guizhou, called a "Night City" in ancient times, is a province with beautiful scenery, a
long history and many nationalities. Our unit has a rich collection of ceramics and bronze
articles of different dynasties; calligraphic works by famous figures and handicrafts of
the minority nationalities. Please contact us for business.
Add: 17-1, Jiefang Rd.(W), Xiashan, zhangjiang City, Guangdong Province
Post Code: 524013
Tel: (0759)2169087
Contacts: Mr. Wu, Miss Li

张伟　《王中王》　　　125cm × 125cm　　　1997 年
Zhang Wei　　"King of the Kings"　　125cm × 125cm　1997

张伟，辽宁省美术家协会会员，沈阳市美术家协会会员。作品多次参加全国美术大展并有获奖。其中《雪融》入选全国第八届美展。擅长工笔画虎、人物。作品在国内外受到好评和被收藏。

宅电：（024）6259107

Zhang Wei is member of Liaoning Artists Association and member of Shenyang Artists Association. His works have been displayed in large -scale national exhibitions and awarded. His "Melting Snow" was selected into the Eighth national Gongbi Painting exhibition. he is an expert in Gongbi paintingtigers and figures. His works receive favorable comments at home and are widely collected.

Tel: (024)-6259107

林明臣　《九鹰图》　国画　480cm × 120cm　1987 年
Lin Ming-chen　"Nine Eagles"　Chinese Painting　480cm × 120cm　1987

林明臣，辽宁美协会员，铁岭市美协会员。作品多次参加国
内外美展。《芦塘双鹭》、《三雄图》、《天山六月》等作品获奖。
部分作品被中外友人收藏。
电话：0410-2650687

Lin Ming-chen is member of Liaoning Artists Association and Tieling Artists
Association, with works on show in many art exhibitions at home and abroad. "Two
Herons in the Reed Marshes", "Three Heroes" and "June on the Tianshan Mountains"
have been prized. A number of is works have been collects by art lovers, domestic and
foreign.
Tel: 0410-2650687

左进伟　《踏雪图》　国画　170cm × 90cm　1997 年
Zuo Jin-wei　"Walking in the Snow"　Chinese Painting　170cm × 90cm　1997

左进伟，辽宁美协会员，沈阳美协会员，作品多次参加国内
外美展。《金秋》、《雪融》、《盼》获奖，连续几年参加北京国
际艺术博览会，97年参加上海首届艺术博览会。作品被中外
友人收藏。
电话：024-8424164

Zuo Jin-wei is member of the Liaoning Artists Association and the Shenyang Artists
Associaiton, with works displayed in many domestic and foreign art exhibitions. He
won prizes for his "Golden Autumn", "Snow Melting", and "Expectation". He took part
in the Beijing International Art Exposition in the past several years and the first Shanghai
Art Exposition as well. Part of his works have been collected by people

崔丕超　《野趣》　国画　　120cm × 120cm　　1997
Cui Pi-chao　"Fun in the Open Country"
Chinese Painting　　120cm × 120cm　　1997

崔丕超，辽宁美术家协会会员，沈阳市美术家协会会员。多
次参加全国及国际大型艺术博览会。《野趣》在全国大型美展
中入选。作品受到专业人士好评。多幅作品被国内外友人收
藏。
电话：024-3232533

Cui Pi-chao, me,ber of the Liaoing Artists Associaiton. He has taken part in many national
and international art expositions. "Fun in the Open Country" was selected into national
grand exhibitions. His works are appreciated by professionalists and many have been
collected by art lovers at home and abroad.
Tel:024-3232533

马波生　《三人行》　　中国画　　42cm × 42cm
Ma Bo-sheng　"Three Walking Together"　Chinese Painting　42cm × 42cm

马波生，曾先后在徐州师范学校、徐州国画院工作。85年入
中央学美院卢沉工作室研修，后为李可染入室弟子。92年任
深圳《中国画坛》主编，现为深圳大学美术系副教授，中国
书法协会会员，广东美协会员。作品多次入选全国和地方美
术出版有《波生中国画作品集》

Ma Bo-sheng worked in the Xuzhou Normal School and then in the Xuzhou Academy
of Chinese Painting. He had research in Lushen Studio of the Central Institute of Fine
Art in 1985 and later became a student of Li Ke-ran. He was editor- in- chief of
"China's World of Painting" in Shenzhen and is now associate professor of the Fine Art
department of Shenzhen University, member of the China Calligraphists Association
and the Guangdong Artists Association. Many of his works have been displayed in
national and local exhibitions. Publication:"Collection of Bo-sheng's Chinese paintings".

高旭奇　　《山鬼》　　　国画　　　200cm × 200cm
Gao Xu-qi　"Mountain Ghost"　Chinese Painting　200cm × 200cm

高旭奇，现任丹东大学美术系讲师。作品多次参加全国和省
市展览并获奖。90年举办"旭奇书法绘画特展"。部分作品被
美国，香港，台湾，日本等地私人收藏。

Gao Xu-qi is lecturer of the Fine Art Department of Dandong University with works
displayed and awarded in antional, provincial and municipal exhibitions. In 1990, he
held a special exhibition of his works. Part of them were collected by people from the
U.S., Japan, Hong Kong, Taiwan and other places.

陈楚波 　《忆江南》　　油画　　100cm × 80cm
Chen Cu-bo 　"Recollection of the South of the Changjiang River"
Oil Painting 　　100cm × 80cm

陈楚波,中国美协湖南分会会员,湖南娄底市文联副秘书长,
副教授。作品发表于全国报刊并参加全国美展。作品《无限
风光在险峰》获中国纪念抗日战争胜利50周年"国际书画大
赛"特等奖。作品艺历入编《世界美术家传》。多幅油画被国
内外人士收藏。

Chen Chu-bo is member of the China Artists Associaiton (Hunan Branch),.vice secretary-general of the Loudi Cultural Federation, Hunan Province and associate professor. His works have been published in the country's newspapers and journals and displayed in national exhibitions."The Unmatched Beauty on the Lofty and Perilous Peak" won a special award in the "Internatianl Painting and Calligraphy Exhibition" in commemoration of the 50th anniversary of the victory of the Anti-Japanese War. His art history is listed in the "Biographies of Fine Artists of the World'" Quite a few of his oil paintings were collected by people at home and abroad.

李伯虎　　《逸趣图》　　国画　　68cm × 48cm　　1997 年
Li Bo-hu　"Comfort and Fun"　Chinese Painting　68cm × 48cm　1997

李伯虎，江苏文艺学院美术系毕业。书法作品入选全国第二届中青年书法篆刻家作品展，中国现代临书大展一等奖。国画入选文化部，中国美协主办的世界华人书画大展。现为江苏花鸟画研究会会员，江苏锡山市云林中国画院院长。

电话：（0510）8151115，8150655

Li Bo-hu graduated from the Jiangsu Institute of Culture and Art. His calligraphic works took part in the Second National Exhibition of Calligraphic and Seal-Cutting Works by Mid-aged and Young Artists". He won a first prize in the China Modern Copied-Calligraphy Exhibition, and had works selected into the "Calligraphy and Painting Exhibition of Works by Artists of Chinese Origin in the World" sponsored by the cultural Ministry and the China Artists Association. He is now member of the Jiangsu Flower-and-Bird Painting Research Society and president of Yunlin Chinese Painting Institute in Xishan City, Jiangsu Province.

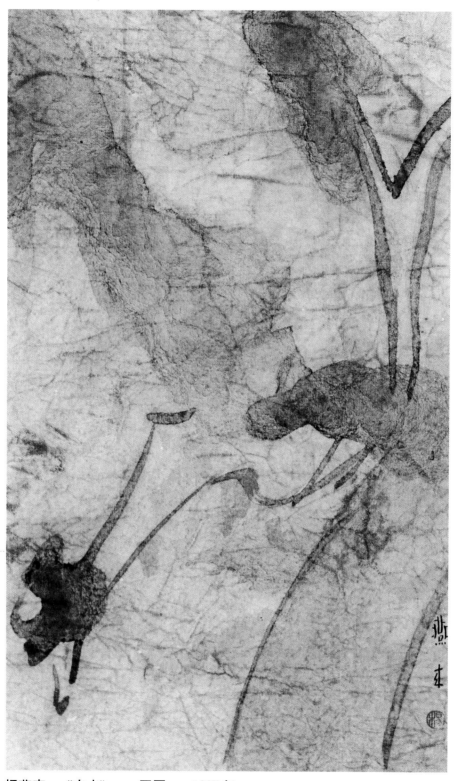

杨燕来　《山水》　　国画　　1997 年
Yang Yan-lai　"Landscape"　Chinese painting　1997

杨燕来，广州画院特聘画家，93 年中央美术学院毕业。96 年在广州举办 "杨燕来中国画展"，97 年在北京举办 "杨燕来中国画展"。作品被国内外收藏家收藏。

Yang Yan-lai, specially engaged painter of the Guangzhou Academy of Painting, a '93 graduate from the Central Institute of Fine Art, held the "Exhibition of Yang Yan-lai's Chinese Paintings" in Guangzhou in 1996 and in Beijing in 1997. His works were collected by art lovers at home and abroad.

杨福音 《人物》 国画 38cm × 157cm 1997年
Yang Fu-yin "Figure"
Chinese Painting 38cm × 157cm 1997

杨福音，广州市书画研究院副院长。曾在香港，台湾，马来西亚举办个展，部分作品被国内外包括欧洲，日本，美国，东南亚收藏家收藏。出版画集两本。

Yang Fu-yin, vice-chairman of the Guangzhou Research Society of Calligraphy and Painting, has held individual exhibitions in Hong Kong, Taiwan, Malysia with part of his works collected by collectors in China the U.S.,Japan, and South-east Asia as well. Two collections of his paintings have been published so far.

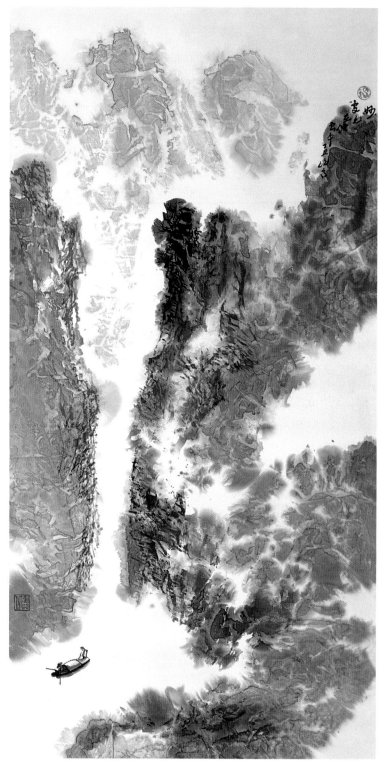

姚伯齐 《妙出原在云中》 国画 134cm × 67cm 1997年
Yao Bo-qi "The Wonder Lies in the Misty Clouds"
Chinese Painting 134cm × 67cm 1997

姚伯齐，荆南书画学院名誉院长，副研究员。国际文人画家总会执行理事（台湾），新加坡新神州艺术院高级名誉顾问。山水画在诸多报刊发表并在国内外画展获奖被收藏。传评入选《世界当代美术家大辞典》等多部辞书。出版《姚伯齐山水画集》。

Yao Bo-qi, honorary president of Jingna Institute of Calligraphy and Painting, associate research follow, executive director of the International General Associstion of Men of Letters and Painters(Taiwan)landscape paintings have been published in dirfferent journals, awarded in exhibitions at home and abroad,and collected as well. His art history has been listed in the "Dictionary of Contemporary Fine Artists of the World"and others.Among his publications is "Collection of Yao Bo-qi's Landscape Paintings"

《清皇帝服》

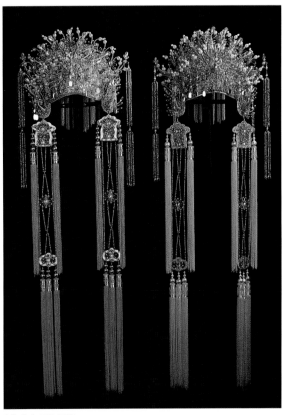

《古代皇后凤冠》

广州市龙凤戏服社，专业设计生产舞台戏剧、电影、电视服装、道具、头饰、头盔及民族服装、工艺品。设计适新、工艺精湛、起货快捷，深受海内外客户青睐。产品远销港、澳、美加、比、荷等20多个国家和地区。

电话：（8620）84982050，81828046

传真：（8620）84615750

Guangzhou Long Feng Stape Costume Factory deals in stage, opera, film, TV costumes,stage proerty,headgears, helmets adn clothes of different nationalities, handicraft. etc. They are warmly welcomed by customers at home and abroad for their designs, workmanship, and quick delivery. Its products sell to more than 20 countries and regions including Hong Kong, Macau, the United States, Canada, Belgium and Holland.

Tel:(8620)84982050,81828046

Fax:(8620)84615750

杨季湘   书法（扇面）   1997 年
Yang Ji-xiang   "Calligraply"   (Fan)   1997

杨季湘，擅各种书法，尤蝇头小楷为工。曾任教师、新闻记者。著有《秋吟集》、《过雁》、《广东名园余荫山与南村邬乐宗族考》。

Yang Ji-xiang, good at different kinds of calligraphy, has kbeen a teacher and a journalist. His publications include "Winter Poems" (2volumes), "Passing Wild Geese", "research on Guangdong's Famous Garden, Yuyinshan and the Wule Clan of Nam Village".

红蓝陶艺 97 系列作品（ 石峰美术陶瓷工艺厂设计生产）
97 of Red & Blue Pottery
(designed and produced by the Shifeng Artistic Pottery and Ceramic Factory)

红蓝陶艺是一群年轻的陶艺设计师拓创的具有传统韵味和时代气息的陶艺作品，熔生活和艺术于一炉。红蓝陶艺多次参加国际艺术博览会，产品远销美，加，法等国及港澳地区。

地址：广州东山区新庆路山河东街 15 号 （510080）

电话：87774945

传真：87662335

联系人：万志强，刘华生

Red & Blue Pottery consists of the pottery works by a group of young artists who have both the characteristics of tradition and the modern age, combining life with art. They have taken part in a number of international expositions and their products sell in the U.S., canada, France as well as Hong Kong and Macau. Product Series

Add: 15, Shanhedong St., Xinqing Rd.,Dongshan District, Guangzhou

Post Code: 510080

Tel: 87774945

Fax: 87662335

Contacts: Wan Zhi-qiang, Liu Hua-sheng

陈玉先　　《长安乐舞》　　国画　　80cm × 58cm　　1996 年
Chen Yu-sian　"Chang'an Dance Accompanied by Music"
Chinese Painting　　80cm × 58cm　　1996

红蓝影视文化有限公司
Red & Blue Film and TV Culture Company
Ltd.

陈玉先，国家一级画家，中国美协会员，《人民日报》神州画
院常务理事，《解放军报》高级编辑。出版《陈玉先画集》，《陈
玉先速写集》等。多次参加全国美展并获奖。先后在新加坡，
马来西亚，日本，台湾地区举办个展和联展。

Chen Yu-xian is state first-class painter, member of China Artists associaiton, standing
director of the Shenzhou Academy of painting under the People's Daily and senior
editor of the PLA Newspaper. Among his publications are "Collection of Chen Yu-
xian's paintings" and "Sketches by Chen Yu-xian". he has taken part and been awarded
many time in national exhibitions. He held solo and joint exhibitions in Singapore,
Malaysia, Japan and Taiwan as well.

陈玉先　　《如愿－香港回归前夕为小平同志传神》　　国画　　232cmX106cm
Chen Yu-xian　　　"Deng Xiao-ing before Hong Kong Returns to the Motherland"
Chinese Painting　　　232mX106m

红蓝影视文化有限公司,致力于海内外文化艺术推广和介绍,
竭诚为中外艺术交流和繁荣文化艺术市场服务,其工艺部经
营书画艺术品,雕塑陶艺及各类工艺美术品。
地址：广州东山区新庆路山沙东街１５号
电话：联系人：王刚、罗国强、王鑫

Red & Blue Film and TV Culture Company Ltd.tries its best to promote and introduce
culture and art both at home and abroad, and to serve artistic exchanges between China
and other countries and work for the prosperity of the market of culture and art. It's
handicraft department deals in books, paintings artistic articles, sculture, pottery etc.
Add: 15, Shanshadong St., Qingshan Rd., Dongshan District, Guangzhou
Tel:020-87774945, 87667516
Contacts: Wang Gang, Luo Guo-qiang, Wang Xin

刘藕生 《虎》 国画 135cm × 68cm 1997 年
Liu Yu-sheng "Tiger" Chinese painting 135cm × 68cm 1997

刘藕生，广州美术学院雕塑系毕业。以国画大写意之精神注入雕塑中，另辟蹊径。书画艺术师承关山月，黎雄才。尤长画虎。

Liu Yu-sheng graduated from the Sculpture Department of the Guangzhou Institute of Fine Art. He puts the spirit of freehand brushwork in traditional Chinese painting into his scultures so as to pave a new path in art creation. He learned painting and calligraphy from Guan Shan-yue and Li Xiong-cai. He is especially good at tiger painting.

权伍松 　《红蜻蜓》 　工笔画 　80cm × 110cm 　　1996 年
Quan Wu-song 　"Red Dragonflies" 　Gongbi Painting 　80cm × 110cm 　　1996

权伍松，哈尔滨画院画家。中国日本"四季"美展《酣秋》蜻
蜓系列获金奖。89，92，94年在韩国举办个展。在加拿大，
台湾等地也举办过个展。96年参加广州国际艺术博览会。

Quan Wu-song is painter of the Harbin Academy of Painting. He won a gold prize in
the Sino-Japanese "Four Seasons" Fine Art Exhibition with his "Deep Autumn"
Dragonflies series. He held solo exhibitions in Korea in 1989, 1992 and 1994 respectively,
and in Canada and Taiwan as well. He was a participant of the '96 Guangzhou
International Art Exposition.

刘声雨　　《高原的母亲》　　油画　　50cm × 60cm
Liu Sheng-yu　　"Mother of the Highland"　　Oil Painting　　50cm × 60cm

刘声雨，国家一级画师，教授。现任职于文化部中国艺术馆
筹备处，中国美协会员，辽宁中国画研究会秘书长。曾获第
六届全国美展铜奖，全国中国画展金奖。作品赴美国，新加
坡，法国，荷兰等地展出。出版《刘声雨画集》。作品被国家
美术馆，钓鱼台国宾馆及美，日，新加坡等收藏。

Liu Sheng-yu, state first-class painter, professor, working of the preparatory
department of China Art Gallery under the Ministry of Culture, member of the China
Artists Associaiton and secretary-general of the Liaoning Research Society of Chinese
Painting. He won a bronze prize in the 6th National Fine Art Exhibition and a gold prize
in the National Chinese Painting Exhibition. His works have been exhibited in the U.S.,
Singapore, France and Holland. His publications include "Collection of Liu sheng-yu's
Paintings" and others. Part of his paintings are collected by the National Gallery,
Diaoyutai State Guest House and by collectors from the U.S., Japan and Singapore.

刘声雨　　《和田女》　　油画　　130cm × 100cm
Liu Sheng-yu　　"Hetian Lady"　　Oil Painting　　130cm × 100cm

张鸿飞　　《律》　　工笔　　67cm × 67cm
Zhang Hong-fei　　"Tone"
Gongbi Paitning　　67cm × 67cm

张鸿飞　　《雪原之子》　　工笔　　67cm × 67cm
Zhang Hong-fei　　"Son of the Snowland"
Gongbi Painting　　67cm × 67cm

张鸿飞，中国美协会员，省美协副主席，国家一级美术师。作品十多次参加国家级美展并多次出国展出。其中获国家级金、银、铜、学术奖六次。多幅作品被中国美术馆收藏，两次获省政府颁发的"长白山文艺奖"并六次获省美展一等奖。被评为省"有突出贡献中青年技术人才"。

Zhang Hong-fei is member of the China Artists Associaiton, vice-chairman of the Provincial Artists Association and state first-class artist. He has taken part in more than ten national exhibitions and had his works exhibited abroad many times. He has so far won six awards of the state level including gold,silver, bronze and academic awards, Quite a number of his works have been collected by the Chinba Gallery of Fine Art. He has also twice won " Changbai Mountain Culture and Art Award " isssued by the provincial government and six first prizes in provincial art exhibitions. He is among the province's mid-aged and young technical talents who have outstanding contributions.

周玉兰 《春光》 国画 83cm × 83cm

王铭 《黄河春早》 国画 13.5cm × 68cm

周玉兰，甘肃省美协会员，中国国画协会会员。作品《仙人球》获"中国石榴节国际书画展"优秀奖；《迎春》入选"中国第四届艺术节"书画展；《春光》入选第八届全国美术展。

王铭，甘肃省美协会员，版协理事。版画《黄土魂》参加中国版画版种大展及全国第五届三版展。扇面《青山叠翠》参加北京首届国际扇面书画艺术展，《瑞雪兆丰年》获首届丰怀北京杯佳作奖。

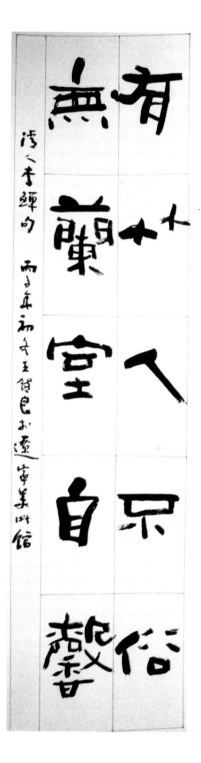

王贺良　　《隶书条幅－－李　句》　　《隶书对联》
Wang He-liang　Calligraphy

王贺良，中国书法家协会会员，辽宁美术馆专业书法家，国家一级美术师，辽宁大学特聘教授。参加全国1-5届书法篆刻展及国内外重要展览。出版《王贺良书法集》。任《中国古代书法经典》编委和隶书卷主编。作品被中南海和美术馆，博物馆收藏。

Wang He-liang, member of China Calligraphists Associaiton, calligraphist of the Liaoning Gallery, state first-class painter, and professor of Liaoning University. He took part in the National Calligraphy and Seal-Cutting Exhibitions(1-5), and other important exhibitions at home and abroad. His has published the "Collection of Wang He-liang's Calligraphic Works" and "Classics of Ancient Chinese Calligraphy". Part of his works have been collected by Zhongnanhai and other museums.

刘胄人　　《雨霁》　　国画　　200cm × 100cm　　1995 年
Liu Zhou-ren　　"The Rain Stops"　　Chinese Painting　　200cm × 100cm　　1995

刘胄人，书画家。广东美协会员，广州青年美术家协会副主席，省书法家协会会员。作品在全国 100 多家报刊发表。96 年作品《着衣的遗憾》在比利时布鲁塞尔书画大展中获奖。

Liu Zhou-ren, calligraphist and painter, is a member of the Guangdong Artists Association, vice-chairman of the Guangzhou Youths Associationof Fine Art, and member of the Provincial Calliographists Associaiton,with works published in over 100 journals of the country. His work"Regret for the Clothes" won an award in Belgium in 1996.

卢望明 《种瓜得瓜》 国画 94cm×44cm 1994年
Lu Wang-ming "One Gets What One Sows"
Chinese Painting 94cm×44cm 1994

卢望明，本科毕业，中国美协会员。主要从事艺术教育和中国画创作。作品多次参加全国美展，并出国巡展。现为华夏禅画院院长、世界禅佛书画家协会副会长。出版《五百罗汉图》，《日月居士卢望明禅画集》。

Lu Wang-ming, a college graduate and a member of the China Artists Associaition, is engaged in art education and the creation of Chinese paintings. His works have been on show many times in national exhibitions and tour exhibitions abroad. He is now president of Huaxia Chan Academy of Painting and vice-president of the World Chan Buddhist Association of Calligraphists and Painters. His publications include "Five Hundred Arhats" and "Lay Buddhist Lu Wang-ming's Chan Buddhist Paintings".

邸立丰　　《大清皇室图》　　油画　　1050cm×250cm　　1996年
Di Li-feng　"The Royal Family of the Qing Dynasty"
Oil Painting　1050cm×250cm　1996

邸立丰，中央美术学院硕士研究生班毕业。多次荣获中国油画大奖。作品广为各地人士收藏。巨作《大清皇室图》、《无邪的东方》轰动北京和香港。现任教于鲁迅美术学院。
工作室：中国沈阳鲁迅美术学院（110003）
电话：（024）3854292

Di Li-feng graduated from the postgraduate class of the Central Institute of Fine Art. He has won many times grand awards for Chinese oil paintings. His works are collected by people over the country. The "Royal Family of the Qing Dynasty" and "The East, Evilless" caused a sensation in Beijing and Hong Kong. He is now a teacher of the Lu Xun Institute of Fine Art.
Tel:(024)3854292

邸立丰 　《大清皇室图》之二 　油画 　1050cm × 250cm 　1996 年
Di Li-feng "The Royal Family of the Qing Dynasty"
Oil Painting 　1050cm × 250cm 1996

邸立丰 《太平乐》 油画 130cm × 130cm 1997 年
Di Li-feng "Peace" Oil Painting 130cm × 130cm 1997

邸立丰　　《上帝的礼物》　　油画　　139cm × 174cm　　　1996 年
Di Li-feng　　"A Gift From God"　　Oil Painting　　139cm × 174cm　　1996

邸立丰　　《丛林中》　　油画　　160cm × 148cm　　1997 年
Di Li-feng "In the Bush"　　Oil Painting　　160cm × 148cm　　1997

邸立丰　　《最深的疲惫》之一　　油画　　139cm × 174cm　　1996 年
Di Li-feng　　"Exhaustion" 1　　Oil Painting　　139cm × 174cm　　1996

邸立丰　　《最深的疲惫》之二　　油画　　130cm×170cm　　1996 年
Di Li-feng　　"Exhaustion" 2　　Oil Painting　　130cm×170cm　　1996

岳青俊 　　　杨英才　　　《晨》　　　陶艺　　　1996 年
Yue Qing-jun　　Yang Ying-cai　　"Morning"　　Pottery　　1996

杨英才，毕业于景德镇瓷学院美术系，获学士学位。96 年参加广州国际艺术博览会。《晨》参加 97 年中国现代陶艺展。

Yang Ying-cai graduated with a BA degree from the Fine Art Departmentof Jingdezhen Porcelain College. He joined the Guangzhou International Art Exposition in 1996. "Morning" was displayed in the '97 China Modern Pottery.

岳青俊，河南大学工艺美术系毕业。作品《远古回忆》入选全国首届现代陶艺展。

地址：广东南海市桂城东二区西约街北十四巷二号（528000）

电话：（0757）6327196

Yue Qing-jun graduated from the Industrial Art Department of Henan University. His "Recalling the Remote Antiquity" was selected into the First National Modern Pottery Exhibition.

Add: 2, 14th Lane (N), Xiyue St. Zone 2 (E), Guicheng, Nanhai City,　Guangdong Province

Post Code: 528000

Tel: 0757-6327196

张建民　　《哦！塞北的雪》　　油画　　82cm × 65cm　　1996年
Zhang Jian-min　　"Oh, the Snow in North of the Great Wall"
Oil Painting　82cm × 65cm　　1996

张建民，９６年入中央美术学院进修。现为甘肃美协会员，中国石油美术家协会理事，中国石油画院一级画师。多次获省，部级银铜牌，并入选全国画展。作品《风》入编《中国当代美术作品集》。部分作品被海内外人士收藏。

Zhang Jian-min had further studies in the CIFA. He is now a member of the Gansu Artists Association, director of the China Petroleum Artists Association and first-class of China Petroleum Academy of Painting. He has won many silver and bronze medals at provincial and ministrial levels and taken part in national exhibitions. His "Wind" was edited into the "Collection of China's Modern Fine Art Works". Part of his paintings have been collected by people in and out of China.

杨德强　《虎》　根书艺术　250cm × 130cm　1995 年
Yang De-qiang　"Tiger"　Root-Carving　250cm × 130cm　1995

杨德强，著名根雕之木家，广西根艺协会会员。将传统书法
艺术运用到根雕上并使之达到至高境界。作品多次获艺术大
奖。

Yang De-qiang, a famous root-carving artist, is a member of the Guangxi Association
of Root-Carving Artists. He applies the traditional calligraphic technique to root-carving,
bringing it to a lofty state. His artworks have won many grand awards.

王晓鹏 《二十世纪。 97》 布面油画 1200cm×300cm
Wang Xiao-peng "The Twentieth Century. '97" Oil on Canvas 1200cm×300cm

王晓鹏 《天涯海角》 布面油画 100cm×80cm
Wang Xiao-peng "The Fartherest Corner of the Earth"
Oil on Canvas 100cm×80cm

王晓鹏 《枯荷．裸女》 布面油画 146cm×114cm
Wang Xiao-peng "Dried Lotus, Nude"
Oil on Canvas 146cm×114cm

王晓鹏，毕业于广西艺术学院美术系。90年进修中央美术学院技术法教研室。现为广西美协会员。作品参加首届全国美术院 校作品展。95年参加台湾桃园市举办的 "中国九人名画家联展"。作品多被台湾，美国，法国，日本等收藏家收藏。

Wang Xiao-peng graduated from the Fine Art Department of Guangxi Institute of Fine Art in 1990, and had refresher courses in the Technique Teaching Unit of the Central Institute of Fine Art. He is now a member of the Guangxi Artists' Association. His participated in the first National Exhibition of Works from Art Schools and Institutes, and the '95 Joint Exhibition of Nine Famous Chinese Artists in Taoyuan, Taiwan. His works have been collected by people from Taiwan, America, France, and Japan.

王双禄　　《古石佛喜迎香港回老家》　　混合材料
Wang Shuang-lu　"The Old Stone Buddha Welcomes the Return of Hong Kong" Mixed Media

王双禄，41年生。自学成材。其作品曾被拍成录像，电台，报
纸等新闻媒体均有报导。96年在广州举办画展。

Wang Shuang-lu born in 1941, a self-taught artist with works made into TV films and
reported by radio stations and journals. He held apainting exhibition in Guangzhou in
1996.

关玉良　　《语》　　彩墨　　68cm × 66cm　　1996 年
Guan Yu-liang　　"Conversation"　　Ink & Color　　68cm × 66cm　　1996

关玉良，任职于深圳大学艺术系，国家一级美术师，中国画研究院特聘画家，美国纽约文化艺术中心东方艺术顾问。哈尔滨师范大学毕业，中央美术学院国画系结业。参加历届中国艺术博览会，广州国际艺术博览会。曾在美国、马来西亚、韩国举办个展。出版《关玉良画集》，《关玉良彩墨艺术》。

Guan Yu-liang, a state first-class artist, is a member of the Fine Art Deaprtment of Shenzhen University, a painter engaged by the Chinese painting Research Institute and an oriental art consultant of the NewYork Center of Art and Culture in the U.S. He graduated from the Harbin Normal University's Art Department and finished his courses in the Chinese Painting Department of the Central Institute of Fine Art. He has participated in the past China Art Expositions and those held in Guangzhou. He has held solo exhibitions in the U.S., Malaysia, Korea.Among his publications are "Collection of Guan Yu-liang's Paintings"and "Guan Yu-liang's Art of Ink & Color".

关玉良　　《和》　　彩墨　　68cm × 66cm　　1996 年
Guan Yu-liang　　"Peace"　　Ink & Color　　68cm × 66cm　　1996

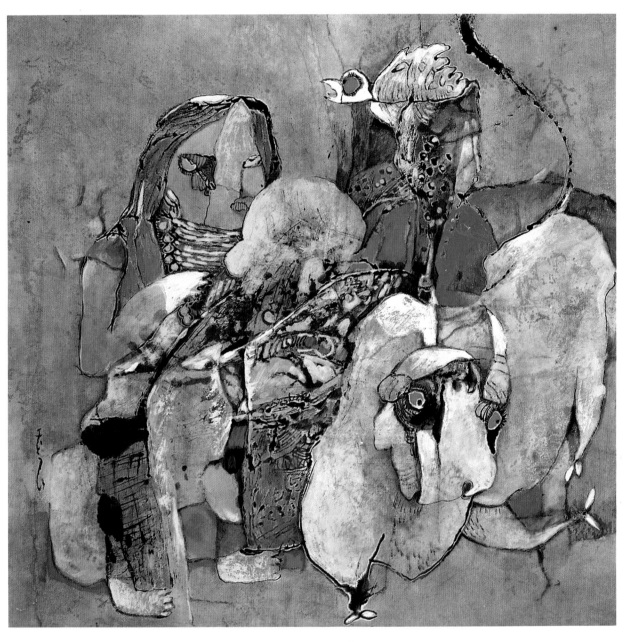

关玉良　《午》　彩墨　68cm × 66cm　1996 年
Guan Yu-liang　"Noon"　Ink & Color　68cm × 66cm　1996

关玉良　　《晨》　彩墨　110cm × 110cm　　1996 年
Guan Yu-liang　"Morning"　Ink & Color　110cm × 110cm　1996

关玉良　　《清》　　彩墨　　54cm × 52cm　　1995 年
Guan Yu-liang　"Clarity"　Ink & Color　54cm × 52cm　1995

关玉良 　《雾》 　彩墨 　110cm × 110cm 　1996 年
Guan Yu-liang 　"Mist" 　Ink & Color 　110cm × 110cm 　1996

海 外 展 厅

统 筹: 澳 门 国 际 视 觉 艺 术 中 心

参 展 画 家

吕风雅	胡文伟	余世坚	香港大一艺术设计院	丘瑞福
王耀麟	蔡逸溪	东南亚美术协会	范子登	白礼仁	何道根
麦少峰	童建颖	李希文	玛利亚	依莎贝	马伟达	吴卫鸣
袁之钦	缪鹏飞	君士坦丁	琥 茹	马维斯	邹中星	马若龙
廖文畅	蔡树荣	黎 鹰	谭可文	罗卓英	冯宝珠	郭 桓
索 文	克丽丝蒂·特侄	西安永生中介介公司		

序 言

　　海外的艺术家在每年一度的艺术博览会上带来了他们各自国家和地区风情的和各具创意的艺术品，给国内观众留下深刻印象。海外艺术家的参展，对促进海内外的文化艺术交流起到十分积极的作用，使艺博会增辉不少。

　　'97广州国际艺术博览会更得到澳门国际视觉艺术中心热情地，积极地统筹了来自俄罗斯，澳大利亚，英国，葡萄牙，新加坡，马来西亚，香港，澳门，等国家和地区的30多位艺术家前来参展。这些具有浓郁异国异地气息的佳作，定会再次受到广大观众的欢迎。在此谨向来自海外的全体参展艺术家表示衷心的感谢，并预祝参展成功！

'97广州国际艺术博览会行政总监　　乐润生

一九九七年十一月

Overseas Artists

Planner:Macau International Visual Arts Centre

Participating artists:

Eddie D. F. N. Lui	Wu Man Wai	Yu Ssi Kin
First Institute of Art And Design, Hong Kong		

South-East Asia Arts Associaition

Fanying Zideng	Robert O'Brien	He Dao Gen
Chieu Shuey Fook	Heng Eow Lin	Chua Ek Kay
Mak Siu Fung	Tong Jian Ying	Mira Dias
Maria Elisa Vilaca	Isabel Candeias	Victor Hugo Marreiros
Un Vai Meng	Un Chi Iam	Mio Pang Fei
Konstantin Bessmertny	Joana Ling	Denis Murrell
Chao Chong Seng	Carlos Marreiros	Liao Wen Chang
Choi Su Weng	Lai Leng	Tan Ke Wen
Jorge Carlos Smith	Anita Fung	Kwok Woom
Sovan Kumur	Kivsti Taxgaard Yongsheng Broker Co. LTD	

Forewords

　　In the Fair each year, overseas artistsa bring with them art works with their local colors and creatvity, which leave a deep impression on the visitors at home. The participation of overseas arttists in the exhibition plays an important part in the exchage of culture and art between China and other countries, and adds lustre to the Fair.

　　Thanks to the enthusastic and acrive arrangement of the Macau International Visual Arts Centre, over thirty artists from Russia, Australia, Britain, Portugal, Singapore, Malysia, Hong Kong and Macau have taken part in the '97 Guangzhou Internationl Art Fair. Their works, with rich local colours, will surely receive warm welcome from the visitors. Here, we express our sincere thanks to all oversas participats and wish them great success!

Le Run-sheng

Chief Administrative Inspector

'97 Guangzhou International Art Fair

Nov. 1997

胡文伟 《我很性感》 大理石 102cm × 31cm × 46cm 1996 年
Wu Wen-wei "I Am Sexy" Marble 102cm × 31cm × 46cm 1996

胡文伟，曾于香港理工学院基本立体设计工作室进修课程，创办艺一画室。95年获美国自由人奖学金。1994年获香港市政府户外雕塑比赛设计奖及梳士巴利公园雕塑奖，89年获香港市政府艺术奖。

Wu Man-wai had courses on basic three-dimensional design extension in Hong Kong Polytech and set up his Yiyi Studio. He won a Freeman fellowship in America in 1995. He won two design awards in the Urban Council Sculpture Design Competition: sculpture champion in the Hong Kong City Hall Garden and sculpture award in Salisbury Garden in 1994, and an Urban Council fine art award in 1989.

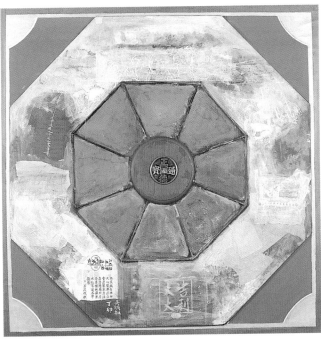

吴珉权　　《节日》　　　120cm × 120cm
Goh beng Kwan　　"Festival"　　120cmX120cm

丰爱伦　　《胡姬花》
Choo Ai Lonn, Angeline　　"Orchids"

东南亚美术协会
South-East Asia Art Association

参展画家：吴珉权、丰爱伦、仁萨、朱庆光
Participating Artists：Gohbeng Kwan, Choo Ai Lonn,
Rearnsak, Choo Keng Kwang.

吴珉权，1962年就读纽约学生联盟学院，1963年获美国福特
奖学金，64年获"波城工作室"奖学金，85年获法国大皇宫
绘画展银奖，89年获新加坡政府颁发文化奖。1965年至1992
年先后十次举办个展。出版《行程》画册。

Goh beng Kwan studied at the Art Students' League of New York in 1962 and joined
the Provincetown Workshop, Ma. USA in 1964. He was awarded Ford Foundation
Scholarship in 1963, and won a first prize in United Overseas Bank Painting of the Year
Competition in Singapore in 1984 and a silver medal in the Salon des Artistes Francais
in France in 1985. He was given a Cultural Medallion Award by the Singapore
Government in 1989. From 1965 to 1992, he held ten one-man exhibitions. Publication:
"Journeys" Picture Album (1992).

丰爱伦，毕业于南洋美专。曾获全国艺术奖及美专校友艺术
展奖牌。新加坡外交部曾购买15幅她的作品作为礼物送给外
国要员。1988年，她代表新加坡艺术家出席日本横槟艺术博
览会。1996年参加总统的慈善艺术展。

Choo Ai Loon, Angeline graduated from the nanyang Academy of Fine Arts (NAFA)
and was awarded the National Art Award and NAFA Old Boy's Art Exhibition Medal.
The Singapore Ministry of Foreign Affairs bought 15 pieces of her artworks to present
to foreign dignitaries. In 1988, she represented Singapore Artists in Yokohama Art Fair
in Japan. In 1996, she also participated in the President's Art Charity Show.

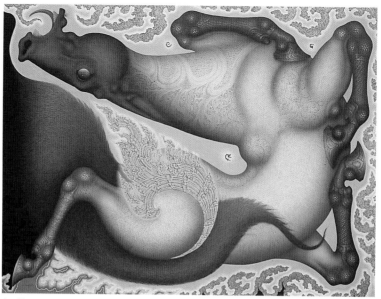

仁萨 《马》
Rearnsak "Horses"

朱庆光 《鹦鹉》
Choo Keng Guang "Parrot"

仁萨，泰国出生，经常活动于新加坡与印尼两地。曾经在伦敦、澳州、日本等地展出。在新加坡获得两项大奖（1991,1992）。善长于油画及胶彩。作品广为日本、印尼、新加坡及泰国收藏家。

Rearngsak Boonyavanishkul, born in Thailand but based in Singapore,became active as an artist after taking part in the Fourth Thai Arts 23in Bankok in 1985. Following that, his works have travelled to manycountries in the world, to the Bhudapadipa Temple in London a yearafter in 1986, the Thai Pavilion at the World Expo 88 in Australia andexhibitions in Osaka, Japan between 1990 and 1991. A winner of severalawards including several in japan and Thailand UOB Painting of the Yaer Competition in 1991 and 1992. His works in oil, watercolour and acrylicare collected by the Bankok Bank, the University of Chulalongkorn, theOsaka Museum as well as several other private and public collectorsboth in Singapore and overseas.

朱庆光，现任东南亚美术协会会长。历任国庆美展评审员。1996年，新加坡政府委任他为加拿大的世界民航总部制作名为"世界和平"的壁画。他首先在新加坡开始总统慈善艺术展。后来，他负责为新加坡总统官邸制作壁画。1976至1986，他因对艺术的贡献而获得新加坡总统颁发的服务勋章。他的作品长期在佳士德和苏富比拍卖行拍卖。

Choo Keng Kwang is the president of South-East Asia Art Association. Heis appointed as a judge for National Day Art Exhibition Yearly. In 1996,the Singapore government commissioned him to do a mural entitled "WorldPeace" for thew World Aviation Headquarters in Canada. He was also thefirst artist to start the president's Art Charity Show in Singapore.Subsequently, he was commissioned to do a mural for the Singaporepresident's official residence. In 1976-1986, he was awarded the PublicService Medal by the president of Singapore for his contributions toart. His artworks are always auctioned at Christie's International andSotheby.

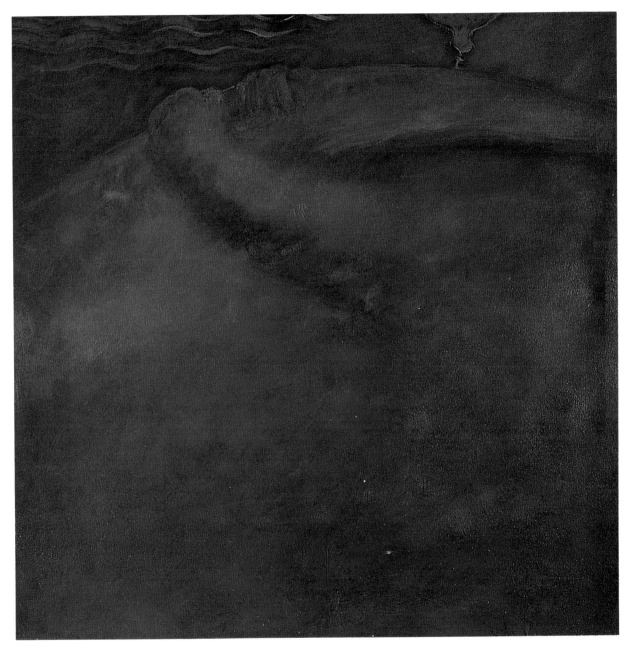

王耀麟　　《吻》　　油画　　123cm × 122cm
Heng Eow Lin　　"The Kiss"　　Oil Painting　　123cm × 122cm

王耀麟，1946 年生于马来西亚，毕业于新加坡南洋美专。他
在新加坡和马来西亚举办过八次个展并参加在瑞士、法国、
菲律宾、美国等地举办的各种美展。

Heng Eow Lin, born in 1946 in Malysia, graduated from the Nanyang A cademy of Fine
Art in Singapore. He has held eight solo exhibitions of painting and sculpture in Singapore
and Malysia and participted in anumber of exhibitions overseas, including Switzerland,
France, the Philippines, the U.S.etc.

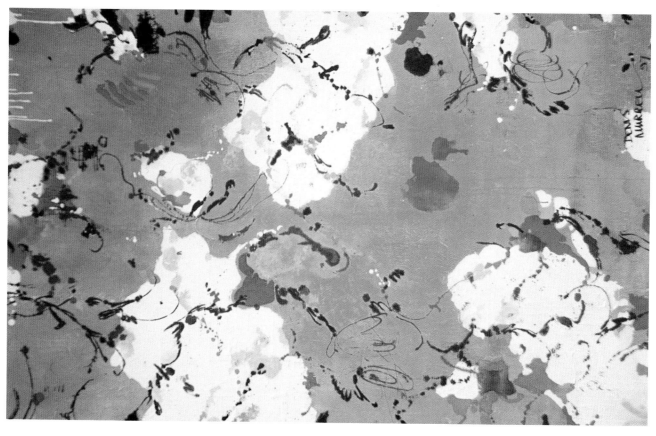

马维斯　　"Leader Quest"　　混合媒材　　112cm × 175cm
Murrell　　"Leader Quest"　　Mixed Media　　112cm × 175cm

马维斯曾参加过巴布亚新几内亚及澳州的多个联展。１９９
５年，他的无题作品获第二届澳门双年展西画组一等奖以及
澳门市政厅赞助的《全澳书画联展》中获冠军。１９９７年，
他参加了八名澳门艺术家联展及第十二届亚洲美术展等。

Denis Murrell won a number of prizes for painting and photography in Papua New Guinea and Australia before coming to live in Macau in 1989. In 1995, his painting "Untitled" was awarded first prize in the Western Painting Section of the 2nd Macau Biennial. In 1996, his painting"Both" was awarded first prize in the Western Painting Section of the Macau Collective Artists Exhibition sponsored by the Leal Senado. In1997 he took part in some group exhibitions including "Eight Macau Contemporary Artists" and the "12th Asian International Art Exhibition".

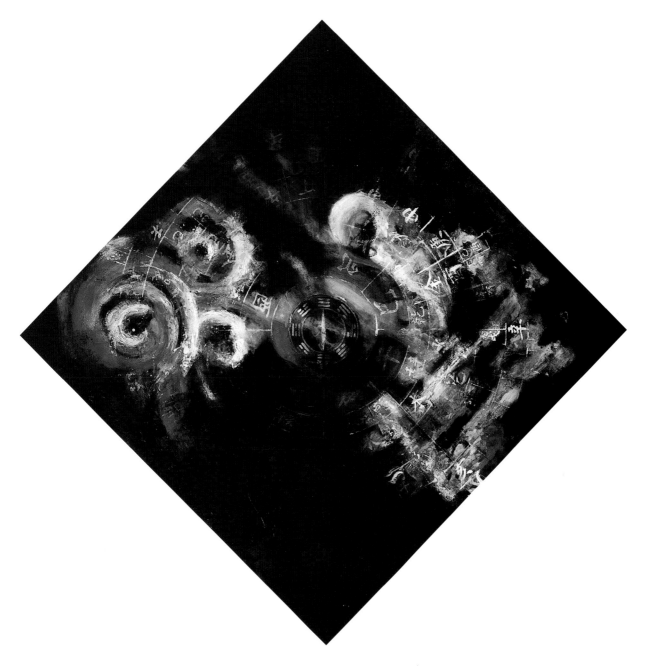

马伟达　《风水》　混合材料　120cm × 120cm
Victor Hugo Marreiros　"FONG SOI"　120cm × 120cm　Mixed Media

马伟达现任澳门文化署美术部主任、文化杂志艺术总监。多
次参加在葡萄牙和澳门举办的摄影展；在澳门、香港、葡萄
牙、新加坡、马来西亚和中国多次举办个展并多次参加联展。
曾获澳门发行机构徽标设计比赛优胜奖；其设计的邮票《澳
门传统竞技》参加意大利《邮票艺术大奖赛》获旅游奖，并
在《第一届澳门设计双年奖》比赛中获一系列奖励。

Victor Hugo Marreiros is head of the Graphic Section at Instituto Cultural de macau
and Art Director of Revista de Cultura. He has participated for many times phto
exhibitions in Portugal and Macau; he has also held solo exhibitions or took part in
collective exhibitions in Macau, Hong Kong, Portugal, Singapore, Malysia and China.
He was winner of the contest regarding the creation of Instituto Emissor de Macau's
logo; the stamps "Macau's Traditional Games" was awarded the Tourism Sector Prize
in the Contest of "PREMIO INTERNAZIONALE ASIAGO D'ARTE FILATELICA"
in Italy and he won a number of prizes in the First Macau Design Contest 94/95.

何道根　　《幽兰》　　国画　　90cm × 47cm
He Dao-gen　"Orchids"　Chinese Painting　　90cm × 47cm

何道根，番禺沙湾人，４３年出生。少师从沈仲强先生画菊。后师从麦华三先生研习书法。６２年移居香港。８３年香港大会堂举办作品展。８５年在台北举办个展。除丹青外喜篆刻。近年致力于研习双勾重彩画法。

He Dao-gen, born in 1943 of Panyu origin, learned chrysanthemum painting under the instruction of Mr. Shen Zhong-qiang in his childhood. Later he learned calligraphy from Mr. Mai Hua-san. He moved to HongKong in 1962. In 1983 he held an exhibition of his works in the HongKong City Hall and in 1985 an individual exhibition in taibei. Besides calligraphy and painting, he is fond of seal cutting. He is engaged in the research of new techniques in his paintings.

丘瑞福　　《欢乐日》　　混合媒体　　152cmX122cm
Chieu Shuey Fook　　"Happy Day"　　Copperplate　　150cmX120cm

丘瑞福1934年生于新加坡，毕业于南洋美专。自１９９３年以来，参加在日本、澳门、新加坡等地举办的各类美展并有作品在广州国际艺术博览会展出。　１９７０年，作品"水屋"获"Instant Asia"艺术大赛一等奖，铝制作品"魔鬼鱼"参加国际广告比赛，在纽约获两个荣誉奖。１９８９年获南洋艺专校友会视觉艺术创作奖。

Chieu Shuey Fook was born in 1934 and graduated from the Nanyang Academy of Fine Art in Singapore. Since 1993, he has taken part in exhibitions in japan, macau and singapore, and he also took part in the Guangzhou International Art Fair. In 1970, his "Water House" won a first prize in the "Instant Asia" Art Competition; his aluminum work "Demon Fish" was selected by ITT for their worldwide advertising campaigns and also won two Citation Awards in New York. In 1989, he won the NAFA Alumi Associaiton Visual Art Creation Award.

冯宝珠　　《孤独的蝎子》　　40cmX48cm　　铜版画
Anti Fung Pou Chu　"Lonely Scorpion"　40cmX48cm　　Copperplate

冯宝珠，现任澳门艺术高等学校课程主任及讲师。93年"第一届澳门艺术双年展"获版画组一等奖。95年获澳门政府奖学金前往英国伦敦大学进修两年纯艺术硕士。作品曾入选展示于日本，英国，法国等二十多次，个展五次。作品120多幅被各地机构或个人收藏。
地址：澳门荷兰园正街15号地下
电话：（853）6820388，353327
传呼机：（853）5010882
电话传真：（853）304305

Anti Fung Pou Chu is currently a coordinator and lecturer at Escola Suoerior de Arttes Macau. In 1993, she won a first prize in printmaking in the 1st Macau Biennial Art Exhibition. From 1995 to 1997, she won a scholarship from ICM to study the Slade School of Fine Art (Master Degree)at the University of London. She has held five individual exhibitions and more than twenty times took part in exhibitions in Macau, London, France, Portugal, Japn, etc.
Add: 15 Ave. C.F. de Almeida, Macau
E-mail: anitafung@ipm.edu.mo
Tel: (853)6820388　727639
Fax: (853)727648

白礼仁　《思家》　　油画　　184cm × 92cm　　1997年
Robert O'Brien　"Thinking of the Wan Family House"　　Oil on Canvas　　184cm × 92cm　　1997

白礼仁1939年生于英国，中央艺术与设计学校舞台设计毕业。从1964年至1975年他分别在伦敦和暮尼黑任全职艺术家。现居香港达22年之久，一直从事中学大学视觉艺术教育。目前在演艺学院任教。他曾在伦敦和香港举办个展8次、联展23次。他的作品为单位及个人收藏。

Robert O'Brien, born in 1939, graduated in Theatre Design from the Central School of Art and Design and worked as a full tiime artist in London and Munich from 1964 to 1975. He has resided in Hong Kong for 22years and had worked as an artist and in visual art educationin the secondary and tertiary sectors. He is currently teaching at the Academy of Performing Arts. Robert has participated in 8 one-man shows in London ans Hong Kong and in 23 group exhibitions. His works are collected by corporate and public collections including the Hong Kong and Regionak Museum of Art.

麦少峰　　《香港 1997》　　水彩　　75cm × 55cm　　1997 年
Mak Siu Fung　"Hong Kong 1997"　Water Colour　75cmX55cm　1997

麦少峰（麦权），生于香港。香港美术专科学校毕业。多次参加海内外联展，举办过两次个展。出版《麦少峰水彩画集》。70 年至 71 年人报纸记者和电视台新闻摄影记者。92 年创办影像制作公司。

Mak Siu Fung (Mak Kuen) graduated from the Hong Kong Fine Arts Academy in 1970. He has participated in numerous local and overseas joint exhibitions. He has held two individual exhibitions and published the "Watercolours By Mak Siu Fung". From 1970 to 1991, Mak worked as a newspaper journalist and later as a television news cameraman. In 1992, he started his own video production company.

余世坚 《瀑》 国画 72.1cm × 142.2cm
Yu Sai Kin "Waterfalls" Chinese Painting 72.1cm × 142.2cm

余世坚　《三峡》　国画　37.5cm × 185.4cm
Yu Sai Kin　"The Changjiang Gorges"　Chinese Painting　37.5cmX185.4cm

余世坚，香港艺术家合作社主席，国际造型艺术家协会创会会员。66年从师吕寿琨习水墨。吕氏在遗作《水墨画讲》评提其画作"不用墨而有水墨味"。69及71年参加香港当代双年展。73年获美国克里夫兰美术学院录取入绘画系四年级。同年获该校学生独立展版画首奖。80年获邀为多伦多佐治罗朗西画廊作开幕首展。85年"水墨的年代"展，88年"ISSPA国际造型艺术协会展"，同年"山水骨风"近作个展，部分作品获选为美国华盛顿香港贸易中心永久藏品。

Yu Sai Kin, chairman of the Artists Co-op of Hong Kong and member of the International Society of Plastic and Audio-Visual Art. In 1966 he followed Lui Sau Kwan to study painting. "Yu Sai Kin's painting uses no Chinese Ink, but gives a feeling of brush and ink painting," Master Lui commented in his last book of Art. In 1969 and 1971, he participated in the "Contemporary Hong Kong Art Biennial". In 1973, he won a first prize in printmaking in the "Students' Independent Show" of Cleveland Institute of Art, Ohio, USA. In 1980, he was invited to show in the Inauguration Exhibition for "George Lorange XX Century Art" in Toranto. In 1997, he held "One-Man Show" of recent works in the Design First Gallery; part of the exhibits were purchased by the Hong Kong Trade House in Washington D.C. as a permanent collection.

Add : 276 Gloucester Road, i/g, Hoi Deen Court, Causeqay Bay, Hong kong
Tel : (852) 28347283
Fax : (852) 28347362

电话: (852) 28347283
传真: (852) 28347362

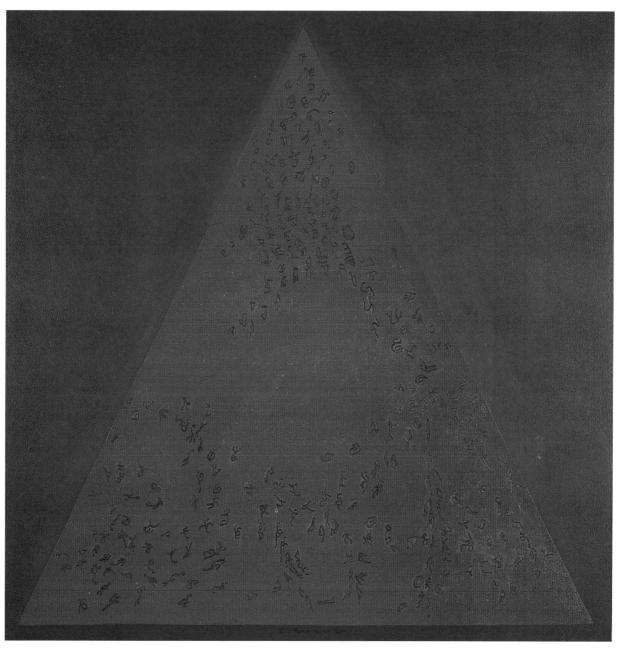

吕丰雅 《万里无云》 布本塑胶彩 122cm × 122cm 1997 年
Eddie D.F.N Lui "Open Sky" Acrylicon Linen 122cm × 122cm 1997

吕丰雅，香港大学艺术及设计证书课程肄业。随后进修一年绘画工作室。在哥德学院举行首次个人画展大获好评。后常参加香港及世界各地重要视觉艺术展览。现主持精雅创作画苑，视觉艺术顾问公司，专注发展其视觉艺术创作事业。

Eddie D. F. N. Lui graduated from the Arts and Design programme at HongKong university in 1972 and completed an additional year in a painting workshop with the university. He held his first one-man exhibition at the Goethe Institue in 1993. His successful show was quickly followed by numerous regional and international exhibitions. Now Lui is focussed on the promotion and enhancement of vsual arts development, with special emphasis on project management, exhibition organization and programming.

蔡逸溪　　《冰河仪舞》　胶彩　29CM × 57CM
Chua Ek Kay　"Ice-Age Ritual"　29cm × 57cm

蔡逸溪，生于４７年，新加坡公民。获澳州塔斯马尼亚大学艺术系学士，西雪梨大学视觉艺术荣誉硕士学位。其创作风格融会中西画法，以水墨技法写新加坡当地街景，一方面保留传统笔墨情趣，一方面开创题材，使作品产生新风格。

Chua Ek Kay, born in 1947, is citizen of Singapore. He studied in Australia and was honoured a Bachelor Degree in Fine Art and a Master Degree in Visual Arts. Ek Kay combines eastern and western styles in his painting. From 1987 onward, he has been trying to use Chinese ink to paint Singapore street scenes, preserving the traditional Chinese painting skills and exploring new methods in his work.

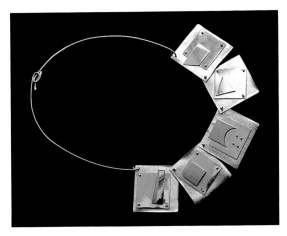

玛利亚．韦丽莎　《首饰》
Maria Elisa Vilaca　"Jewellery"

李希文　《无题》　95cm × 83cm
Mira Dias　"Untitled"
Oil painting　95cm × 83cm

李希文，现为中学美术教师，在澳门视觉艺术学院学习。作品曾参加港澳女子书画联展，摄影比赛，并于澳门旅游司举办《情思》双人画展。96 年参与 JUM 在澳门陆军俱乐部和广州国际艺术博览会画展，在葡萄牙各省举办《依莎贝－李希文双人油画展。97 年在葡萄牙再次举办双人画展，参加 "澳门视觉艺术" 举办的两次画展，及入选本年度澳门艺术双年展。

Mira Dias is a teacher of fine art, with works participating in the Collective Exhibition of Female Artists' Calligraphy and Paintings, "Phtography Competition" and a two-person exhibition in the Gallery of Macau Tourist Office. In 1996, she took part in the collective Exhibition of J.U.M Painting Association in the Gallery of Macau Military Club, the Guangzhou International Art Exposition and held the "Isabel-Mira Dias" Oil Painting Exhibition in Portugal. In 1997, she held once again a two-person exhibition around Portugal, took part in two exhibitions in the Internaional Centre of Visual Arts of Macau.

依莎贝，任职教师。作品曾参加《现代画联展》、第二届澳门艺术双年展、广州国际艺术博览会、葡国各省及澳门所举办的各项画展。在葡国举办《依莎贝、李希文》油画展和多次双人展并参加第十二届全澳书画联展。

Isabel Candeias is a teacher, with works participating in the "Joint Exhibition of Modern Paintings", the Second Macau Biennial Art Exhibition, the Guangzhou International Art Exposition and exhibitions in Portugal and Macau. She held the "Isabel-Mira Dias" Oil Painting Exhibition several two-person shows in Portugal and took part in the 12th Macau Joint Exhibition of Calligraphy and Painting.

Maria Elisa Vilaca was born in 1955. She has lived in Macau since 1982 and now works as a kindergarten teacher. From 1987 to 1990, she studied Chinese Ceramics under Master Lai Kuai Peng in a course organized by the Macau Education and Youth Department. She has taken a variety of courses at the Macau Academy of Visual Arts. From 1991 to 1992, she attended the Jewellery Course taught by Manuela Sousa. In March 1994 she held a joint exhibition of Jewllery with Teresa Santos in the Exhibition Gallery of the Macau Government Tourist Office."

范婴子登　　《山水》　　国画　　141cm × 68cm
Fanying Zideng　　"Landscape"　　Chinese Painting　　141cm × 68cm

范婴子登。所作墨荷，气势壮润灵动，自成一家。享有国际声誉，被尊称为写意画大师。作品在美，加，星，马，港及深圳等地展出，屡获免审殊荣。作品参与中国海外艺术家联展，97首届中国邀请展等，被罗马教廷美术博物馆，罗马圣母总院美术馆，新加坡国立大学李光前文物馆，台国立历史博物馆，马来西亚艺术学院收藏。私人藏者遍及世界各地。现为香港拥翠画院院长，香港国际艺术家联合会会长。
画室地址：香港九龙 官塘道 55A，启德大厦第 4 座，1 号 5F

Fanying Zideng is a world famous master of art, soecially good at ink-painting of Lotus. His works have been exhibited in the U.S., Canada, Singapore, Malysia and Shenzhen and highly praised. He also participated in the China Joint Exhibition of Works by Overseas Artists, the first China Invitation Exhibition, etc. His works have been collected by institutions in Rome, Singapore, Taiwan, Malaysia and by private collectors all over the world. Mr. Fan is president of Yongcui Academy in Hong Kong and chairman of the Hong Kong International Artists Union.
Studio Add: 5f No.1, Block 4, Kai Tak Mansion, 55A Kwun Tong Rd., Kowloon

童建颖 《文字彩拓》 宣纸彩拓 70cm × 70cm 1997 年
Tong Jian-ying "Characters Color Printing" Xuan Paper 70cm × 70cm 1997

童建颖，江西文艺学校美术专业毕业，浙江美术学校油画系进修。获奖多次。88 年于上海美术馆举办个人抽象绘画展，开始《文字彩拓》系列的创作。为中国美协会员，上海美协会员。入编《世界华人艺术家成就博览大典》。加入澳门美协。作品参加澳门国际视觉艺术中心现代画家邀请展，第 12 届亚细亚国际美术展览会，并个展于 97 广州国际艺术博览会。

Tong Jian-ying, a graduate of Jiangxi Art School, had further studies in the Oil Department of Zhejiang Institute of Fine Art. He has won awards of different kinds several times. In 1988 he held a solo exhibition of abstract painting in the Shanghai Art Gallery and began his Characters Color Printing series. He is a member of the China Artists Association and the Shanghai Artists Association. His name is listed in the Dictionary of Achievements by the World's Chinese Artists. He is also a member of the Macau Artists Association, with works displayed in the Invitation Exhibition of Modern Painters at the Macau International Visual Arts Centre, the 12th Asia International Exhibition of Fine Art. In 1997, he held a solo show in the '97 Guangzhou International Art Fair.

马若龙　　《太后》　　混合媒材　　120cm × 190cm　　1995 年
Carlos Marreiros　"Empress Dowager"
Mixed Media　120cm × 190cm　1995

马若龙，现任建筑师。毕业于里斯本大学建筑系。在德国修
读都市重整规划课程。在瑞士学习环境工程并在里斯本美术
学院修读艺术课程。曾为杂志作插图，发表对艺术，建筑和
文物有关的评论文章。与菲基立建筑师合作出版《澳门建筑
文物》一书。87 年起任《文化杂志》副总编辑，同年获澳门
颁发文化功绩勋章。曾出任澳门文化司署司长。参与德国，新
加坡，比利时，中国，日本等的美术联展。获第 二届全澳书
画联展西画冠军，首届澳门造型艺术双年展素描组冠军。澳
门文化体现代画会创会成员，当选首任主席至今，并受聘为
上海大学美术学院客座教授。

电话：（853）785725，555055

Carlos Marreiros is an architect. He graduated from the architecture department of Lisbon
University and took courses on city redevelopmentin Germany, environmental
engineering in Switzerland and art courses inLisbon Art Institute. He has made
illustrations for magazines,published articles on art and architecture and
"HistoricalArchitectural Relics in Macau" (Co-author). From 1978 on, he has beendeputy
editor-in-chief and art director of "Cultural Magazine". He wasawarded a Medal of
Cultural Merit in 1978. Between 1989 and 1992, hewas president of the Cultural Institute
of macau.He has taken part in exhibitions in Germany, Singapore, Belgium, China,
Japan, etc. He won aspecial prize for creativity in the 2nd Macau Exhibition of
Calligraphyand Painting, a first prize in Western Painting Section in the 4thMacau
Exhibition of Calligraphy and Painting and a first prize in thein the Drawing Section in
the First Biennial of Art of Macau. He was oneof the founders of the Circle of Friends of
Culture of macau and hasbeen its president of the group since. Besides, he is guest
professorof the Fine Art College of Shanghai University.
Tel: (853)785725, 555055

邹中星　　《五千年来的人间色相》　　混合材料　183cm × 122cm　　1997 年
Chao Chong Seng　"Different Looks in the Past Five Thousand Years"
Mixed Media 183cm × 122cm　　1997

邹中星，参加多届澳门美协主办的全澳美展。国际青年年美
术作品展获优秀奖。入选多届全澳书画联展。加入澳门文化
体，现代书会。参加"视觉艺术学员展"获西画组冠军。参
加联展包括澳门文化体现代画会八周年展，韩国亚洲美展，
葡萄牙学会联展等。
电话：(853) 764133

Chao Chong Seng has participated in such exhibitions as the Macau Fine Art Exhibition,
the International Young Artists Exhibition, the Macau Artists Collective Exhibition. He
is a member of the Macau Friends of Culture, Modern Painting. He won a first prize in
the Western Painting Section of the Exhibition of Students Visual Art Works. The
collective exhibitions he has taken part in include the 8th anniversary of the Macau
Friends Culture,Modern Painting, Asian Art Exhibition in Korea and the association
collective exhibition in Portugal.
Tel: (853)764133

琥茹　《傩文化的迷惑》系列　　纸本压克力　　79cm × 79cm
Joana Ling　　"Puzzles of the Culture of Evil Driving"
Series Acrylic on Paper　79cm × 79cm

琥茹,1994年出生于新加坡,1971年毕业于新加坡师范学校。80年移居澳门。1989年获澳门东方基金会奖学金到葡萄牙里斯本A.R.C.O.艺术学院进修现代造型艺术。至今举办个展六次、双人展七次,多次参加国际联展。她是澳门文化体成员之一。

Joana Ling was born in 1949 in Singapore. She graduated from the Singapore Ministry of Education Teacher Training College in 1971. In1980, she came to live in Macau. In 1989 she won a scholarship from the Orien Foundation to study at A.R.C.O. Centre of Visual Art and Communication in Lisbon. She has held six individual exhibitions, the first in Casa garden Gallery and the last in Club Milita. She is currently a member of Macau Friends of Cilture and she has participatedin various collective international exhibitions.

康斯坦丁　《梦解》　压克力　145cm × 206cm　1996年
Konstandin Bessmertnyi　　"Explanatory of Night Dreams"
Acrylic on Canvas　145cm × 206cm　1996

康斯坦丁，1964年出生于前苏联的布拉戈维申斯克并在该地的美术学校学习。从1978年开始，参加国在俄罗斯举办的美展。自1993年以来，分别在俄罗斯、日本、澳门、香港、葡萄牙、德国和丹麦展出。

Konstantin Bessmertny was born in Blagovesthensk U.S.S.R. and educated at the Fine Art School there. Beginning from 1978, he had participated in several exhibitions in Russia and from 1993 on, his works have been exhibited in Russia, jaopn, Macau, Hong Kong, Portugal, Germany and Denmark.

缪鹏飞 《水浒绣像图》 混合媒材 240cm × 1296cm 1996 年
Mio Pang Fei "Embroidered Figures of the WATER MARGIN"
Mixed Media 240cm × 1296cm 1996

缪鹏飞，福建师范学院美术系毕业。曾在澳大利亚、比利时、葡萄牙、印度等地举办个展和联展。受聘为上海大学美术系客座教授，东方文化艺术学院客座教授，和上海工艺美术学校客座教授。曾获 CASINO ESTORIL 艺术画廊 "秋之沙龙" 大奖，全澳书画联展构图褒奖，和第一届全澳双年展银奖。入编 1994 年《世界华人艺术家成就博览大典》。

Mio Pang Fei graduated from the Fine Art Department of Fujian Normal College. He has held solo and joint exhibitions in Australia, Belgium, Portugal, India, etc. He is guest professor of the Art College of Shanghai University, the Beijing Academy of Oriental Culture and Art and the Shanghai Art and Craft School. He has won awards in the 1st Macau Biennial Art Exhibition, the Macau Artists Collective Exhibition and the October Salon at the Estoril Casino in Portugal. His name is listed in the Dictionary of the Achievements of the World's Chinese Artists.

袁之钦　　《道民》　　国画　　65cm×65cm　　1997年
Un Chi Iam "Pedestrains"　Chinese painting　65cm×65cm　1997

袁之钦，南京艺术学院美术系毕业。曾在新加坡，马来西亚，墨尔本，日本，印度，韩国等地举办个展。曾获第二届全澳书画联展创作褒奖，第五届全澳书画联展国画冠军，第六届全澳书画联展国画冠军，和第一届澳门艺术双年展荣誉奖。

Un Chi Iam graduated from the Fine Art Department of Nanjing Art Institute. She has held solo exhibtions in Singapore, Malaysia, Australia, Japan, India and South Korea. She won an award of creation in the 2nd Macau Collective Exhibition of Calligraphy and Painting, and was champion in Chinese painting in the 5th and the 6th. She was awarded an honored prize in the first Macau Biennial Art Exhibition.

吴卫鸣　　《大地之子》　　电子媒材　　102cm × 75cm　　1997 年
Ung Vai Meng　"Son of the Earth"　Electronic Media　102cm × 75cm　1997

吴卫鸣1986年获澳门文化司署助学金前往波尔图高等美术学院学习绘画及版画。1989年获《第六届全澳书画联展》西画组冠军及《澳门中央图书馆壁画设计比赛》冠军。1995 年获《第二届澳门艺术双年展》装置组冠军。自 1995 年起，在澳门及国内和海外美术设计比赛获奖四十多项。此外，他还在各地多次举办个展。

Ung Vai Meng won a scholarship from the Cultural Institute of Macau to study painting and print-making in Oporto's College of Fine Art in 1986. He was champion of the Western Painting Section in the 6th Macau Collective Exhibition of Calligraphy and Painting and champion in the"Mural Design Contest for the Macau Central Library" in 1989; and champion in the Facility Section of the 2nd Macau Biennial Art Exhibiton. Beginning from 1995, he has won more than forty awards in Macau and the Mainland of China. And he has held many solo exhibitions in and out of Macau.

廖文畅 　《后院》　　**压克力**　　184cm × 120cm
Liao Wen-chang　"Backyard"　Acrylic　184cm × 120cm

廖文畅，现为澳门美协理事，畅意画室专业画家。作品入选
第六届，第八届全国美展。曾获澳门青年美展优秀奖，第11、
12届全澳书画联展西画组最佳作品奖，第2届澳门艺术双年
展西画第2名，"中国仙人"和"澳门庙宇"邮票设计获"最
佳澳门邮票艺术奖"两项冠军。

Liao Wen-chang is director of Macau Artists Association and a professional painter of
"Changyi Studio". His artworks have been shown in the 6th and 8th China Exhibition of
Fine Art and won an excellence prize in the Macau Youths Art Exhibition, "The Best
Work in Western Style" in the 11th and 12th Macau Joint Exhibition of Calligraphy and
Painting, a second prize in the 2nd Macau Biennial Art Exhibition, an "art award for the
best Macau stamps" for stamp design. "Chinese Celestial Beings" and "Temples in
Macau" both won the first place.

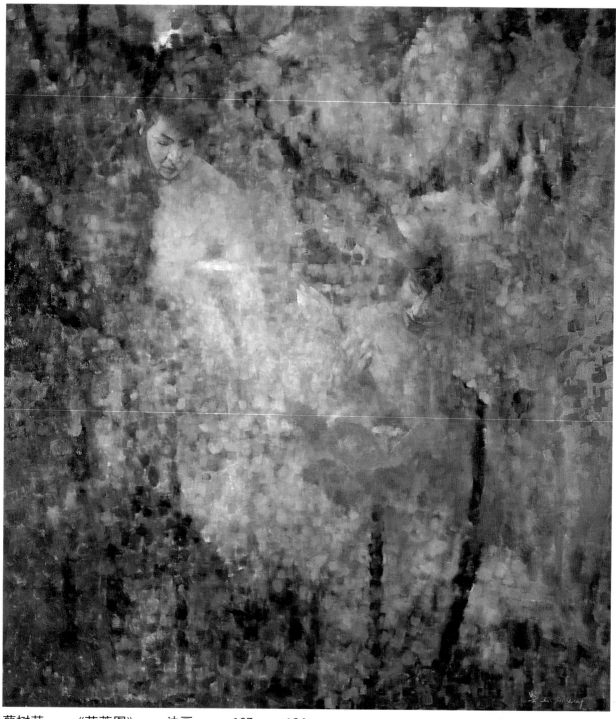

蔡树荣   《芙蓉图》   油画   137cm × 184cm
Choi Su Weng   "Cottonrose Hibiscus"   Oil Painting   137cm × 184cm

蔡树荣，52 年出生于澳门，从事美术创作多年。展出于加拿
大，葡萄牙，北京，广州，香港。作品入选第七届全国美展。
电话：(853) 719173

Choi Su Weng, born in Australia in 1952, has been engaged in fine artcreation for many
years with works exhibited in Canada, Portuga,Beijing, Guangzhou, and Hong Kong.
He also took part in the 7thNational Exhibition of Fine Art.
Fax: (853)719173

黎鹰　《节日》　油画　120cm × 80cm　1997 年
Lai Leng　"Festival"　Oil Painting　120cm × 80cm　1997

黎鹰，澳门出生。擅长水彩，油画，曾展出加拿大，葡萄牙，
北京，香港，澳门。作品入选第六届和第七届全国美展。
电话：719439
传真：(853) 719173

Lai Leng, born in Macau, is good at watercolor and oil painting. Hisartworks have been
displayed in Canada, Portugal, Beijing, Hong Kongand Macau. And some were selected
into the 6th and 7th Nationakl FineArt Exhibitions.
Add: Av. Venceslau De Morais S/N 3 Andar-D Edif. Ind. Fu Tai Macau
Tel: 719439
Fax: (853)719173

谭可文　《山水》　国画　68cm × 67cm
Tan Ke-wen　"Landscape"　Chinese Painting　68cm × 67cm

谭可文，澳门美协会员，澳门书法家协会理事。作品多次参加澳门市政厅举办的全澳书画联展。澳门第二届艺术双年展。作品《黄山图》获澳门青年美展优良奖。篆刻作品获第二届王子杯海峡两岸书画大赛金奖。
地址：澳门雅廉访马路46-48号雅廉花园5楼L座

Tan Ke-wen, member of Macau Artists Associatio and director of Macau Calligraphists Association. His works participated many times in the Macau Exhibition of Calligraphy and Painting sponsored by the City Hall.His "Huangshan Mountains" won an excellence prize for young artistsat the Macau Biennial Art Exhibition, and his seal-cutting work won agold prize at the second "Prince Cup" Calligraphy and Painting Competition Between the Straights.
Add: Edificio Nga Lim Avn. Ouvidor Arriaga, No. 46-48 Andar 5 (L) Macau

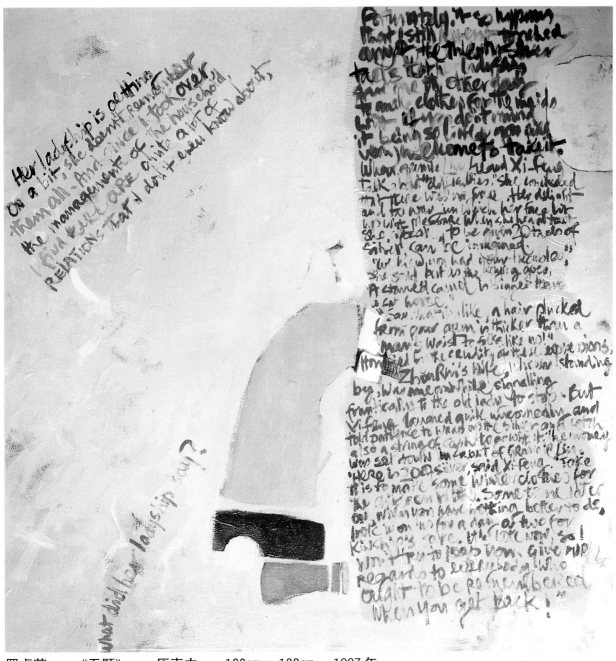

罗卓英 　《无题》 　压克力 　100cm × 100cm 　1997 年
Jorge Carlos Smith 　"Untitled" 　Acrylic 　100cm × 100cm 　1997

罗卓英（若热史密斯），9岁移居葡萄牙，两年后赴英国留学。16岁在当时就读学校首次获艺术奖。一年后转校。曾参与舞台设计，集体绘画联展等多项艺术活动。96年在澳门葡文书局画廊举办首次个人作品展览。

Jorge Smith was born in Mozambique in 1965. He studied in Portagul and England and completed a course in hotel management. He participated at the age of 16 in the first collective exhibition at Corfes School in condres. He was a street portraitist for two years. In 1966, he had his first solo exhibition at the Gallery of the Portuguese Bookshop in Macau.

郭桓 《律动的风采》 木板混合材料 111cm × 78cm 1997 年
Kwok Woon "The Grace of Rhythm" Mixed Media 111cm × 78cm 1997

郭桓　《梦幻东方》　混合媒材拼贴　85cm × 85cm　1997 年
Kwok Woon　"Dreams of the East"　Mixed Media　85cm × 85cm　1997

郭桓，全职专业画家，至今个展十回，双人展七回，联展超
过百回。作品经常展出于世界各地。澳门文化体，现代画会
成员，广州国际艺术博览会艺委会委员，负责海外招展，统
筹国际展区。97 年创立"澳门国际视觉艺术中心"。曾获第 2
五届"全澳书画联展"西画组金奖，第四届"中国藏书票"优
秀奖。95 年"新加坡美术奖"荣誉表扬奖。94 年编入《世界
华人艺术家成就博览大典》。出版个人画集七册，双人画集三
册。

Kwok Woon, a professional artist. Up to now he has held ten individual exhibitions,
seven two-person exhibitons and joined more than a hundred joint exhibitions. His works
have been displayed all over the world. He is a member of the Macau Friends of Culture
-- Modern Art Section, member of the art committee of the Guangzhou International Art
Exposition. He founded the "Macau International Visual Art Centre" in 1997. He won a
gold medal for painting in the 5th Macau Artists Collective Exhibition, an excellence
prize in the 4th China National Exlibris Exhibition and an honored prize of Singapore
Arts Award in 1995. His name was included in the "Dictionary of Achievements of
Chinese Artistsin the World". He has so far published seven individual painting albums
and three two-epople albums.

郭桓 《幻化的足迹》 环保物质－废料混合 205cm × 202cm 1996年
Kwok Woon "Illusive Footprints"
Mixed Waste Materials 205cm × 202cm 1996

澳门国际视觉艺术中心
Macau International Visual Arts Centre
Centro Internacional De Artes Visuais de Macau
澳门连胜街2号G座
Rua de Coelho do Amaral 2-G,MACAU
Tel：(853) 324504
Fax：(853) 557147

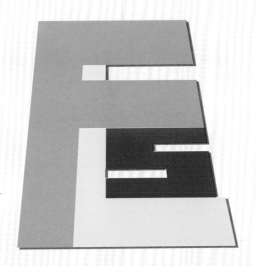

FENG LIN SHAN

风 林 山

自96广州国际艺术博览会后，今年又以更多的参展画家的支持再与观众见面。风林山画廊的宗旨是，以国际性画廊的操作方式，现代的装裱手段和力所能及的宣传力度为画家提供一个与收藏家接触的场地，同时又为收藏家提供风林山的艺术精品推介。

创办一个具有自己特色的，集现代与传统装裱技术于一身的实体。是我在日本获得一级装裱师后的第一个念头。现代国际上，对艺术品的装裱分现代传统两大类。现代装裱是以现代机械与技术、材料、美学等综合因素，对每一件艺术品，根据不同的环境及场合进行装饰，其优点在于合理、简明及运用先进的工艺，对艺术品的包装，方便快捷规范，能与现代的环境及国际展览规定接轨，对于提高中国画的现代装裱工艺及进入各种展示空间提供了特殊的展示魅力。因此，我在创办风林山艺术装饰厂的开始就以：高、专、精为发展方向，即采用高品质的原料，包括各国知名厂家的高级材质，结合国际最先进的专业技术和加工机械设备，最后实现作品在工艺装饰完成后，达到完美的效果。传统装裱是我国独有的一种书画保护、装饰、修复技术，它分为新画的装裱和古画的修复两类。它主要的对象是中国传统书法、绘画作品。其形式分为立轴、册页、手卷镜片等，它的最大优点是易于保存、便于携带、方便张挂展示，利于日后的修复。无论现代、传统装裱，我在二十年来的学习和国外游历中发现二者的优点和区别。两种不同的东、西方文化、新科技的应用及对艺术作品的审美与制作工艺方面均可以互补长短。更能适应艺术市场的需求。

近年来，在艺术市场中发现，传统的装裱，有所停滞而难于满足社会的需求。特别是在古画修复方面，更是没有一个专门的修复专业店，因此在大力发展现代装裱的同时用自己所学的专长开设一个较完善的传统装裱及古画修复中心，为有需要的人士服务，更是我创办风林山的另一个愿望。

风林山
郑于民

FENG LIN SHAN
风 林 山

《人 体》

杨 之 光　　1930年生于上海，广东揭西县人

48年就读南中美术院（即前春睡画院）为高剑父入室弟子，50年读中央美术学院受徐悲鸿指导。54年《一辈了第一回》入选首届全国美展（中国美术馆藏），59年《雪夜送饭》获七届世界青年联欢节金奖（中国美术馆藏），62年《浴日图》开现代大写意人物的先声，71年《矿山新兵》将逆光带入中国写意人物画。84年《儿子》入选六届全国美展并为优秀作品。91年获美国纽约国际文化艺术中心颁发"中国画杰出成就奖"，93年获美国加州及旧金山市政府荣誉奖状。97年画家将其毕生的精品1000幅分别赠给中国美术馆、广东省美术馆及广州市美术馆收藏，实现了画 家"来之于人民，还之于人民。"的崇高愿望。画家曾任广州美院国画系主任、副院长。现为中国美术家协会理事，广东美协常务理事，出版画集九册。

《明天会更好》82年作

鸥 洋　1937年生，江西龙南县人。

60年毕业于广州美术学院油画系。85年在法国受赵无极大师的指导，回国后潜心探索具有东方印象主义风貌的意象油画及彩墨画。代表作品：中国画《雏鹰展翅》、《新课堂》等入选全国美展。水粉画《五爱》获取广东少年题材创作一等奖，《金色的秋天》获中国水彩、水粉大展优秀奖。彩墨画《池韵》获取现代中国画展荣誉奖。油画《冬天里的春》获中日联展之"四季画展"银奖。其作品分别被中国美术馆、中国军事美术馆、日本美术馆等机构收藏。编著有《水粉画写生技法》、《现代绘画形式与技巧》，出版个人画集数册，现为广州美术学院教授，中国美术家协会会员。

FENG LIN SHAN
风 林 山

《 脸 谱 》

许 固 令　字白父，1943年生，广东汕尾市人。

64年毕业于广州美术学院附中。80年移居香港，90年移居台湾。为港台著名的彩墨大师。91年获全日本收藏家联盟金赏，92年获韩国国际现代水墨邀请展优秀作品奖，93年获德国法兰克福（中国水墨大展）荣誉奖。作品分别被香港港督府，　德国法兰克福艺术馆，日本大阪美术馆，日本奈良博物馆，加拿大多伦多美术馆，美国圣约翰大学美术馆，　澳大利亚新洲美术馆，新西兰美术馆，中国美术馆等机构收藏。　曾在香港、韩国、台湾、日本、加拿大、德国、法国、美国、　新加坡、澳大利亚、广州等地区举办个人画展十八回。出版画集多本。

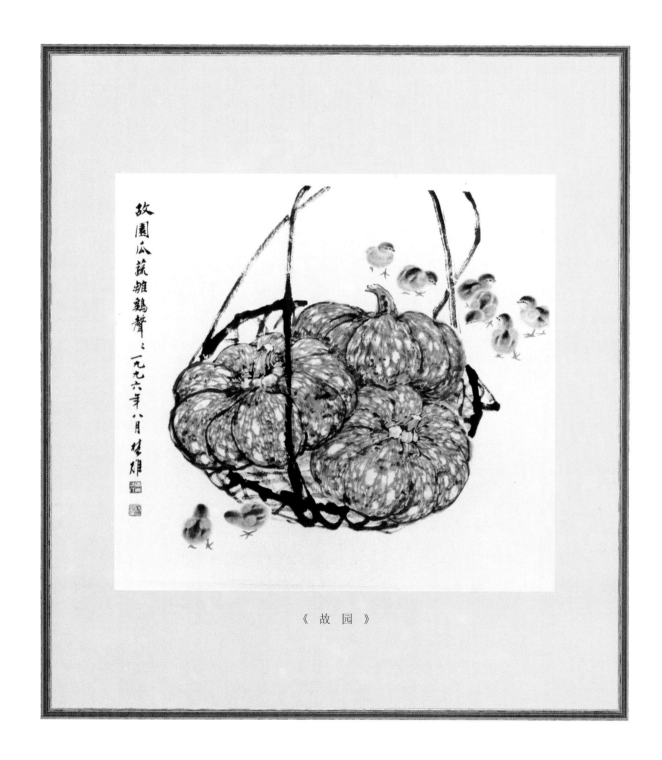

《 故 园 》

方 楚 雄 1950生于汕头市，广东普宁县人。55年从王兰若学画，少年时作品多次被选送出国展览并发表。
78年毕业于广州美术学院并留校任教至今。作品入选第六、七、八届全国美展。 先后在新加坡、澳大利亚、纽西兰、台湾、香港、
上海、南京、广州、汕头等地举办个人画展，其作品被北京人民大会堂，全国政协，中南海，钓鱼台国宾馆、军事博物馆 及各地美
术馆、博物馆收藏。 出版有《动物画谱》、《画好小动物》、《方楚雄画选》、《方楚雄画集》多册。 现为中国美术家协会会员、
广东美术家协会常务理 事。广州美术学院国画系副主任、副教授。

FENG LIN SHAN

风 林 山

《秋山行旅》局部

李劲堃　　1958年生于广州，广东南海市人。

87年毕业于广州美术学院中国画系研究生班，获硕士学位。作品分别入选广东青年美展（获铜奖）、第七、八届全国美展，《大漠之暮》获第七届全国美展铜奖"容奇杯奖"，和建党七十周年全国美展（获铜奖）。作品曾在广州、新加坡等地举办个人展画，出版有《李劲堃近作集》。现为中国美术家协会会员，广东省美协理事，广州美术学院国画系副主任、副教授。

《马到天明》局部

董帜强 1958年生于广州，广东省番禺市人。
就读中国艺术研究院和广州美术学院。享受政府优秀专家待遇。作品分别入选第八届全国美展、全国山水画展、纪念长征胜利全国美展。 其作品分别被江苏美术馆、广州美术馆、中国军事博物馆和联合国等机构收藏。 分别在广州、台湾、香港、南韩、新加坡、美国等地区举办个人画展， 并被邀请赴美国、俄罗斯、法国、荷兰、西班牙等10多个国家地区访问及进行艺术交流活动，出版有画集三册。现为广东美术家协会会员。

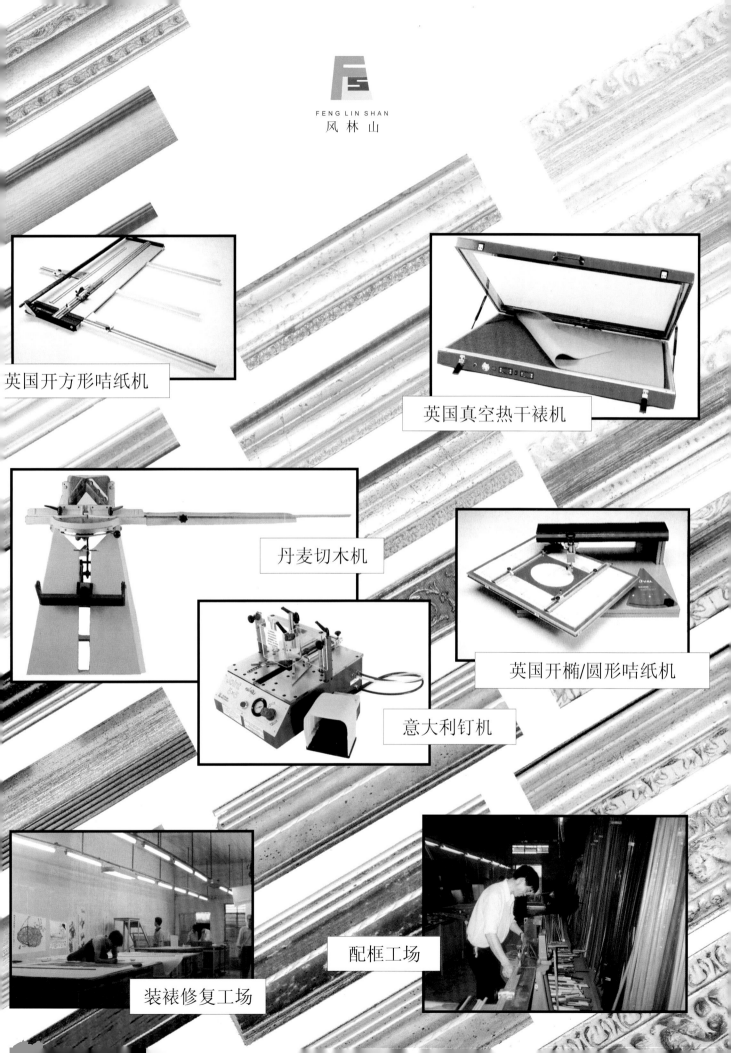

英国开方形咭纸机

英国真空热干裱机

丹麦切木机

英国开椭/圆形咭纸机

意大利钉机

装裱修复工场

配框工场

代理国际知名厂家的设备 材料 配件

书画装裱

古画修复

框艺配装

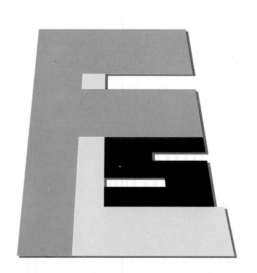

FENG LIN SHAN

风 林 山

艺术装饰厂

电话 84344047 传真 84344047 邮编 510285

厂址 广州市工业大道中庄头福南五巷十八号 通信 广州市工业大道中庄头福南五巷四号

西藏艺术博览之窗

主办单位：拉萨市人民政府　　中国市长艺术博览会组委会　　广州市文学艺术届联合会

承办单位：拉萨市文化局　　广州市新光太广告策划制作中心

协办单位：万宝电器工业公司　　拉萨市经贸委　　拉萨市工艺美术厂

在蓝天和白云下面，有一片最高寒的雪山群大陆，人们称它为地球第三极，它就是西藏。西藏，悠远而博大，神秘而神圣……

一个善良智慧、勤劳勇敢的民族世世代代地生活在这里，以特有的生存方式在这片高大陆创造了独具特色的文明，不仅丰富了中华民族的文化宝贵，也令世人仰首高望。

神奇的雪域文化称漫并沉潜在多姿多彩的高原生活之中，它的魅力正吸引着世界上更多人们的向往。改革开放使西藏高原尤其拉萨圣城厚重的文化积淀焕发了勃勃生机和前所未有的机遇，酝酿已久的"西藏热"正在逐步推向高潮。西藏高原的海拨每上升一个高度都具有新的文化意义，我们通过这个窗口介绍神秘而独具魅力的藏文化艺术。

布达拉宫　Potala Palace

位于拉萨市中心的红山上，是我国著名的宫堡式建筑群。为公元7世纪松赞干布迎取文成公文而建。17世纪，五世达赖扩建重修，历时50年始具今日规模，后为历代达赖喇嘛的冬宫。布达拉宫分为红宫和白宫两部分，红宫为历代达赖灵塔殿和各类佛堂，白宫系达赖生活和政务活动的场所。全部建筑依山势而建，为石木结构，宫殿主楼13层，高117.19米，东西长400米，南北宽约350米。五层宫顶覆盖金瓦，外观雄伟，建筑艺术别具一格，是藏汉文化的结晶，藏族建筑艺术的精华。如今也是西藏最大的文物博物馆。

Potala palace is the famous palatial architecture group of our county.The whole palace is built against the mountain slops in stone and wood constructure.The main building of 13 storeies is 117.9 meters high and 400 meters long from the east to the west and 350 meters from the south to the north.There are five layers of the palace roof covered with gold tiles. The whole Palace appears magnificant and of extraordinary style of architecture arts.

体 现 西 藏 宗 教 建 筑 特 色 的 布 达 拉 宫 宫 门 之 一

Gate of Potala Palace, presenting the unique construction style of Tibetan religion

天和地的交合处，生命在跳舞......

在晒佛节，展佛（唐卡的一种）被挂在寺院高墙上或铺展在山坡上供万人瞻仰、朝拜，它展示了西藏的绘画艺术和缝制工艺。

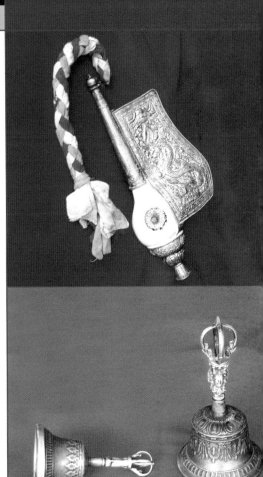

西藏人民在这片高大陆创造了独具特色的文明，其中西藏古乐器就有着一千多年的悠久历史。在一些宗教节日的佛事活动中，在寺庙的祭祀仪式上，以及在民间藏戏演唱时，人们敲打吹奏着古乐器，使气氛更为浓烈，民族色彩更为浓郁。

主要的西藏古乐器有长号角、钹、法螺、长柄鼓、羲鼓、佛铃、哨呐、木笛、胫骨号筒等等几十种。

阳光明媚，绿树成荫。
节日里，勤劳的藏族儿女唱出了心中的歌，跳起了欢乐的舞。

色彩绚烂、独具民族特色的地毯从
这里铺向国内外。

藏族民居内的佛龛。

嶺南美術出版社

LINGNAN ART PUBLISHING HOUSE

社长：曹利祥
地址：广州市水荫路 11 号 9、10 楼
邮政编码：510075
电话：87768688 转　传真：87771049

岭南美术出版社成立于 1981 年 1 月，是广东省唯一的美术专业出版社。出版各类美术、摄影画册、美术史论、连环画、年画、美术教材，以及《周末画报》和《画廊》等期刊。

岭南美术出版社建社以来，不断开拓，积极进取，成为一个颇具规模，富于特色并较有影响的出版社。现有员工逾百，获高级职称者 18 人，中级职称者 21 人。

岭南美术出版社建社 15 年来，出书近 5 000 种，其中在全国、中南地区及全省评比中获奖达 150 多项，众多读物深受广大读者的喜爱。《岭南名画家画丛》分别为明清以来的林良、苏六朋、陈树人、何香凝等立传，记录了岭南画派的崛起。又将一批闻名遐迩的艺术大师的精品结集，出版了大型豪华画册《高剑父画集》、《黎雄才画集》、《关山月》、《李铁夫》、《邓白画集》等，《石湾艺术陶器》更以其浓郁的地方特色和精美的印刷荣获首届全国优秀美术图书评比银奖。《画廊》杂志、《周末画报》作为广东的重点报刊，历来得到海内外同行的赞许和读者的青睐。岭南版的读物多层次多方位地揭示了岭南文化的光彩与品格，成为博大精深的中华文化不可缺少的篇章。

嶺南美術出版社
LINGNAN ART PUBLISHING HOUSE

社长: 曹利祥
地址: 广州市水荫路 11 号 9、10 楼
邮政编码: 510075
电话: 87768688 转 传真: 87771049

岭南美术出版社
全体员工
祝

'97 广州
国际艺术博览会

圆满成功!

 廣州博雅藝術有限公司
GUANGZHOU POK ART CO. LTD.

博雅簡介

　　廣州博雅藝術有限公司是由深圳博雅藝術公司和廣州市文物總店聯合開辦的文化企業，"博雅"文化企業自1981年在深圳特區建立以來，一直至力于介紹和推廣海內外先進的科教文儀，美術設計用品，并率先創辦首屆《深圳書市》，多年來深受廣大文化、教育、藝術、廣告界人士歡迎，1988年得到了中央文化部、財政部授予《全國以文補文先進單位》稱號；今年又被全國美術出版協會評為"全國十佳美術圖書銷售單位"。

　　廣州博雅藝術有限公司是繼深圳、中山、北京后于今年建立的新型文化企業，商場面積800平方米，經營各類文化、藝術類產品二萬多種，并輔設代客加工、大宗商品送貨上門服務，多功能展廳定期舉辦各種商品展示和推界，商場貨物95％以上采用敞開式銷售，"博雅"將繼續本着建設社會主義精神文明的宗旨，謁誠為中外文化交流和繁榮文化市場服務。

地址：廣州市文德北路170號　　電話：(020)83196401　83196325
傳眞：(020)83196362　　　　　郵政編碼：510030

經營項目

美術廣告設計用品

音像制品及樂器

藝術部類圖書畫冊

文化辦公用品

中外美術用品

中外鐳射唱片

藝術圖書

辦公用品

各類樂器　　　　各類設計用品

裝飾用紙、卡紙板

鏡框裝配

學生文具

財務賬册

科教文儀用品

賀卡、郵集

| 香港 | 香港中環城多利皇后街號中商大廈六樓 電話：(852) 2526 1816 2526 2431 傳眞：(852) | 深圳 | 深圳市羅湖區立新路1號羅湖商業大廈 電話：(755) 222 9508 220 5038 傳眞：(755) 222 2378 | 蛇口 | 蛇口興華路海濱花園高層裙樓B座一層 電話：(755) 6684113 傳眞：(755) 6884113 | 中山 | 中山市石岐華柚路7號 電話：(760) 8851367 傳眞：(760) 8851149 |

迅 匯 國 際 洋 行 有 限 公 司
EXPRESS TRADE INTERNATIONAL COMPANY LTD.

香港沙田火炭坳背灣街61－63號盈力工業中心13樓23室
ROOM 23, 13/FL., YALE INDUSTRIAL CENTRE, 61-63 AU PUI WAN STREET, FOTAN, SHATIN, N.T., HONG KONG.　TEL: (852) 2601 5105 (3 LINES)　FAX: (852) 2693 0142

EDDING
德国（威迪）专业美术设计麦克笔用品

德国（威迪）专业美术设计麦克笔用品，产品优良，系列繁多，色彩丰富，向誉欧州市场。

产品种类：设计麦克笔，移印纸，美工笔，绘图针笔，漆油笔，水彩笔，砌割刀，砌割胶垫板等。

HANSA
德国（汉沙）专业喷绘用品

德国（汉沙）专业喷绘产品系列，素以品质优良，种类齐全，深得专业人仕选用。

产品种类：喷笔，气压泵，遮挡纸，喷绘液体，塑胶彩（丙稀）颜料等。

RICH
日本（一池）专业喷绘用品

日本（一池）专业喷绘用品，品质优良，款式齐全，深受专业人仕信用。

产品种类：喷笔，气压泵等。

ROYAL TALENS
荷兰（泰伦斯）专业美术颜料及设计用品

荷兰（泰伦斯）专业美术颜料及设计用品，历史悠久，品质优越，种类繁多，向誉全球，更委任为荷兰皇室及国家博物馆顾问荣誉。

产品种类：油彩，水彩，塑胶彩（丙稀），广告彩，粉彩，油性粉彩，媒剂，光油，画笔画刀，画架，画布，画纸，玻璃彩，染布彩，美工塑泥及颜料等。

迅汇国际洋行有限公司代理世界各地著名优质专业之美术颜料，喷绘及设计用品，货类多达数千，以便提供专业美术，喷绘及设计人仕创作所需求。

特约经销

廣州博雅藝術有限公司
GUANGZHOU POK ART CO., LTD.

广州市文德北路172号
46, YONGXIN ST., RELEASE RD., SHENZHEN.
电话：319 6401　传真：3196 325

深圳博雅藝術公司
SHENZHEN POK ART HOUSE

深圳市解放路永新街46号
46, YONGXIN ST., RELEASE RD., SHENZHEN.
电话：220 5038，222 2082　传真：0755-222 2378
邮政编码：518001

中山博雅藝術有限公司
ZHONG SHAN POK ART CO. LTD.

广东中山市石岐华柏路七号
7 HUA BAI ROAD, SHI QI, ZHONG SHAN CITY, GUANG DONG.
电话：883 0067，885 1367　传真：(0760) 885

大一藝術設計學院是由名藝術設計教育家呂立勛院長於一九七零年創辦，至今已逾二十八載。多年來為香港培育了超過八萬多名藝術設計學生，成績裴然，其中許多已在香港或海外取得超卓成就。一直以來，本院跟內地的藝術學院有很密切的交流活動。早於一九七九年，呂立勛院長便應邀前往北京中央工藝美術學院講學，其後更先後到廣州美術學院，南京美術學院、上海、杭州、浙江、和成都等地作講學和學術交流訪問。現任院長呂歐陽麗堃女士亦秉承

呂立勛院長的精神，除繼續推廣藝術設計教育、培育藝術設計人才外，更與內地、英國、美國、澳洲、意大利、紐西蘭、馬來西亞、日本、韓國等地不斷加強教學交流。本院現提供工商設計、室內環境設計、時裝設計、產品設計、插圖設計、專業攝影、純藝術和漫畫等八個專業文憑課程。隨著科技的進步，現更在工商設計文憑內增設了專業電腦設計課程。大一藝術設計學院是香港最負盛名和規模最大的藝術設計學院。

大一藝術設計學院
First Institute of Art and Design

耕耘廿八載　培育八萬才

校址：香港銅鑼灣蓮花宮東街 1-9 號

電話：（852）2806 0228

傳真：（852）2806 1221

广州市红印品章有限公司

本公司建于五十年代，积累了四十多年刻章经验，拥有一支从事刻章专业技术人材及高素质的员工队伍，在广州市是唯一的刻章老企业。也是经广州市公安机关批准指定刻制公章之专业定点单位。

本公司采用国际先进的电脑激光刻制印章技术，其具有质量优良，保密性强，以便公安机关终端联网的特点。

本公司内部管理严谨，可靠性强，并具备服务至上的经营原则，市内分布各区共有十个业务网点。

本公司除刻制公章之外还兼营印刷、商标、装璜、表格、钢印、机械、模具、刻字，金、银箔加工业务。

公司地址　广州市人民南状元坊七十六号

电话　八一八八三九四六
八一八四九四七九

法人代表：项善麟

富丽家园 广州南部崛起的一座滨江新城市

占地三千余亩·逾十三年开发建设·拥有2公里黄金海岸风景线·超6000户广州地区人家入住

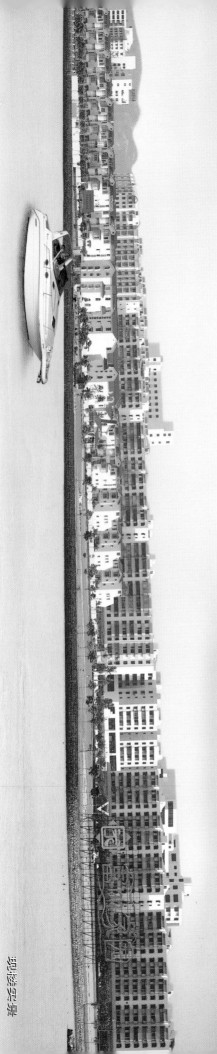

现代临江美景

'97 广 州 国 际

艺术博览会

GUANGZHOU INTERNATIONAL ART FAIR

主 办 单 位 ：广 州 市 人 民 政 府

承 办 单 位 ：广 州 市 文 化 局

日 期 ： 1 9 9 7 年 1 2 月 6 日 至 1 2 月 1 0 日

地 点 ： 广 州 、 中 国 出 口 商 品 交 易 会 大 厦

Time:From December 6th 1997 to December 10th 1997

Address:Guangzhou China Import & Export Commodity Fair's Hall

SPONSORS: GUANGZHOU MUNICIPAL PEOPLES GOVERNMENT

UNDER TAKER: GUANGZHOU CULTURAL BUREAU

* EUROPEAN ARTISTIC COLLECTION *

1. Italian artistic statues.
   (DEAR, ISAC collection)
2. Italian artistic porttery.
   (PALLADIO, TIGROTTO, ACF collection)
3. Italian artistic resin.
   (ARFEFICE, CERERIA RONCA collection)

4. Italian artistic crystals.
   (VETRARTI, VNASON & C, BARBINI collection)
5. Belgean artistic crystals.
   (VAL SAINT LAMBERT collection)
6. Spainish artistic statues.
   (ITALICA collection)

荟萃欧洲艺术极品 共赏名师经典之作

* 本公司经销欧洲艺术精品系列 *

1. 意大利雕塑工艺品
   (DEAR, ISAC系列)
2. 意大利陶器工艺品
   (PALLADIO, TIGROTTO, ACF系列)
3. 意大利树脂工艺品
   (ARFEFICE, CERERIA RONCA系列)

4. 意大利水晶玻璃工艺品
   (VETRARTI, VNASON & C, BARBINI系列)
5. 比利时水晶工艺品
   (VAL SAINT LAMBERT系列)
6. 西班牙雕塑工艺品
   (ITALICA系列)

SWAROVSKI TRADE, CO.LTD.

思 华 乐 贸 易 有 限 公 司

ADD:1F Of NO.53, 3th Building Of Trade Market, Shilong Town, Dongguan, Guangdong, China. TEL: (0769)6613344 FAX: (0769)6613803 P.C.: 511721

地址：中国广东省东莞市石龙镇商贸市场第三栋53号地下 电话：(0769)6613344 传真：(0769)6613803 邮编：511721

深圳卷烟厂祝贺'97广州

深圳卷烟厂　　　　地址：深圳市水贝工业区太宁路　　　　电话：5533525　　　　传真：5533525

尽情 享受 精彩人生

国际艺术博览会圆满成功

吸烟有害健康

广州白云房地产开发总公司

公司简介

　　广州白云房地产开发总公司成立于一九八六年，是具有独立法人资格的全民所有制经济实体，主要经营房地产开发和销售、兼营物业管理、建筑材料和装饰材料等业务，经广州市城乡建设委员会审核批准为城市综合开发二级公司。

　　本公司经济技术力量雄厚，管理经验丰富，有着良好的社会信誉。公司成立以来，锐意进取，不断开拓，先后建设开发商品房和城区搬迁用房逾四十万平方米。主要有项目：广源路云苑直街小区、交电新村小区、河南沙路村凤阳小区、同德围侨德花园小区以及利源大厦、群英大厦、远景大厦、远景市场、豪贤苑、中意花园、富业苑等，为改善市民居住环境作出了贡献。取得了良好经济效益和社会效益，多次被市建设银行评为"信用一等企业"。

　　本公司坚持"信誉第一、质量第一、服务第一"的原则，热诚欢迎海内外商客及各界人士前来购房置业和投资合作。

法人代表：总经理刘文雄

地址：广州市下塘西路13号之二

邮政编码：510091

电话：83501668

传真：83505049

中意花园

凤阳苑

豪贤苑、聚豪楼

侨德花园

南航大酒店

广州新苑

房地产开发有限公司

广州新苑房地产开发公司直属于广州新苑企业集团有限公司，成立多年以来，开发了大量质优楼盘，其中包括拥有38栋大型住宅小区的远景新村，建筑面积达30000平方米的黄石大楼和同乐楼八万平方米的园林住宅晓景苑。本年初开发的苏州园林式御景花园更是本公司代表之作，多年来本公司紧抱开拓、求实、进取的态度经营，将业务多元化，属下企业分别包括加油站，土石方运输车队，物业管理公司，各项企业均取得了良好的经济效益。现本公司更准备开发位于广花二路矿泉别墅附近，总建筑面积达十多万平方米的大型广场住宅，入住后，必然成为北区楼盘的榜样，加上本公司精良的销售队伍和采用多方面的销售策划，介时必然轰动全城，带动北区楼市的活跃性。继后本公司凭着实力会继续前进，竭力为社会作出贡献。

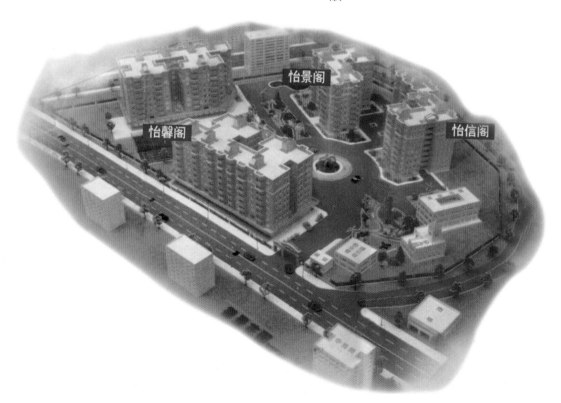

怡景阁

怡馨阁

怡信阁

广州新苑房地产开发有限公司

地址：广花3路98号之一3楼负责人欧静海

电话：86631819
8650909
86639238

负责人：欧静海

宝利来实业有限公司主要生产近年来畅销俄罗斯的ＶＩＴＯＲ（伟涛）针织服装系列及被受国内消费者青睐的针织休闲服装系列。同时，以设计精制影视戏剧服装、头盔、头饰、道具、工艺品、旅游产品而著称。

宝利来

针织休闲服　新潮得体
影视戏剧服　美轮美奂

地址：中国广东省东莞市城旗峰路浩宇工业区座五楼　　邮编：511700　　电话：(0769)2483626　　传真：(0769)2483623

广州电影书店

经营范围 书籍、文具、音像
邮品、收藏品
挂历、吊画
台历、福
牌

广州电影书店成立于一九八七年，是一家由中国电影出版社和广州市文联共同经营的企业，十年的努力，书店已发展成为广为人知、享有盛誉的报刊、书籍、挂历、画册的发行单位，并相继在深圳及广州分别成立了颇具规模的"深圳大志成实业有限公司（图片库）"和"广州市华达利彩色印务有限公司"，在九七年六月又建立了邮品、收藏品服务部，形成了摄影、租赁、设计、制版、印刷、生产、销售及拍卖一条龙服务。把国内摄影师画家等艺术家的作品制作成挂历、吊轴画、台历、吊历、邮品、收藏品等成为大众喜爱的生活文化艺术品，进入千家万户，使艺术家们在增加知名度的同时提高了社会效益和经济效益。为艺术和经济架桥，同时拓展了祖国的文化艺术领域。

书店及华达利公司经营部地址：广州市广卫路九号之三
邮编： 510030
电话： 8338189 83371457
传真： 83190006

大志成提供图片，华达利印制，书店销售的部分产品

大志成正片 内容包罗万象：

自然景观、静物、动物、植物、国内外的建筑、风光、美女、情侣、居室装饰家庭、民俗风情、交通工具⋯⋯。

是您出版发行的好选择

公司地址：深圳市上步中路4号深勘大厦706室　邮政编码：518028　电话：(0755)3234761

超越传统

树立精致典范

雅昌彩印

///IRTRON

深圳雅昌彩色印刷有限公司

广东拍卖业事务公司
广东古今艺术品拍卖有限公司

　　广东省拍卖业事务公司和广东省古今艺术品拍卖有限公司是广东省贸易委员会属下公司。其职能是接受卖买双方之委托组织拍卖活动。于每年春、夏、秋、冬四季举办四届大型拍卖会《中国艺术珍品广东拍卖会》和每月两场的《中国艺术珍品广东巡回拍卖会》.

　　公司长年征集拍卖会拍品。范围包括：近、现代名人书画、陶瓷、玉器、工艺品等项目。

　　有意委托拍卖者，请将拍卖品送至本公司：

深圳市华强北路新世纪酒店14楼

邮编：518028

电话：0755-3234493

传真：0755-3234494

广州市人民北路616号粤广商业中心202室本公司广州征集处

邮编：510180

电话：020-81365741　　90790859

　　　　1392280075　　1392281362

广州市天河区协昌装饰
工程公司
　邮政编码:510500
　传真电话:8770 5097
　业务范围:室内装饰设计,承接水电安装、空调、铝合
　金门窗
　广州市沙河愚东西路 27 号
　………………………………………… 8770 2455
　………………………………………… 8770 2617

广州海外中国文化传播中心
　邮政编码:510030
　传真电话:8335 4237
　广州市文德路 81 号
　………………………………………… 8335 4237
　………………………………………… 8330 1055

广州市少年宫
　邮政编码:510170
　广州市东风西路 167 号
　………………………………………… 8136 1483

广东省集美设计工程第六公司
　邮政编码:510030
　广州市河南昌岗东路 257 号
　………………………………………… 8441 3224

广州美术学院附属中专
　邮政编码:510261
　广州市河南昌岗东路 257 号
　………………………………………… 8444 1752

广东省集美设计工程第五公司
　邮政编码:510261
　广州美术学院内
　………………………………………… 8442 9430

南海石油广州服务总公司
南油大厦
　邮政编码:510170
　广州市东风西路 142 号
　………………………………………… 8136 2125

南海石油广州服务总公司
　邮政编码:510170
　广州市东风西路 142 号
　………………………………………… 8136 3259

广州市天河工艺美术发展部
　邮政编码:510170
　广州市东风西路鸟苑正街 3 号
　………………………………………… 8138 6304

香港柏姬婚纱晚装公司
　邮政编码:510130
　批发零售婚纱、晚装等珠绣系列
　广州市人民南路 224 号 2 楼
　………………………………………… 8188 0063

天河影视霓虹灯广告中心
　邮政编码:510405
　广州市机场路 92 号东座
　………………………………………… 8659 0731

采石家
　邮政编码:510405
　以石会友、至诚于石文化交流、研究开拓,本馆收藏各
　类天然奇石,承办奇石馆及园林艺术
　广州市机场南金钟横路 36 号 402 室
　………………………………………… 8657 5821
　………………………………………… 9902 - 988930

广州美术学院石膏门市部
　邮政编码:510261
　广州市海珠区昌岗东路 257 号
　………………………………………… 8425 5551

广州美术学院综艺美术
用品门市部
　邮政编码:510261

批零国内外美术绘画用品,书籍;现代美术
设计用品,各类美术用纸塑料及文化办公用
品
广州市昌岗东 257 号
　………………………………………… 8444 1753
　………………………………………… 1305161393

广州市海珠区艺林美术专门店
　邮政编码:510260
　传真电话:8425 1409
　总经销:英国"威美"、日本"好品"、美国"泰
　华"设计、美术用品;各国名牌喷绘、裱画、卡
　纸、色纸、测绘工具及美术画册、设计图书
　等。
　广州市河南昌岗东 257 号
　………………………………………… 8425 1409

广州市东山区文华广告公司
　邮政编码:510080
　传真电话:8776 4473
　创新设计吊牌月历、台历、挂历、台垫、年历;
　电脑设计、彩色印刷;欢迎洽谈
　广州市东山区烟墩路 33 号 2 楼(培正小学侧门)
　………………………………………… 8776 4473
　………………………………………… 8766 5770

博艺
　邮政编码:510140
　广州市长寿西路新胜街 46 号
　………………………………………… 8139 1872

石湾美术陶瓷厂
　邮政编码:528031
　佛山市石湾镇东风路 17 号
　………………………………… 0757 - 2715039

广东教育书店
　邮政编码:510030
　广州市文德北路 69 号
　………………………………………… 8339 3802

广州钢琴厂贸易服务部
　邮政编码:510170
　广州市中山七路王家园上街 34 号
　………………………………………… 8188 3343
　………………………………………… 8191 3070

广东省工艺美术总公司
珍品馆
　广州市东风东路 840 号艺苑大厦五楼
　………………………… 87777612 - 254(245)

广东省文化厅
　邮政编码:510080
　广州市培正一横路 8 号
　………………………………………… 8776 5002

广东达裕实业有限公司
　邮政编码:510080
　加工、销售工艺美术品、装潢设计、文化用品
　广州市东山区达道路 5 号(八一学校旁)
　………………………………………… 8776 6197
　………………………………………… 8776 9083

四海灯画
　邮政编码:510030
　批发零售纸画、灯画、动感画框、粉彩画、进
　口铝合金
　广州市文德北路 83 号
　………………………………………… 8334 0454
　………………………………………… 1393059085

广州市芳村永利综合购销部
　邮政编码:510030
　批发、零售各种进口白木、红木镜料画框、画
　纸
　广州市文德北路 79 号
　………………………………………… 8333 3853

广州见山墙画彩印有限公司
　邮政编码:510115
　承印各种规格大型墙画,生产销售本公司产
　品

广州市起义路 120 号
　………………………………………… 8333 8854

广州市东山区通兴塑料
镜框经销部
　邮政编码:510030
　批发、零售各种塑料镜框,装饰塑料画框
　广州市文德北路 146 号北侧
　………………………………………… 8338 3805

广州市美图画业设计工程公司
　邮政编码:510260
　批发、零售各种进口框条,欧美名画,现代饰
　画
　广州市河南康乐西约新区海关前 14 号 2 楼
　………………………………………… 8419 9200
　………………………………………… 8331 1326

瑞隆贸易发展公司
源远办公用品贸易行
　邮政编码:510060
　传真电话:8332 4123
　经营:西德"利是"金笔,办公用品,帐册凭
　证,会计用品,电脑用品,各类纸品,文件柜,
　代理各国名牌文具
　广州市越秀北 102 号
　………………………………………… 8380 7890

广州恒兴工艺实业公司
　邮政编码:510260
　经营项目:礼品、奖品、工艺旅游品、超塑合
　金产品
　广州市泰沙路瑞宝南约西街 46 - 48 号
　………………………………………… 8431 8986

广州香雪书画社
　邮政编码:510500
　中国书画、专业裱画、中国书画创作、交流;
　专业裱画
　广州市先烈东路 137 号
　………………………………………… 8772 2446

广州美术馆
　邮政编码:510040
　广州市越秀山镇海路
　………………………………………… 8319 7252
　………………………………………… 8354 1016

广州市文史研究馆
　邮政编码:510600
　广州市广州大道中 39 号 2 楼
　………………………………………… 8737 9520

广州市春苑工艺美术品
经营部
　邮政编码:510030
　各类油、画、墙、布画,加工各种铝合金、木、
　塑、胶字画、相框等
　广州市文德中路 39 号(中国人民建设银行旁)
　………………………………………… 8330 4291

红印印章有限公司
　邮政编码:510120
　广州市人民南路状元坊 76 号
　………………………………………… 8184 9479

中盈企业有限公司石韵音响
　邮政编码:510220
　石韵牌系列,工艺石音箱,达到了石材工艺
　与音响技术的完美结合,国内首创,造艺精
　湛。
　广州市同福东路 640 号(市二宫文苑内)
　………………………………………… 8423 8546

天意礼品工艺厂
　专业生产水晶胶广告匙扣
　广州市滨江中三巷 27 号
　………………………………………… 8444 6680
　………………………………………… 01392222851

印 出 自 然 色 彩

永利发

彩印印有限公司

WINFRNE PRINTINE CO.LTD

本印刷公司是一間具有一定
規模與實力的印刷公司，采用
先進的海德堡四色電腦酒精印
刷機和ＮＡＮ７四色機，最大
印刷版面１００Ｘ１５０ＣＭ。

高質素的專業設計和精湛
的印刷技術，從設計到印刷一
條龍服務，以優質的服務和優
惠的價格贏得了新舊客户的廣
泛好評和信賴。

电话：84418650 84357107 邮编：510250
地址：广州市昌岗中路昌岗大街 35 号

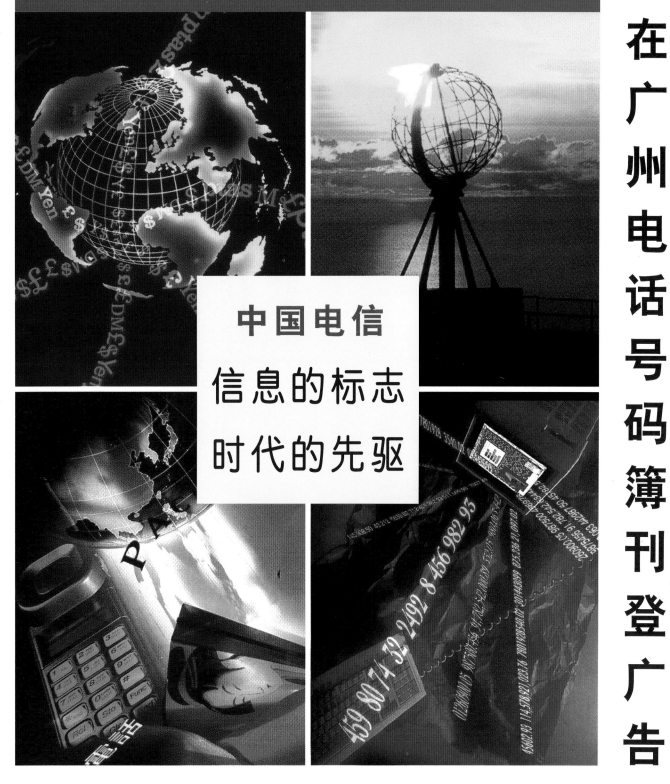

目录
CONTENT

组委会名单
Namelist of the Organizing Committee

艺委会名单
Namelist of the Art Committee

组委会办公室成员名单
Namelist of the General Office of the Organizing Committee

图录编辑人员名单
Namelist of the Catalogue Editorial Stoff

致词
Mesage

参展画廊 / 单位、画家及作品
Participating Galleries / Units Artists & Works

广告
Advertisements

参展画廊 / 单位、画家及索引
Index of Participating Galleries / Units &Artists

参展画廊 / 单位、画家及索引
Participating Galleries / Units
Artists & Index

赖征云　　　　　　　　　　　　　　　1
LAI ZHENG-YUN

叶献民　　　　　　　　　　　　　　　2
YE XIAN-MIN

吴海鹰　　　　　　　　　　　　　　　3
WU HAI-YING

张 伟　　　　　　　　　　　　　　　4
ZHANG WEI

陈 铿　　　　　　　　　　　　　　　5
CHEN KENG

熊德琴　　　　　　　　　　　　　　　6
XIONG DE-QIN

黄坤源　　　　　　　　　　　　　　　7
HUANG KUN-YUAN

何坚宁　　　　　　　　　　　　　　　8
HE JIAN-NING

徐兆前　　　　　　　　　　　　　　　9
XU ZHAO-QIAN

何 东　　　　　　　　　　　　　　　10
HE DONG

醉墨堂画廊　　　　　　　　　　　　　11
SHOW-HALL OF ZUI MO TANG ART GALLERY

卢津艺　　　　　　　　　　　　　　　12
LU JIN-YI

王根生、王山岭　　　　　　　　　　　13
WANG GEN-SHENG、Wang Shan-ling

纪荣耀、杨乾亮　　　　　　　　　　　14
JI RONG-YAO、Yang Qian-liang

王全力　　　　　　　　　　　　　　　15
WANG QUAN-LI

史 玉、高学年　　　　　　　　　　　16
SHI YU、GAO XUE-NIAN

王惠民、陈学周　　　　　　　　　　　17
WANG HUI-MIN、CHEN XUE-ZHOU

张文君　　　　　　　　　　　　　　　18
ZHANG WEN-JUN

武剑飞　　　　　　　　　　　　　　　19
WU JIAN-FEI

黄克中、龚东庆　　　　　　　　　　　20
HUANG KE-ZHONG、GONG DONG-QING

叶永青　　　　　　　　　　　　　　　21
YE YONG-QING

杨天生　　　　　　　　　　　　　　　22
YANG TIAN-SHENG

陈春勇　　　　　　　　　　　　　　　23
CHEN CHUN-YONG

刘宗久　　　　　　　　　　　　　　　24
LIU ZONG-JIU

刘家振　　　　　　　　　　　　　　　25
LIU JIA-ZHEN

乔卫明　　　　　　　　　　　　　　　26
QIAO WEI-MING

张惠斌　　　　　　　　　　　　　　　27
ZHANG HUI-BIN

陈炳佳　　　　　　　　　　　　　　　28
CHEN BING-JIA

陈炳佳　　　　　　　　　　　　　　　29
CHEN BING-JIA

壁 光　　　　　　　　　　　　　　　30
BI GUANG

陈英灿　　　　　　　　　　　　　　　31
CHEN YING CAN

杨 明　　　　　　　　　　　　　　　32
YANG MING

赵永家　　　　　　　　　　　　　　　33
ZHAO YONG-JIA

马松林　　　　　　　　　　　　　　　34
MA XONG-LIN

陈 晶　　　　　　　　　　　　　　　35
CHEN JING

宋克冰　　　　　　　　　　　　　　　36
SONG KE-BING

吴松山　　　　　　　　　　　　　　　37
WU SONG-SHAN

徐勤军　　　　　　　　　　　　　　　38
XU QIN-JUN

陈义水　　　　　　　　　　　　　　　39
CHEN YI-SHUI

祁 峰　　　　　　　　　　　　　　　40
QI FENG

李 富　　　　　　　　　　　　　　　41
LI FU

陈韵竹　　　　　　　　　　　　　　　42
CHEN YU-ZHU

墨 丁　　　　　　　　　　　　　　　43
MO DING

代书斌　　　　　　　　　　　　　　　44
DAI SHU-BIN

孟祥顺　　　　　　　　　　　　　　　45
MENG XIANG-SHUN

陈建功　　　　　　　　　　　　　　　46
CHEN JIAN-GONG

邓子欣、王伟　　　　　　　　　　　　47
DEN ZI-XIN、Wang Wei

薛军、董才、鲁峰　　　　　　　　　　48
XUE JUN、DONG CAI、LU FENG

黄廷海 HUANG TING-HAI	49	乔玉川 QIAO YU-CHUAN	78
林玉宇 LIN YU-YU	50	梁根祥 LIANG GEN-XIANG	79
黄继明 HUANG JI-MING	51	罗志奇 LUO ZHI-QI	80
王靖忠、聂振基 WANG JING-ZHONG、Nie Zhen-ji	52	真言雕艺工作室 ZHENYAN STUDIO OF SCULPTURE ART	81
罗锦雯 LUO JIN-WEN	53	朱全增 ZHU QUAN-ZENG	82
李少桦 Li SHAO-HUA	54	朱全增 ZHU QUAN-ZENG	83
李少桦 Li SHAO-HUA	55	柳之雄 LIU ZHI-XIONG	84
康宏博 KANG HONG-BO	56	克丽丝蒂．特佳 KIRSTI TAXGAARD	85
路仁茂 LU REN-MAO	57	戴恩．维拉 DEAN VELLA	86
韩浪的陶艺 HAN LANG'S POTTERY ART	58	雷蒙．饶可让 RAYMOND GEORAGEIN	87
千艺美术陶瓷厂 QIANYI FACTORY OF ARTISTIC	59	帕拉．杰立佛 PALLA JEROFF	88
卢 秋 LU QIU	60	索文．库玛尔 SOVAN KUMAR	89
陈少梅 CHEN SHAO MEI	61	郑发祥 ZHENG FA-XIANG	90
周韶华 ZHOU SHAO-HUA	62	郑发祥 ZHENG FA-XIANG	91
于景才 YU JING-CAI	63	董俊启 DONG JUN-QI	92
张黎明、赵 净 ZHANG LI-MING、ZHAO JING	64	孟庆一 MENG QING-YI	93
郭同江 GUO TONG-JIANG	65	左正尧 ZUO ZHENG-YAO	94
青岛市雅族陶艺工作室 QINGDAO YAZU POTTERY ART WORKSHOP	66	莫建文 MO JIAN-WEN	95
张平树 ZHANG PING-SHU	67	陈子文，朱海军 CHEN ZI-WEN AND ZHU HAI-JUN	96
王俊英、刘勐 WANG JUN-YING、LIU MENG	68	王光辉 WANG GUANG-HUI	97
亚 英 YA YING	69	陈正清 CHEN ZHENG-QING	98
李晓林 LI XIAO-LIN	70	陈正清 CHEN ZHENG-QING	99
戚大成 QI DA-CHENG	71	陈宜明 CHEN YI-MING	100
杜兴久 DU XING-JIU	72	杨孝军、杨敬仲 YANG XIAO-JUN、YANG JING-ZHONG	101
陈为中 CHENG WEI-ZHONG	73	李伟钦 LI WEI-QING	102
李 跃 LI YUE	74	黄向卫、黄向阳 HUANG XIANG-WEI、HUANG XIANG-YANG	103
聂天雄 NIE TIAN-XIONG	75	李连信 LI LIAN-XIN	104
封 尘 FENG CHEN	76	黄诗筠 HUANG SHI-YUN	105
王有政 WANG YOU-ZHENG	77	刘穗艳 LIU SUI-YAN	106

梁明明	107	邓福林	147
LIANG MING-MING		Deng Fu-lin	
刘学峰	108	黎雄才	148
LUI XUE-FENG		Li Xiong-cai	
广州金夫人婚纱影楼	109	佟雨	149
GUANGZHOU MADAME JIN'S WEDDING-DRESS STUDIO		Tong Yu	
天一庄文化艺术有限公司	110	江云龙	150
TIANYI ZHUANG GULTURAL & ART COMPANY LTD.		Jiang Yun-long	
羊 羔	111	许荣	151
YANG GAO		Xu Rong	
张广志	112	张石培	152
ZHANG GUANG-ZHI		Zhang Shi-pei	
曾道宗	113	许喜裕	153
ZENG DAO-ZONG		Xu Xi-yu	
黄 兵	114	倪秋汉	154
HUANG BING		Ni Qiu-han	
七星名砚工艺厂	115	李金明	155
SEVEN-STAR INKSLAB FACTORY		Li Jin-ming	
叶秀炯	116	李正天	156
YE XIU-JIONG		Li Zheng-tian	
韦正彬	117	李正天	157
WEI ZHENG-BIN		Li Zheng-tian	
艺兰轩画廊	118	艾欣	158
YILAN XUAN GALLERY		Ai Xing	
范京生	119	艾欣	160
FAN JING-SHENG		Ai Xing	
黄树德	120	豪美墙画彩印有限公司	161
GUANG SHU-DE		Haomei Wall-painting	
程 辉	121	地丁	162
CHENG HUI		Di Ding	
董毓明	122	杨伟	163
DONG YU-MING		Yang Wei	
牛亚平	123	深圳市怡家印饰品有限公司	164
NIU YA-PING		Shenzhen IGA Household Decoration	
李东伟	124	孔凡超	165
LI DONG-WEI		Kong Fan-chao	
李东伟	128	石里溪	166
LI DONG-WEI		Shi Li-xi	
花都市福星工艺有限公司	129	孙成斌	167
GUANGZHOU FR STAR CRAFT FACTORY		Sun Cheng-bin	
花都市福星工艺有限公司	130	袁学君	168
GUANGZHOU FR STAR CRAFT FACTORY		Yuan Xue-jun	
陈永锵	131	田婕	169
CHEN YONG-QIANG		Tian Jie	
陈永锵	133	张向军	170
CHEN YONG-QIANG		Zhang Xiang-Jun	
谭伟成	134	南岭梅	171
TAN WEI-CHENG		Nan Ling-mei	
赖建成	135	杜浩	172
LAI JAIN-CHENG		Du Hao	
范贯忠	136	张桥	173
FAN GUAN-ZHONG		Zhang Qiao	
蔡 超	137	孙黎	174
CAI CHAO		Sun Li	
叶 泉	138	王豫湘	175
YE QUAN		Wang Yu-xiang	
叶 泉	146	张洪亮	176
YE QUAN		Zhang Hong-liang	

石萍 Shi Ping	177	刘秦生 Liu Qin-sheng	207
庄小尖 Zhuang Xiao-jian	178	邹莉 Zhou Li	208
庄小尖 Zhuang Xiao-jian	180	黎明晖 Li Ming-hui	209
邓崇龙 Deng Chong-long	181	谢桂森 Xie Gui-sen	210
邓崇龙 Deng Chong-long	182	梁国荣 Liang Guo-rong	211
张秋华 Zhang Qiu-hua	183	高伟彬 Gao Wei-bin	212
王 盛 Wang Sheng	184	林子超 Lin Zi-chao	213
王首麟 Wang Shou-lin	185	李任孚 Li Ren-fu	214
耿郁文 Geng Yu-wen	186	杜炜 Du Wei	215
刘增孝 Liu Zeng-Xiao	187	广东省丝绸进出口（集团）公司 Guangdong Silk Imp.& Exp.Corp. (Group)	216
苟正翔 Gou Zheng-xiang	188	广东省丝绸进出口（集团）公司 Guangdong Silk Imp.& Exp.Corp. (Group)	217
傅文刚 Fu Wen-gang	189	黄乘黄 Huang Cheng-huang	218
王长明 Wang Chang-ming	190	逯树林 Lu Shu-lin	219
刘老五 Liu Lao-wu	191	符超军 Fu Chao-jun	220
季智俞 JI Zhi-yu	192	甘迎祥 Gan Ying-xing	221
田应福、程其德 TIAN YING-FU、Cheng Qi-de	193	黄战生 Huang zhan-sheng	222
陈艳梅 Chen Yan-mei	194	甘丹 Gan Dan	223
深圳市福传工艺制作有限公司 Shenzhen Fuchuan Industrial Manufacture	195	胡锦雄 HU Jin-xiong	224
纪淑文 Ji Shu-wen	196	广东粤广工艺彩瓷公司 Guangdong Yueguang Artistic Colored Ceramics Company	225
纪淑文 Ji Shu-wen	197	蒋嫒 Jiang Yuan	226
王锦清 Wang Jin-qing	198	博雅画艺饰品中心 Boya Oainting and Decoration Items Centre	227
陈圻 Chen Qi	199	于文江 Yu Wen-jiang	228
许如秀 Xu Ru-xiu	200	柳月良 Liu Yue-liang	229
张红曼 Zhang Hong-man	201	刘振铎 Liu Zhen-duo	230
梁少兴 LIang Shao-xing	202	白靖夫 Bai Jing-fu	231
吴荣文 Wu Rong-wen	203	刘诗东 Liu Shi-dong	232
王衡鉴 Wang Heng-jian	204	曾嵘 Zeng Rong	233
陈恺 Chen Kai	205	邓铭 Deng Ming	234
吴贤淳 Wu Xian-chun	206	广州新星投资顾问工程公司 Newstar Investments and Projects Consultand Co.	235

萧荣　　236
Xiao Rong

萧荣　　241
Xiao Rong

国祥了静　　242
Devotee Guoxiang Liao,jing

国祥了静　　243
Devotee Guoxiang Liao,jing

石湾美术陶瓷厂　　244
Shiwan Fine Art Ceramics Factory

张玉茂　　245
Zhang Yu-mao

王义胜　　246
Wang Yi-sheng

张智量　　247
Zhang Zhi-liang

Key Yakushiji　　248
Key Yakushiji

刘长福　　249
Liu Chang-fu

叶志华　　250
Ye Zhi-hua

柳根青　　251
Liu Gen-qing

肖广成　　252
Xiao Guang-cheng

马艺星　　253
Ma Yi-xing

广州星月木雕工艺美术品有限公司　　254
Guangzhou Star-Moon Wood-Carving Industrial
Handicraft Corporation Ltd.

张燕根　　255
Zhang Yan-gen

陈可之　　256
Chen Ke-zhi

蔡圣委　　257
Cai Sheng-wei

梁业鸿　　258
Liang Ye-hong

梁业鸿　　259
Liang Ye-hong

古原　　260
Gu Yuan

古原　　264
Gu Yuan

贵州省人民政府驻湛江办事处　　265
Zhangjiang Agency of the Guizhou Provincial People Government

张伟　　266
Zhang Wei

林明臣　　267
Lin Ming-chen

左进伟　　268
Zuo Jin-wei

崔丕超　　269
Cui Pi-chao

马波生　　270
Ma Bo-sheng

高旭奇　　271
Gao Xu-qi

陈楚波　　272
Chen Chu-bo

李伯虎　　273
Li Bo-hu

杨燕来　　274
Yang Yan-lai

杨福音　　275
Yang Fu-yin

姚伯齐　　276
Yao Bo-qi

广州市龙凤戏服社　　277
Guangzhou Long Feng Stape Costume Factory deals in stage

杨季湘　　278
Yang Ji-xiang

红蓝陶艺　　279
Red & Blue comsists

红蓝影视文化有限公司　　280
Red & blue Film and TV Culture Company

陈玉先　　281
Chen Yu-sian

刘藕生　　282
LIu Yu-sheng

权伍松　　283
Quan Wu-song

刘声雨　　284
Liu Sheng-yu

刘声雨　　285
Liu Sheng-yu

张鸿飞　　286
Zhang Hong-fei

周玉兰、王铭　　287
Zhou Yu-Lan、Huan Ming

王贺良　　288
Wang He-liang

刘胄人　　289
Liu Zhou -ren

卢望明　　290
Lu Wang-ming

邸立丰　　291
Di Li-feng

邸立丰　　297
Di Li-feng

岳青俊、杨英才　　298
Yue Qing-jun、Yang Ying-cai

张建民　　299
Zhang Jian-min

杨德强　　300
Yang De-qiang

王晓鹏　　301
Wang Xiao-peng

王双禄　　302
Wang Shuang-lu

关玉良　　303
Guan Yu-liang

关玉良　　308
Guan Yu-liang

胡文伟　　310
Wu Wen-wei

吴珉权、丰爱伦 311
Goh beng Kwan、Choo Ai Lonn

仁萨、朱庆光 312
Rearnsak、Choo Keng Guang

王耀麟 313
Heng Eow Lin

马维斯 314
Murrell

马伟达 315
Victor Hugo Marreiros

何道根 316
He Dao-gen

丘瑞福 317
Chieu Shuey Fook

冯宝珠 318
Anti Fung Pou Chu

白礼仁 319
Robert O'Brien

麦少峰 320
Mak Siu Fung

余世坚 321
Yu Sai Kin

余世坚 322
Yu Sai Kin

吕丰雅 323
Eddie D.F.N Lui

蔡逸溪 324
Chua Ek kay

玛利亚·韦丽莎、李希文、依莎贝 325
Maria Elisa Vilaca、Mira Dais、Isabel

范婴子登 326
Fanying Zideng

童建颖 327
Tong Jian-ying

马若龙 328
Carlos Marreiros

邹中星 329
Chao Chong Seng

琥茹 330
Joana Ling

康斯坦丁 331
Konstandin Bessmeertnyi

缪鹏飞 332
Mio Pang Fei

袁之钦 333
Un Chi Iam

吴卫鸣 334
Ung Vai Meng

廖文畅 335
Liao Wen-chang

蔡树荣 336
Choi Su Weng

黎鹰 337
Lai Leng

谭可文 338
Tan Ke-wen

罗卓英 339
Jorge Carlos Smith

郭桓 340
Kwok Woon

郭桓 342
Kwok Woon

风林山
Feng Lin Shan

西藏艺术博览之窗

ART FAIR

广州国际艺术博览会

'97 广州国际艺术博览会会刊编辑人员
Editorial Staff of the Catalogue

主 编	**Chief Eiditor**
曾石龙	Zeng Shi-long
副主编	**Deputy Chief Editors**
刘长安 ---- 陈永锵 --- 乐润生	Liu Chang-an ---- Chen Yong-qiang --- Le Run-sheng
编 审	**Copy Editor**
黎服兵 ---- 王璜生	Li Fu-bing ---- Wang Huang-sheng
责任编辑	**Duty Editor**
李健军	Li Jian-jun
英文翻译	**English Translator**
区慧坚	Ou Hui-jian ---- Ou Wei-guang
会徽设计	**Emblem Designer**
陈志超	Chen Zhi-chao
设计制作	**Cover Design**
广东占美广告有限公司	Jami Advertising Company
装帧设计	**Binding and Layout Design**
陈志超 ---- 梁丽红	Chen Zhi-chao ---- Liang Li-hong
梁锦威 ---- 梁鼎莹	Liang Zhen-wei ---- Liang Ding-ying
艺术总监	**Chief Art Inspector**
陈永锵	Chen Yong-qiang
设计总监	**Chief Design Inspector**
黄雄伟	Huang Xiong-wei
中文校对	**Chinese Proof**
高 玲 ---- 张 捷	Gao Ling ---- Zhang Jie
英文校对	**English Ptoof**
区炜光 ---- 高 玲	Ou Wei-guang ---- Gao Ling

书　　　名：'97广州国际艺术博览会
编　　　辑：'97广州国际艺术博览会会刊编辑部
责任编辑：李健军
责任技编：乐润生
责任校对：张　捷

'97广州国际艺术博览会

出版发行：岭南美术出版社

电分制版：锦兴电子分色制版有限公司

印　　刷：广东新华印刷厂

印刷协力：永利发印刷有限公司

版　　次：1997年11月第一版 1997年11月第一次印刷

印　　数：1-1000册

开　　本：787×1092毫米　1/16 印张 25

书　　号：ISBN-5362-1723-4 / J · 1563

定　　价：280元